Angels and Shadows

By K. L. Stewart

Copyright © 2012

Cover art by

K. L. Stewart 2012

Map of Sark by Robert Mozingo

Published By Reimann Books

Published September 2012

2nd edition

ISBN 978-1-938743-01-6

Printed in the U.S.A.

Angels and Shadows

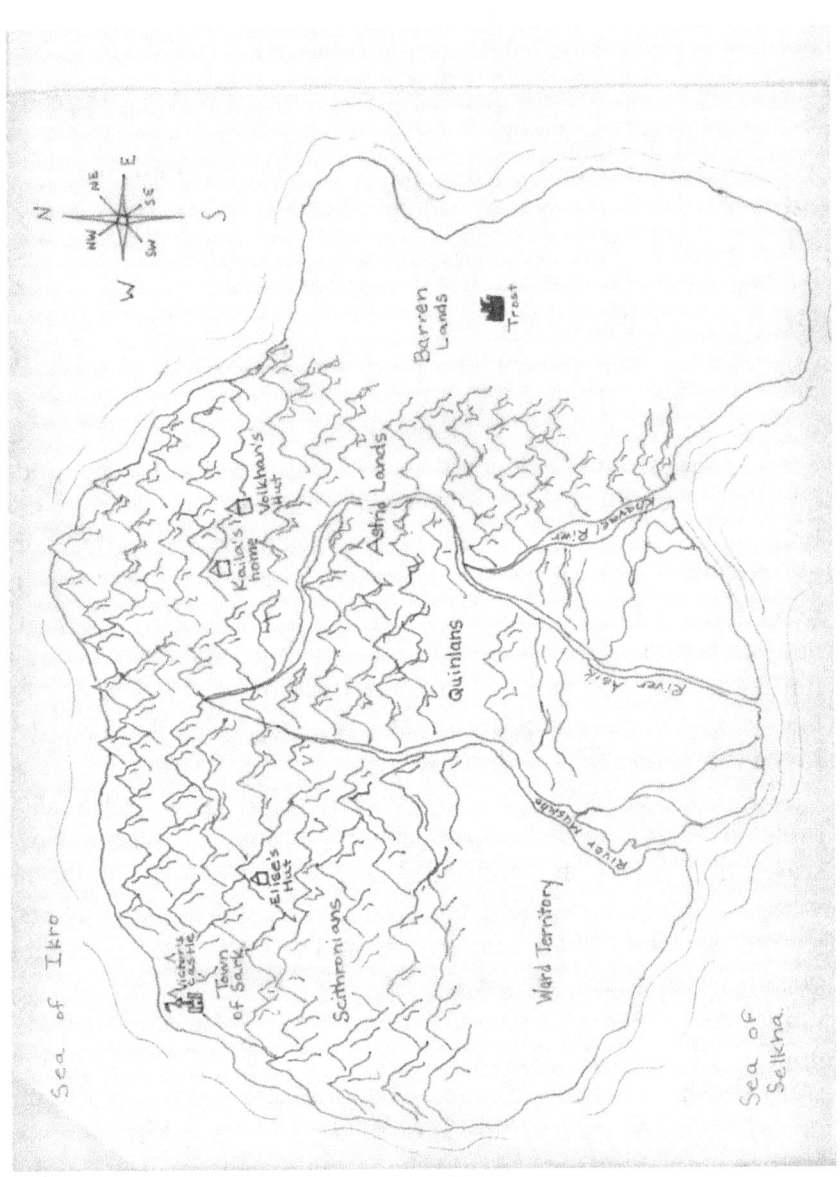

I

A Mother's Plan

Shea, castle of Kristiniva

Morning had come again with its illusions, its deceptions of light, and the dread that had come with every other morning that had preceded it. Celeste lay hanging to the lasting comfort of the dream that she had awakened from. She lay under the golden silk blankets woven by the Quirials, the elves of the sky. She dared not stir, for the fear of waking to face the day ahead. She dreaded the mornings; for they brought a deep sadness and longing that she could often forget as she slept at night. When darkness fell she could sleep, and dream of her husband, and her old life, and live where she belonged. Now there were times when her old life, her rightful life, seemed so far away that she often tried to tell herself that it was a fantasy, but then she would look at her daughter, and be reminded that such a beautiful angel could not come from her alone. She carried so much of her father in her, that he could not be forgotten. He was a man that Celeste loved too much to have dreamed up.

The feeling of anxiety was overpowering her. She dreaded to live, to wake, but what choice did she have? She was a dark angel, an immortal being who could not die, but who was also separated from the land in which her powers should be used. Here, her powers had always been different, because they were not really needed. Her daughter, being only seven, was an angel of light, being bred of two dark angels. It seemed appropriate for her to be born here in the skies of Shea, where the moon filled the sky with silvery light during the darkness, and the sun filled everything with shining brilliance in the day. Angelik had never seen her true home, and Celeste felt this could be for the best. She was unsure if her child's powers would be different there, in Sark, but she

3

knew that it was a possibility. Then again, how would she ever know if her daughter was better off here, if never given the opportunity to live in her true home?

As she lay pondering this, there were footsteps in the nearby rooms. They were lightweight, yet full of a subtle power. It was the sound of her captor's footsteps as she prepared for the morning. Kristiniva was both her captor and savior. When her own people betrayed her, she had been burnt alive, but since she could not die, Kristiniva took pity on the angel. She sent rain down on the land, and a deep raging storm swept through Sark, melting the snow, and flooding the valleys. When the fire was extinguished, Kristiniva gathered Celeste's pregnant, burnt body in her arms, and carried her back to the hidden land of Shea, where she nursed her back to health, and helped deliver Angelik into the world.

There were laws in Shea that kept Celeste here. It had been seven years that Celeste lived in Shea, and because Kristiniva had saved her, Celeste was indebted to the sky goddess. She owed her ten years of service. Five were hers, and the others were her daughters. Her daughter would be free of a servant's life, but because she was not grown, she had to be left with her mother, and was not allowed to return to her homeland.

She was treated more as a friend than a servant, but Celeste was kept from her duties to her god, the duties to her kingdom, all of her friends, but most painful to her was being kept from her husband, who no doubt had been searching for her these seven years. She had often thought of running away, but she did not know how to get back to her homeland, and the sky goddess, although kind, and pleasant, could be one of the most wrathful creatures that Celeste had ever encountered.

She laid thinking, as she did every morning, and she realized what she must do and how she must do it. It had come to her in a dream. She knew that it might not work, but she also knew that it was probably the only chance of seeing her husband again. Kristiniva feared the angels, but none more so than Victor, the angel of justice. Celeste would have to make her believe that he was trying to force his way into the land. In her dream she had been shown how to make the goddess believe he was coming. She lay preparing her emotions for the day ahead.

Her eyes were closed, but the subtle footsteps of her captor were coming closer now, then into her room, and to the bedside. The gentle weight of the goddess sitting on the edge of the bed shifted the blankets, and Celeste faced what she dreaded more than anything. She opened her eyes, pretending to awaken.

"Celeste," Kristiniva's voice flowed like a light wind. The dark angel opened her eyes, and felt the familiar warmth of blood swelling in her tear glands. She wiped the blood away as she sat up, careful to use a gentle hand on the right side of her face, where the scars of fire still ached and burned in a horrible disfigurement. She was sure that if she were in her homeland, she would have already healed, but things were different here.

She forced a sideways smile at Kristiniva. The right side of her face would not allow a smile. Instead, it hung limp and swollen in a constant frown.

"Did you sleep well?" The goddess asked with her usual concern.

Celeste only nodded her head in reply.

When she thought about it, she realized that she had slept very well. The riddle in dream she had been having for the past two weeks had been solved. She knew what must be done, and felt an anxious wave pass over her with the realization that it had to be done today. She knew now that she was the weakness of her captor. Kristiniva couldn't deny that she had wronged the angels, and she feared the wrath of Victor, the angel of justice above all else.

Kristiniva smiled; her face smooth and white as the brightest clouds of the summer sky. Her eyes reflected her mood, mirroring the morning sunshine that was getting brighter as the minutes passed. Her bright blue hair was down this morning, flowing as if in a breeze. Kristiniva reached a long, thin arm out to the angel, caressing her face in a gesture that Celeste had always thought was meant to comfort her. Lately, though, she felt that Kristiniva's touch was taking power from her, like a morning ritual to drain her of strength.

The goddess spoke with a light voice, "I am glad that you are feeling well this morning. Our meal is waiting if you feel hungry."

"Yes, I'll be there in a moment," Celeste said, straining to speak. Speech was still difficult because the side of her face burned with each word she spoke.

Kristiniva stood, towering to her full height of six and a half feet. "I'm sure that Angelik is hungry. She has been up for hours already." The goddess turned to exit the room; her flowing purple robes billowed out behind her as she glided breezily out of the door.

Minutes passed with only the sounds of muffled voices, and light breezes blowing through the castle. Celeste smiled, hearing her daughter's footsteps approach the door. Angelik's footsteps had a distinctly light and springy pace. The sound came closer, and there was a sudden burst of energy as Angelik ran through the door, her arms outstretched to her mother. Angelik's golden curls bounced with each step she took. She had a sweet grin on her face. It was a smile that only the innocent could possess. Celeste threw her arms around her daughter, embracing her tightly and pulling her onto the bed. The small angel let out a squeal of delight.

"And what have you been doing this morning?" Celeste asked.

"I've been playing with my new friend. His name is Raffie, and he's a Pegasus...a very beautiful one. He wants to take me flying one day. Can I go flying with him one day?" A silence followed. Great anguish overcame Celeste, making her doubt the meaning of her dream... or at least the courage to follow through with her plan. Her daughter looked back with a stare of undeniable comprehension. She knew what her mother felt, her angelic gift allowed her to feel the emotions of others.

"You want me to go away?" she asked, reading her mother's feelings, and thoughts.

"Shhh..." Celeste carefully and silently placed a finger over her scarred lips, leaning in closer to her daughter. Angelik came closer until their faces were almost touching. Celeste's eyes were suddenly intense, "Darling, if you can read my soul, then you'd know the last thing I could ever want would be for you to depart from me." Celeste lowered her voice to such a small whisper that only an angel could hear it. "The time has come for us to leave Shea. We need to go home. It is the only way that I will ever truly heal, and the only way that you will meet your father. Now understand, and listen carefully." The angel took her daughter's hand, and whispered so low that not even Kristiniva could have eavesdropped.

"I cannot leave. I am bound here by the laws of this land, and it would make Kristiniva very sad if I were to leave her at the moment. You don't want her to be sad, do you?" Angelik shook her head, and looked back at her mother attentively, with shining blue eyes.

"You have to go home, and find your father. He will be able to come here and get me. I can't make any promises about how you will find him. He is a dark angel just as I am and will be able to read your soul, if you let him in. You must tell him where I am, and have him come find me. Can you do this, Angelik?"

The small angel felt a rush of excitement pass through her. "Do you mean that you are sending me back to him? I'm going to meet him?" Angelik whispered back, a little louder than her mother had. Celeste put her finger over her own lips, reminding the child to keep her volume low.

Celeste nodded her head in reply. Angelik looked into her mother's emerald green eyes, and saw determination shining with a new light of purpose.

"Yes, mother." Angelik nodded as she spoke in a voice that was just as hushed as her mother's.

Celeste looked back at Angelik with an expression that her daughter could not comprehend. The child could feel the weight of her mother's emotion bearing down on her own soul. "This is going to be harder than it sounds, honey. Things in Sark are not the same as they are in Shea. Even your gifts will be different."

"I can do it, mommy!" Angelik exclaimed. Celeste put her finger to the child's lips.

"Then here is my plan. Listen carefully, because we have no time to waste. We must begin now, at breakfast. We don't want to upset Kristiniva by telling her that we are leaving, so you must not speak a word to her about it. We must get her to agree to send you to your father. We can only do this by making it look both necessary and unplanned. I need you to pretend that you are linked to your father through a soul connection. She has seen us do it before, so you must make it look believable. You must pretend that your father is talking to you. Pretend that he is coming here to get you. Act like you are sick. Pass out! Make it as believable as you can. You see, this will make her fear that your father is coming here. If you play your part well, she will believe that it is necessary to send you back to him. When you find him, you must tell him where I am. You must help him find me. It is the only way our family will be together again."

The small angel reached out, comforting her mother with an embrace. "I understand mother, but I will miss you while I am away."

"I will miss you more." Celeste smiled out of habit from this game, but this time she meant it like never before.

II

Shekley and the Shadow

Tahln

David sat waiting in the sands of Tahln. His brown hair ruffled in the hot breeze that swept across the rocks. Sweat poured from his brow, and his breathing was labored from heat and exhaustion. His skin had been blackened by falling ashes and smoke. He looked down at Michael. It was hard to take in the sight of his friend, so weak and helpless. Michael was short, muscular, stronger than most men his size. He was the last person that David had expected to find in this condition. Yet, here they both were, stranded on the outskirts of Trost, his brother's city. The remains of his brother's creatures lay scattered on the ground. Wire, metal, and human body parts littered the earth. The stench was becoming unbearable, but David had to stay, for Michael's sake. He was worried that his friend wouldn't last much longer.

David and his friend were both selbdes, so they could see into each other's thoughts. David could sense that his friend was alive, but sleeping. Michael had been wounded in several places, but the worst was a deep puncture to his gut. David wasn't going to leave his friend's side. He knew that he was close to the point of giving up, but David had no intention of letting that happen. He had bandaged Michael's wound, but it was deep, and without medicine, it was harder to heal. Hopefully, one of the healers would find them soon.

Trost, inside the city

Shiana had become an expert at staying hidden. She had veiled her dark, red hair with a black wig. She looked out at the courtyard. There, she saw a man working. He was wearing tan coveralls, and steel toed work boots. He had been at work for hours, and she had patiently watched with interest.

9

To anyone who didn't know, he seemed nothing more than a worker, but she knew better. She knew it was Shekley. He was supposed to be hiding in his fortress, wrapped in his metal armor, but something had possessed him to come out into the open to build…what was it that he was building? She couldn't read his thoughts. They were being hidden in darkness. She continued to watch. After a few hours, he sat back, and stared at his work.

The Shadow was gone, and she was able now to see his thoughts, which were always hard to read, but she did manage to figure out what he was building. The idea of what he was planning terrified her.

Trost, outside the city walls

Some time had elapsed. David was confused about exactly how much of it had slipped by, but the important thing was that they had been found by a healer, who had heard their cries for help in his mind. The healer was James, a skinny, brown haired man. He sat now, with his hands pressed to the wound. Both he and Michael were locked in their own thoughts. David couldn't enter even if he tried. That's how healers had to work, though. His mind was free to wander now across the sands, and into Trost. Shiana was there, unseen so far. Shiana was David's girlfriend, and the one person he loved more than anyone else. He could almost see her red, flowing hair and blue eyes as he listened to her thoughts. When she knew he was listening, she sent a message to him.

David, you have to come see what Shekley is planning. His plans have gone far beyond what we imagined. You have to come. He's built a new kind of machine, and he's going to use it to leave our world. He needs more resources, and the Shadow has shown him a way to get them by traveling to other realms. David, we have to try and follow him, but there isn't much time. You must gather as many of our forces as you can, and head to the center of the city. That's where you'll find your brother, and that's where the machine is.

Shiana edged carefully to the alley where she planned to meet David. One of Shekley's creatures, the Mahldrusecs, patrolled the area around the machine. It was Xandra. She was Shekley's girlfriend, and first experiment. Shiana hoped to slip past her unseen. Xandra wore black military clothes, and the parts of her, skin that showed were no longer skin, but shiny silver metal. Her face only resembled that of a woman. Her eyes were no longer her own, but computerized lenses. Her hair ran from her forehead to her neck in one thin long stripe down the middle of her head. She stopped suddenly, facing Shiana. Her right arm slowly morphed into a long, metal spear with several, small clicks and then she stood there, motionless. Shiana stared back, still for a moment and then she ran into the doorway of a nearby building. She expected Xandra to follow, but when she looked out of the window, Xandra walked around the machine as before. The spear now replaced yet again with a shiny metal hand.

David was in the city now, afraid that he would be seen. He had managed to pull together what was left of his friends. They were headed now to the center of Trost, to try and stop Shekley from using the machine to reach another world. Shiana left to meet up with them as soon as she sensed that they were coming. Now they were split up, all moving toward the same objective, but coming from different directions. Michael had insisted on coming, but he was lagging behind. The healer James was close beside him. They were resting in an alley at the moment. There were other teammates close by, all trying to converge on Shekley at once, but then there was a numbing feeling. Suddenly, there was a rip in space and time. The selbdes could all feel it. It threw all of their senses off, and they knew that they were too late. Shekley was successful. They could no longer hear each others thoughts. There was a loud pulsating sound, and then a bright electric fog rolled through the air. There was a sound like static, and then they felt themselves being pulled up from the concrete, sleep taking hold of them.

Sark, The Barren Lands

Wind whistled in Shekley's ear, and the heat seared his flesh. He tried to see, but the sun forced his eyelids shut. He felt weak, but he summoned enough strength to roll over in the sand, so that the light didn't seem as bright. As always, Xandra was there with him. She seemed to shine with an intensity that blinded him, like the goddess had been before the Shadow imprisoned her. He closed his eyes and sat up, feeling tired and thin. He placed his palms over his eyes, forcing darkness, cool comfort upon his burning vision.

"Where are we?" His voice sounded as two now, the shadow was with him.

"You have been successful. We have found a new world." Xandra replied. Her voice was still her own, and some part of him was glad that he had left it so, but the Shadow urged him to change it as soon as there was time.

With a whispery command, the Shadow spoke into Shekley's ear. "There are more important things at the moment. You must let her lead you back to safety. The sunlight must be harnessed if we are going to continue our dominance. The light is hurting me. Make Xandra take you." The Shadow spoke in his thoughts, and Shekley did just as the Shadow ordered him, and grabbed his girlfriend by her metal arm, regretting it as soon as his skin made contact.

"It's too hot!" He screamed at the Shadow, in his own mind. "I have to let go!" He screamed aloud as he fell into the sand, turning up dust as Xandra pulled him along. "Please! I am burning!"

She stopped and looked down at him. "Grab me with your other hand, Shekley. You will not feel the pain of the sunlight." Xandra spoke words meant to comfort him, as always. She tried to let go, but his hand was sticking to her, sizzling in the heat of the desert.

The Shadow laughed at him, and gripped her more firmly; the smell of cooking flesh excited him, and the joy of making Shekley flail around in pain, uncertain and blind entertained him, as he had not been for many months. The Shadow laughed gleefully as Shekley writhed on his knees, screaming and twisting. Xandra's stride forced his body forward uncontrollably.

When Shekley was finally allowed to release Xandra's arm, he fell to the floor, weak and defeated, clutching his burnt and bleeding hand. He simultaneously looked around him at what remained of the citadel, frowning under the dominating collapse of everything he had worked so hard for. He was suddenly being scolded by the Shadow for his failures and he knew now why his hand burnt like it did. He wanted to get away, but he knew that he could not. He set his jaw against the pain, and looked up. The roof of the main entrance was caved in, and none of the equipment seemed to be functioning. It would take months to rebuild this. He had not taken into account just how much would be destroyed by traveling to a new world.

He frowned as he turned to Xandra. She was covered in a dark shadow, but he knew that it was her. "You will be the one to help me." He said. "You will be the one to begin the repairs. No one else is as reliable as you are. I need you to get started collecting the materials for solar panels. We'll harness the sunlight for our power. There seems to be a great abundance of that here."

Xandra gave no sign that she had heard what he said, she only walked away to do as she had been told.

Sark, barren lands, later

Shekley examined the solar panels. All of them seemed to be working, and Xandra was still working to make

13

more of them. He now had some electricity flowing through the building. This was good. Things were starting to turn in his favor.

He felt the Shadow then. It was with him again. Its voice and presence were cold, and filled with a patient glee. "We could have willing servants if you play your part well."

"What do you mean?" He asked aloud.

The Shadow answered in a whisper. "There are mighty, evil souls, hunters they are, and they will pledge loyalty to me if you gamble with them. I will show you. Bring your woman. She may be useful in this matter, for they crave the flesh of a woman always." It laughed again, and again, louder and louder.

"She has no flesh left!" Shekley protested, and in some way he started to feel jealousy at any one else craving anything that belonged to him, especially Xandra.

"Ah, Shekley, this is precisely why I chose you." The cold laughter continued, and then the Shadow spoke again, this time with urgency. "Quickly! You must do as I tell you, if you want to rebuild Trost, and release the goddess." At the mention of the goddess, Shekley turned to Xandra, willing to obey.

"Come with me!" He demanded as he held his hand out for her to take. "You have a very important job to help me with. We are to find willing servants."

"We cannot rebuild this whole station by ourselves. It will take too long." The Shadow said into his mind.

"We cannot rebuild this whole station by ourselves. It will take too long." Shekley echoed the Shadows thoughts aloud, as he took hold of Xandra's metal hand with his now bandaged and gloved hand.

III

Conspiracies

Shea, Kristiniva's palace

The dining hall was blinding in the morning sun. Angelik always loved the mornings. The white halls sparkled. Rays of sunlight streamed through the open windows. There was always a refreshing breeze whispering through the halls, filling them with a song of new beginning. On this particular morning, the round crystalline table had been filled with a sweet smelling breakfast.

Angelik peered over the edge of the table spying sky flower petals in her mother's usual place. Her mother's favorite flowers were soft, sugary, and came in all the colors that the Shean sky could conjure. Angelik looked at the plate in front of Kristiniva, and saw that she would be eating a pastry with a creamy filling. In Angelik's own plate there was sweet bread seasoned with bits of sky fruit. Each blue goblet contained juice made from morning mist and sky flower nectar. Kristiniva called it shareen. A vapor wafted up from the goblets, creating a mist over the table. Rainbow colors danced around the shimmering glass as the sunlight cascaded into the room.

Kristiniva and Celeste soon entered the room. They all took their places and began their morning meal. Celeste ate slowly, the muscles in her face aching with each bite. Kristiniva was eating just as slowly, but there was no cause for it, other than to appear more refined. Angelik ate her breakfast as quickly as she could, butterflies fluttering in her stomach. She did so wish to please her mother and hoped that Kristiniva didn't suspect anything unusual. Angelik kept glancing at the goddess, but Kristiniva's eyes were hard to read when they were misted over.

Angelik realized that this may be the last morning she

would have that was filled with such comfort and pleasure, but she knew what she had to do. As soon as she had her fill, she hesitated only a moment before putting her mother's plan into action. As she finished her last morning roll, she felt a twinge of anxiety shoot through her stomach. She still wished to go through with the plan, but now that it came to it, she felt a terrible dread. It was a fear of what lay before her. She feared separation from her mother and what the future might hold. Negative emotions were not spoken of in Shea, so Angelik had no way to define the feelings twisting inside of her. She only knew that Celeste needed her, and she knew what she must do to help.

She glanced at her mother, and pushed aside the feelings that were keeping her from carrying out her plan. She knew that the dark angel could no longer live in this place which was, to Celeste, a prison.

"Mother..." Angelik put her small hand to her forehead and groaned. "I do not feel well," she said in a dry, weak voice.

Celeste looked at her daughter sternly.

"Angelik!" she exclaimed. "Play of this kind is not very funny."

The child began to breathe heavily, as if it pained her. Kristiniva looked at her, confused. Suddenly, Angelik stopped the breathing entirely, and slipped from her chair with a groan. She fell to the floor with a light thud.

"He calls to me," she whispered frantically and feverishly as her mother leaned over her. With wide wild eyes, she cried out, "He's searching for me!" Her voice fell again, "He is coming to find me!"

Kristiniva stood up and came around the table to kneel over the child. With a panicked voice, she asked, "Who calls to you? Who is trying to enter here? Who is in your mind?" With each question, Kristiniva's voice became more raised until she was shouting. She placed her hands on the child to demand an answer, but Angelik would not respond. She only screamed and writhed on the floor as if in great torment.

Celeste held fast to her daughter, even when Kristiniva let go, stood up, and backed away in fear.

"Angelik!" Celeste cried. "Angelik! Stop this! Stop!"

Kristiniva spoke, in a hushed whisper. "I do not think that the child is playing. We must send her away. Someone wants her, and I believe it is her father. He wants her back. I'm certain of it. We must send her back to him. She has to go away, before…" Kristiniva had a cold look in her eyes, and the light cascading into the castle suddenly dimmed. "She'll have to go alone. You are still not well." Celeste had never heard the goddess express such fear and panic.

"No, not Angelik! You can't send her out alone, and without me. Please do not make me part from my daughter. I am all that she has ever had. She could not survive without me!" the angel pleaded to the goddess.

"I will be back. Do not move from this place!" Kristiniva demanded, throwing her hands into the air. Suddenly the sun was covered in a great gray cloud. Thunder rumbled throughout the castle. The goddess' eyes flashed with bright electricity, and she vanished in a bolt of lightning. A moment of stillness passed over mother and daughter as the sound of the storm rumbled around them in the darkening day.

Angelik looked at her mother. Red tears were tracing down the dark angel's face. The child reached out a hand to wipe them away.

"Don't cry, mother." she whispered.

Celeste stopped her daughter's hand and held it in her own. "It's okay," the dark angel sobbed. "It's only for pretend, remember? Now lie down. Kristiniva will be back soon."

Angelik did as her mother told her, but she knew… she could feel that the tears were real. They sat there in a silent goodbye until Kristiniva returned.

When she came back, there were others with her. Angelik could not see them, her eyes remained closed.

However, she could feel their presence. They were unlike anything she had ever felt before. They were light, but filled with a dark beauty.

She heard Kristiniva's voice, filling the room with thunder, "We must send her to Sark, Celeste. It is the only way."

"Why? Please, Kristiniva, this is my daughter. I cannot part from her. I am all that she has ever had!" Celeste pleaded.

"She is disturbed with darkness, no doubt from Sark. The only creatures that can reach her here would be other angels. Her father wants her."

"Is it necessary to send her away?"

"We must do this!" Kristiniva declared.

Suddenly, a new voice spoke, coming nearer from across the room. "Do not worry. We know the way to Sark, and we can lead her safely home."

The voice was that of Arik, the prince of the moon elves. Like all moon elves, his complexion shone with a dim light, but his waist-length hair was as black as the darkest night. His eyes were deep purple. He stepped toward Celeste to take Angelik, and Celeste momentarily feared he would find the child was only pretending. The elf had a look on his face that told Celeste that he knew her secret. He turned so his back was to the goddess, smiled at the angel and winked an eye as he lifted the child.

"Kristiniva,' he said, "I believe that you are right. Whatever is hurting the child cannot be cured. Perhaps her father can heal her. We will see to it that she gets to Sark."

Angelik felt like she had been lowered onto a soft, cushioned bed. There followed a snapping sound, and a darkening. She risked opening her eyes to see that she had been laid in a basket, no doubt woven by the elves, and it had a rounded cover, so that it resembled an egg. She had been laid on blankets with spells woven into them. She could already feel a numbing sense of sleep taking hold of her. She barely heard the rest of the conversation as she was being lulled into dreams of things beautiful, dark, mysterious, and light.

Arik turned to Celeste, with an expression that held all the splendor of the night sky. "This will not be our last meeting, dark angel. Do not let this separation from your child fill you with emptiness. Be glad, rather, that she is safe." He smiled as he spoke the words. They were words meant only for Celeste, spoken to her in her mind, and with the words, she felt a peace wash over her.

Sark, northwestern forests

Angelik awoke to the swinging sensation that seemed to be moving her, even in her dreams. It was the back and forth motion of the basket being carried. Along with the movement there were voices, which she was faintly coming to realize were actually real, and not in her dreams at all. The effects of the spell were starting to wear off. Darkness had come. She knew it even before her eyes were open. She could feel the element as she never had before, and the rhythm of the swaying basket was not helping her to stay awake. She was almost asleep again, when the basket suddenly stopped.

She started to open her eyes, but shut them quickly when the cover started to come off of the basket. Arik had opened it, and she heard his voice, as she felt the weight of something small being set beside her.

"Here, in the forests of Sark, we must all agree to an oath never to tell Kristiniva what we have done. We will only speak of it while in Sark, and we will not mention it to anyone else, even if we trust them. For, in laying this small trinket into this basket, we risk our very lives...or worse fates. She must never know."

Angelik heard each of the other three elves agree in their rightful turn to the oath. They each swore on the name of Selfirin, the Shean God of creation that they would never speak of it; unless it was to each other and even then only if it

19

was spoken in the realm of Sark.

Angelik could sense all four elves crowding close to the basket. A light voice now spoke. It belonged to a female elf, and her words flowed as if they had been caught in a stream of trickling water. "She is a real angel of light. She shines with the Saigolai's blessed light." She leaned down kissing Angelik on the forehead.

Then, another voice was heard, serene, and filled with the sound of a welcome rest. "May the Holy One be with her, for this is as far as we can take her." She felt the hand of this elf as he took hold of hers. "Innocence is her quality. It is that which radiates from her. May she be blessed to always wield such a powerful weapon."

The fourth elf touched her forehead, and he spoke in a language that not even she could understand. She knew no words to describe the way that his voice sounded, or the beauty of his language. It was deep, like the night, filled with wisdom and foreknowledge from many thousands of years. It was weighed down with magic, and sounded all at once like the thunderstorm, and it seemed bigger than a mountain, yet it did this in a whisper which shivered, as if it were a star.

Then the first elf spoke again. "May you sleep, and have beautiful dreams." With these words, Angelik felt heaviness over her eyelids, and she fell into a long slumber of dreams that were filled with her mother, and her father, and an overwhelming happiness."

IV

The New Land

Shea, the summer forest

Shiana awoke, feeling strangely good. She felt well rested, and healthier than she had felt for many weeks, though her relief was shadowed with dread and fear. She looked around, realizing with a sick feeling in her gut, that Shekley had succeeded. Never had she wanted to see the dark land of Tahln spread out around her, but she wanted it now. It would have meant Shekley's failure, but it was not to be. She looked around at the new land that surrounded her. Tall green leafed trees swayed lazily in a breeze that blew around them, curling her red hair around her face. She looked out to see thriving vegetation sprawled over the floor of the forest, lush and flowering, with all sizes and colors of blossoms. She even thought that she heard the faint trickle of water nearby. She looked over at her teammates, a group now reduced to only about thirty, who lay scattered around her. The fusion of particles as they raced through time and space should have damaged them physically, but her friends seemed to mirror the good health that she felt in her own body. All their scars had repaired themselves, even the wounds that had been making Michael lag behind were now completely gone. Sassy lay nearby, resting peacefully at the root of a tall, budding tree. Her true form had been restored, and she seemed a young woman, still in her teens, with long blond hair. Shiana smiled as she remembered Sassy telling her about her nickname.

"My momma calls me Sassy, because I talk back so much. She says that my sass is only going to make life hard. I don't call it sassing, I call it voicing my opinion." Shiana laughed aloud as the memory came to her.

They had stayed friends for many years. Sassy was a Selbdes who could change her appearance, just by imagining she looked different. She had come under the protection of David and Shiana after her parents had been violently carried away by the Mahldrusecs. She had never let her opinion, or her undeterred independence wear her down. She was one of the most persistent members to their cause. Now, she lay so peacefully, that it seemed to Shiana that she was that young woman all over again. Her burdens seemed lighter, as she snoozed in the grass.

Shiana pulled herself into a stand, and let her mind scan what was around her. She couldn't help but to smile. It seemed that they lay in an untouched land. Everything was pure and natural. There was a breeze swaying the tree branches and she sniffed the air. It was fragrant, something that she was not used to. She couldn't place the smell, but she wished to find what it was. She followed the sound of the trickling water. There was a small shallow stream rippling through the woods not too far from where they all lay. She cupped her hands. Reaching down, she let the cool water into her palms, then, raising them to her lips, she drank. It was the most refreshed she had felt since before the war had started. She stared into the reflections of the trees in the water, and then she did something that she had not allowed herself to do very often. She let a tear slide down her face. It was a good cry. She did not recall ever having one of those, and wasn't quite sure what to do about it. She splashed water on her face, washing away the tears, and then wiped the water away with her shirt. She was just glad that she was away from her team mates. She did not want them to see signs of weakness in her.

Shiana was so into her own thoughts at the moment that she did not see the head pop up from the water, but she was brought to attention when she heard a woman's voice. It was soft, and barely audible.

"Oh, why are you crying in my stream?" She looked over, and saw a woman under the water. She could do nothing but stare for a moment. Was there really someone there? It was hard to tell. The movements of the water, and the reflections of light and shadow as the trees swayed made her second guess what she had seen and her wellness at the moment, but her mind reached out, and there was no doubt about it. There was someone in the water.

"Hello?" she asked. There was no answer. She waited, until she started to think she was crazy, and then she decided that she better get back to where her friends lay in their restful states of mind. Wiping another tear away, she made her way over to where they lay sleeping peacefully.

David awoke at the sound of her approaching footsteps. He looked around with a wondering smile, his hair was sticking up, and he had a red spot on his face where he had been resting his head on his arm. He smiled at her as she came towards him. She smiled back, loving him even more when he seemed so human.

"I wonder where we are," he said to her.

"I don't know, but apparently, there is no doubt that Shekley has succeeded." She reached out, smoothing his hair down. "We have to find him."

There was a silence between them, they were thinking similar thoughts, and they were the same hopes and fears that they had felt for so long. She sat with her red hair slumping over her shoulders, and him with his brown hair ruffling in the breeze. Then there were sounds of movement as Sassy stirred. She sat up groggily.

"So it worked," she said, yawning, and stretching her arms into the air. "I hope that we don't ever have to go back!" she exclaimed, "but one thing is for sure, I feel better. I can't exactly explain it, but I feel really good."

"Strangely good?" Shiana asked.

"Yes, you could say that." Sassy said. "Hey, they even have real vegetation," she said as she looked around her. "Do you think that they have any food, you know, like it used to be? Like...oh, I'd almost kill for an apple. My mom used to give me those to get rid of loose teeth. I loved them, but I can't even remember the last one I had. I wish they had them here. It would be good to have one, even if I never have another one."

"Well, we could take the time to search the area..." David started.

"I've already started. There is a stream right over there." Shiana pointed to a place where the undergrowth seemed to be a little heavier.

"The water is real, and drinkable."

"Well, let us wake the others, and start searching the area." David said. The others agreed in their minds, and quickly set to waking their teammates.

Sigh Reen, the faerie of the summer stream watched the salty tear as it dissolved into the water around her. She didn't understand why someone would do this to her water. They had taken all of their weariness and upset thoughts, and dumped them into her very clear running stream. She cupped her hands, and reached carefully out until she felt the salt from the tear, and then she licked it from her palms. It was not from any creature that she recognized. There must be strangers here. She pulled herself from the stream, and was astounded at just how many actually were here. What should she do about it? She should do something. Strangers were not allowed in here, unless they were invited, or brought by the elves. These creatures seemed to have neither the invite, nor the elf. She thought about it for a moment, and then decided to go to the forest elves. Perhaps they would know what to do, and they may even know who these creatures were that cried into her stream.

The faerie descended into the water, and let the currents slide her downstream until she reached the pool in the fen, then she emerged, and stepped onto the grass. Invisible though she was, the elves realized that she was there. Malah, the queen of the forest elves, turned to where she stood. She was camouflaged in the leaves of the undergrowth, lying in a bed of fragrant summer flowers. Only her eyes set her apart from the leaves. They were a dark brown, but the movement as she opened them caused them to stand out.

"Fausti, Sigh Reen," she said, greeting her formally as she turned to the faerie, who was wavering in and out of the visible spectrum.

"Who are the creatures taking water from my stream?" She asked the elves.

"Whatever do you mean?" asked another voice. This one came from higher up. The king of the forest elves, Mondlif, was seen as he emerged from what seemed to be the very bark of an old oak tree. His face was even covered in a wooden mask of oak tree bark.

"What creature could it be?" He addressed the faerie.

"I have never seen them, but they lie at the feet of the poplar trees. They cried tears into my stream. I heard them talking, and they seem to be lost. I thought that perhaps you would know from whence they came." The faerie's voice wavered as she spoke. She appeared, and disappeared in pale shimmers as the sunlight shone through the treetops, highlighting her figure.

"Take us to them," pleaded the king.

"Follow me," said Sigh Reen, the faerie of the stream. "I will show you them." She then stepped back into the stream, and the elves walked beside the stream, as the faerie led them to the feet of the poplar trees. They stared before them in shock. Much to their surprise, there was a group of visitors, and they were stealing water, and pears, and fruits from all the trees in the forest.

"What should we do about this?" asked the queen, gripping her husband by his arm, feeling already what would come about if they could not explain this to the gods.

"Perhaps the water elves gave them passage. We should speak to them about it," decided Mondlif.

"Look at this!" exclaimed Michael. "I haven't seen these in a long time," he said as he plucked an apple from the tree branch.

"Well, Sassy will be delighted." Shiana said. "I wonder what they're finding on the other side of the forest."

"Hopefully, it is something that is just as good." He laughed with wonder as he pulled more apples, stuffing them into a bag he had made from his jacket. "If not, though, I am happy with this. It's amazing, isn't it?"

Shiana nodded her head in agreement. "Yes, but we mustn't forget that Shekley is responsible for destroying another land that was once just as beautiful as this. We have to stop him before this land is destroyed by the Shadow as well."

"Yeah, we better get back, besides, my jacket is full."

They started walking back to where they had awakened, when they both stopped. They had heard something. It sounded like someone whispering another language. They sat silently for a moment.

"What was that?" Michael asked, whispering.

"I don't know. I've never heard anything like that before."

They stood there for a moment longer, and then Shiana asked, "Who's there?" There was no response. The woman in the stream was remembered now, but Shiana pushed the memory away, questioning her sanity. They were both reaching out with their minds, but neither of them got any response. "Let's just get back," Shiana said. Michael nodded. So, the two Selbdes headed to the clearing to meet with the others.

In the clearing, they all put down the fruits that they had gathered. Shiana smiled as she handed Sassy an apple. "Looks like you won't have to kill for one." Sassy let out a sigh of delight as she took it, with a smile of disbelief spreading across her face.

"Oh, thank you so much. Look what we found. We have pears, and figs."

"Okay, look," said David. "We don't have any bags to carry this stuff in, so let us all take our jackets off, like Michael has done, and make a bag that we can sling over our shoulders. That way we can carry it with us while we walk. We'll divide up the fruit as evenly as we can. Then we'll follow the stream until we get some sort of idea of where we are. That way, we won't be far from the water if we need it. Sound okay?"

There was nodding and agreement all around, and even some "agreed" voices sounding in his mind. They all watched and followed as Michael instructed them on how to tie up their jackets like he had done.

There was a rustling of leaves nearby, and they all turned in unison to see what it was. A deer stood quietly by a tree. It stared at them for a moment, and then walked away.

"What was that?" asked Sassy, never having seen an animal quite so large.

"I think it was some sort of animal," replied Kim, a tall brown skinned girl who was sitting beside her.

"It was a deer," Shiana replied. "We used to have them, a long time ago. I remember seeing them on the edge of the forest, when we still had one."

They all sat in silence for a moment. "Let's hurry up," David announced, "I don't want this to take too long. We are still in a hurry to find Shekley and implement a plan to stop him.

When all the fruit had been sorted, and everyone had taken a quick drink of water from the stream, they all began following David and Shiana as they walked beside the stream. For a while, there wasn't much talking, just the wonder of the forest filling all of their senses. Every once in a while, they thought that they heard a sound, but then they would turn, and find that nothing was there, or see a small animal that would quickly scurry away. Sassy and some of the others were a little afraid, but they were okay when they compared it to the darkness they had lived in before. They were hoping in a way to never find Shekley, to be able to live in this land forever. They were unaware that they had been spotted by many creatures that were not animals. All of the creatures acted as the faerie had, and simply told another creature, for they were not used to seeing the likes of this new species trekking about in their summer forest.

They were also unaware that they were headed to the mushroom garden. There was a very brave and good sensed gnome who had been living there among the mushrooms for many years. He was very inquisitive when it came to new things, and so when he saw these new creatures walking toward him, he quickly stood up and planted himself in front of them. He stood with one hand balled into a fist on his hip, and the other gripped his smoking pipe. He watched them with his wrinkled old face. They did not see him, and would have stepped on him if he wouldn't have shouted.

"Fausti! Gazevi! Zouphi!" He had gotten their attention, but they didn't respond.

When they looked down, they saw what looked like a tiny old man, about a foot tall with a very long white beard and mustache. He wore long brown trousers, and a white shirt that laced up in the front with an open brown jacket that matched his pants. One of his eyes didn't open as far as the other, but he had rosy cheeks, and so it gave the impression that he was smiling sideways all the time. He had a prominent nose, and he wore a brown hat with matching boots that came up to his knees.

"I think this creature is trying to speak to us!" Shiana exclaimed into David's mind.

"What is it?" he asked.

"I don't know. Let us get someone who is good with interpretation." They both turned to Teri, a psychic with almond shaped eyes and long straight black hair. Realizing what they wanted without asking, she walked up to the front of the line, and looked down at the little gnome. He had his arms folded, and was tapping his foot impatiently on the ground.

"Hello?" she asked him, and then she could understand what he said as he spoke.

"Oh, hello, I am Noggle, a gnome, and what are you creatures, and how did you gain passage into the forest?" He asked them.

"We are Selbdes. We come from another land, and we are lost. Someone else came with us, and he means to do harm to your world. We need to stop him before he can succeed. Can you help us?" She sat down on the ground, and then leaned toward him until their faces were eye level.

"Well," said the gnome, "I see what you're saying, but it did not answer my question. I asked you how you managed to gain passage into our lands."

"We arrived here by following the one who means to do your planet harm. He travels with a great shadow of evil. He destroyed our home, and we need to stop him before he manages to destroy yours as well."

"So how did he gain passage?" Noggle asked.

"We're not sure. He just came here with a machine that he built. We were going to stop him, and then something happened. We were brought here by a great force. We traveled through time and space, and woke up in this forest," Teri explained.

The gnome didn't answer. He was lost in thought. Small wisps of smoke were released from the pipe as he puffed. After a moment, he lifted up his hand and walked a short distance. When he came back, he motioned for them all to sit down. "You may stay here, until I get you help, but the only help that I know to offer you is to get you to the castle of my king. Kialo may be able to help you, but I don't know. You see, we monitor our borders, and the fact that you are here baffles me, and will no doubt baffle him as well. He may see you as a threat. I hope that he can help you. Just wait here, and when I get back I will have some help for you." He turned towards the pile of white mushrooms growing around a stump, and then he climbed down a hole nearby.

Teri took this time to explain to the others all that Noggle had said. Shiana looked relieved. "Maybe we will be able to get down to business quicker than I thought," she said.

No one noticed a brown rabbit scurrying quickly away with a small roll of paper tied to its neck with a bit of ivy.

They sat in the shade of the summer forest, and waited for the gnome to return, enjoying the beauty of the new land.

Then suddenly, as if springing from the forest itself, came tall, human-like creatures camouflaged to the trees, and the undergrowth. They seemed to spring to life all around them, and encircle them. Some of the Selbdes had fallen asleep while waiting, and now they were quickly awakened.

"Fausti!" One of them exclaimed, as he came into the center of the circle. He removed his mask, and the psychics saw what looked like a brown skinned man with long curling hair filled with bits of bark and leaves. He wore a long robe of dark brown. "We were told to escort you to our king. He is awaiting your arrival. He wishes to speak to all of you. Come with us, and we will show you the way."

"Thank you," responded Shiana, surprised that she was able to understand his thoughts, as she motioned for her team mates to do as they were told. They all followed, hoping that this would give them the upper hand on Shekley, and some much needed help.

V

Angelik's Journey

Sark, northwestern forest

Angelik was dreaming. It was a beautiful dream, with songs woven into it by the elves' magic. She had been happy. Laughter was filtered through the peace that filled her soul, but then she awoke, and all light faded. All warmth left her, and her memories started to come back. She had willingly put herself here, leaving her mother behind.

She pulled herself into a sitting position, fighting the heavy drowsiness that she felt. She shook off the numbing effects of sleep as the reality of her separation sank into her soul. She was alone and colder than she could ever remember. She shivered as a biting, winter wind whistled through the tiny holes in the weave of the basket.

Why would she abandon her mother? The thought came to her now as she faced a dark, unknown world ahead. She had been so sure, so confident in the bright sunlight of the Shean morning. When there was only possibility and no danger to be seen, she had been excited, but now there was fear, which was one of the emotions that she could not define. Being raised in Shea, she had never been allowed to feel it.

She wished that someone could help her. She wanted a sign or something to show her where to go and what to do. There was no map, no guiding star, nothing to lead her in a direction to anything. There was not even her mother to steer her onto the path with a smile and a kind word. Worst of all, she was not there to tell her mother that everything would be okay. She had left her in Shea where there was no hope for her. Hopelessness... it was another new feeling. She had heard her mother mention it, but could never feel it herself until now.

She pulled at the part of her mother that was in her

31

own soul, and reached out, searching. Searching for anything, any trace of her to let her know that she was not alone. She expanded her mind stretching it as far as she could, but nothing was returned. Her mother was gone, lost, as Angelik was without her. The elves had abandoned her, in the darkness and the cold. She knew no name for what she felt, but could not stop the emotion from turning itself into tears that began to slowly trace down her face. She pulled her blanket close around her, and cried like she never had. If light had allowed her to distinguish color in the void of darkness, then she would have seen the blankets were not just getting wet, but they were being stained with red...red blood that could only come from the tears of an angel's pain.

Sark, the king's castle

Victor sat alone, staring at the dying embers of the fire. He was seated in his red armchair. It was the only decoration in the room of gray stone besides the red carpet that had been woven by the artisans of the western lands across the seas. It had been a gift from his marriage to Celeste, and the continued unity of his people. All of it was for nothing, he thought to himself, sourly.

His gray hair slid long and smooth around his youthful face and down the back of his neck. His clothes were black, simple designs made from the soft, but tough fabric of the Kial fibers. He sat as he usually did. He was sideways in the chair with his right leg thrown over the right arm of the chair, and his left elbow resting on the left arm of the chair, where his cheek lay on his palm.

His thoughts were of his past tonight. Ghosts hovered all around him, never giving him a moment of peace. His wife seemed to be lingering in the very stones of the castle, as if she were still there, but out of reach. Every sound and spoken word seemed to sing of her essence, and remind him that he was alone. She was not there, and may not ever be again. She had been lost for too long, and the pain of separation stung at his soul, unceasing. Red tears trickled from his gray eyes, forming deep rivers into his pale skin as he gave in yet again to the deep pain of emptiness and loss burrowing ever deeper into his soul.

Some nights had not been too bad. Belle always tried her best to brighten the castle and bring cheer to all who had remained there, but even her smiles had seemed to be mocking him tonight, so Victor had locked himself in his chambers to drown himself in the hopelessness that he felt. Hollowness that had started to fill with the company of his close friends in the castle had been newly dug tonight. They had passed a girl in the street. She had been playing with her father on the walkway by the inn, and Victor had been reminded of all that he had lost.

The hunters had stolen his wife and unborn child. He had searched everywhere he knew to look. His angelic senses had deadened, and there was no trace of Celeste or his child anywhere in his kingdom. He wondered if there was a little girl somewhere that should be calling him father. He imagined how she might look. Victor had heard her heartbeat before. He remembered when Celeste had laid on the bed, and he had placed his head to her belly, listening to the beautiful little rhythm. He wondered if she was out there, and if she knew how much he wanted to know her.

While his past consumed his thoughts, he had emptied an entire bottle of Kial brew. He threw it into the fireplace, watching the fire suddenly blaze brighter while he ignored Belle's consistent knocks, Carmina's scribbled messages sliding under the door and even Slatkin's repeated requests that he join them outside. Victor did not wish to join them, for he was sure his mood would dampen whatever his friends were doing to entertain themselves.

There really was nothing to do but drain the Kial brew and then make his way to bed. He lay in the chilled room where quiet and shadows reminded him that his life had been emptied, void. It would be until his wife's return...if she ever did return.

Sark, northwestern forest

Angelik had cried until she had no more tears to shed. She sobbed dryly into the blankets. Exhaustion had come over her, draining all of her energy and she felt like sleeping. She fought it back, remembering that she had to find her father. She had to please her mother, reunite her family and erase all of her mother's scars. *The elves left me here for a reason.* She thought to herself. *My father must be close by.* The small angel sighed deeply, and then gathering her strength, she pulled back the cover of the basket, ready to face the challenges that lay before her in the darkness.

She was unprepared for the winter of Sark. It swirled around her, and she could hardly breathe as the wind assaulted her face, battering her skin with pellets of ice. Her golden curls were thrown about, slashing at her eyes and whipping her neck and face. She tried to open her eyes against the forces throwing themselves at her, but she could not. Blindly, she felt around her, pulling her blanket close around her. She stretched it over her head to shield her eyes. She squinted as she looked for any sign of shelter, but she could see nothing in the grayness of winter.

With her hope quickly fading, and her body shivering beyond control, she managed to pull herself upright, and ready herself to step over the edge of the basket and walk. Through deep stabbing pains with each of her shallow breaths, she managed to grip the side of the basket, and haul her leg over the edge.

Her small feet disappeared under the ankle deep snow. The cold stabbed deeper, aching into her very bones. She felt the pain, so hard and biting, enough so that she never felt the wetness of the snow seeping through her lightly slippered feet.

She pulled her right foot forward, bracing herself against the wind which blew from one direction, and then another with unerring force. *Well, this is the only way,* she thought to herself, *one foot at a time.*

When she was sure that she could do it, she stepped with the other foot, her determination building.

Sark, the king's castle

Victor awoke suddenly. He had been dreaming, but as he came to, the dream slipped away, leaving only a feeling of urgency. It was a nagging emotion, a call to action he couldn't place. He threw off the blankets, and dressed quickly. As he walked into his sitting room, he glanced out the window at the East tower. He was relieved to find the torches were still burning brightly. He would see to it that they remained that way until his wife's return...whenever that would be. He knew that despite his emotions of the previous night there would be hope tonight, for he knew Celeste was a dark angel, and dark angels cannot be killed. They simply exist, always.

When he was ready, he walked with his lengthy stride quickly down the long corridor, to the spiraling staircase leading to the kitchen. Belle sat by the hearth in her red sleeping gown and a black fur. She did not hear him enter, for she was only mortal and her ears were not attuned to the subtle movements of the angels she shared a home with. She sat reading her ancient cookbook. She looked up as Victor walked over to the table. She smiled and sat the book down, after marking her place. She then hastened to try and ready breakfast.

"You're up early!" she exclaimed. "I mean the light of day has barely left the sky, if we could have even seen it today. Winter's come in strong. It will not be one of our days for outdoor adventures." She reached for the pot heating over the hearth. With an exasperated sigh, she put her hands on her hips and turned to look at Victor. "It's not hot yet," she said. "You'll just have to wait for it to heat up."

"That's alright, Belle," he said. "I'm not ready for breakfast anyway. I need to go...somewhere." Victor was already slipping on his black coat lined with gray fur when Belle moved closer to protest his actions.

"Did you not hear me? The winter has come in. It will be bad this year. The winds will be washing the waves halfway up the cliffs. There will be no way to reach the town by now. There's already ice on the ground and by the end of the night, I suspect we'll be completely snowed inside." She looked frantic as her words came at him.

Victor smiled at her with his youthful face, as he slipped his hands into his gloves then pulled his hood over his gray hair. "I'll be fine, Belle, you forget who you are talking to. Don't worry. I'm only going for a walk." He opened the door then to the howling winds and swirling snows that were becoming grey and blurred with the fading light of day. "Besides," he added, "I have something to do."

Belle pulled the black fur wrap closer around her shoulders and watched as he disappeared into the swirling snow. She couldn't help but to send words of caution out the door to him. "Don't be going down to the beaches. They'll be flooded." Her voice became louder with each step he took. "...and stay away from the cliffs, they're too slippery! Oh, and Victor don't forget..."

Victor was almost to the gate before her shouts of concern faded behind him. He smiled at her comments, almost laughing, his face seeming more youthful than it had been in a while. When one was immortal there was little need to worry over such things. She was right though, about winter. He tried to remember what it was like to be mortal, to fear for your own safety, to have a need to worry over such things, but all his memories of childhood had been faded and worn until they seemed only a dream to him.

He found himself heading down the south side of the mountain, towards the wilderness of the Sarkian forests. Perhaps this sense of urgency could be shaken when he had walked enough to clear his mind. He was used to feelings of urgency when he hunted down souls of the unjust, but this feeling was different and it was sending his angelic senses into a state of frenzied confusion. The feeling pulled him forward, and his thoughts wandered until they settled on his wife. He smiled grimly. The youthful glow faded into the coldness of his thoughts. Even when he tried not to think of her, she would be there turning his emotions, pulling them along. First, there would be tormenting grief and then unrelenting hope...maybe tonight would be different. He hoped that it would be.

Sark, northwestern forest

Angelik could not tell the amount of time she had been struggling, numbly pressing on; one foot after the other. She continued to trudge through the deepening snow, pulling the elven blanket tightly around her. The tall, ancient trees provided shelter from the bitter wind as she walked. They seemed strong, stifling the wind, but the cold still found ways to get through their sweeping boughs. Snow was up to her knees now, and her journey was getting more difficult.

She knew that there was only one hope, and that would be to lie under a tree, and let the heat coming from it warm her. Using her arms, she pulled herself forward, towards the nearest tree. It was warm, with rough black bark as hard as stone. It spiraled above her farther than she could see and its twisted arms circled around her, protecting her from the violent winds. Angelik lay as close as she could to it, wrapping the blood soaked blanket around her. She knew failure now, and it made her want to cry, but she was too exhausted to go any further. The young angel knew not what was to become of her, but she knew lying here was her only chance. She didn't know exactly what it was that made her believe this. She just knew it from within her soul. Her thoughts turned to her mother as she slept under the tree, and the rapidly descending snow began to cover her in a white blanket as winter greedily claimed this child that had defied her.

Victor didn't realize how far he had walked, until he came to the sea cliffs. He walked to the edge, and peered over the side. For a mortal, it was no doubt one of death's traps. The ocean waves were shielded in a layer of thick fog and snow as the waves crashed against the cliffs. The storm surge was tremendous. The valleys would already be flooded. He smiled as he remembered the warnings Belle had thrown at him. She knew the ways of nature far better than any angel. She had made a lifelong study of how to harness its magic. It was this that never ceased to amuse Victor when he thought of her. She was always willing to explain to anyone how it was not magic, it was practicality, but they all still called it magic...his thoughts were cut off by a sound behind him. It was not part of nature's song, it was something he could not place...it was something he had heard once before, but could not remember. It was rhythmical and beautiful. He listened intently. It was a song...a heartbeat...the heartbeat of a child...his child.

His thoughts had been wandering, but now he came to his senses, sharply and suddenly. He turned to the sound. Something was happening that he did not understand. He heard his own daughter's heartbeat, and the panic in his soul made him feel that he had to get to her. She was near. He had to find her, and now it was clear to him why he had been awakened early and lured out here. His dark vision took away the blur of winter as each snowflake that fell seemed to slow and present itself to him in perfect clarity. The darkness of night was no hindrance, as it separated all shapes and pushed them into his line of sight.

The trees were suddenly thumping with their own pulses, full of life and fiery veins tracing throughout the kial bark, throbbing to restrain the heat locked inside of them.

He stepped cautiously forward through the snow. Surely, if she were here, then he would see her, but there was no one, so he walked away from the edge of the cliffs, and deeper into the forest. He now ran, trying to reach the sound before it stopped. He hoped that it was real, and that he was not falling into madness. Deeper into the tangled mess of trees he ran, snow was almost up to his waist in some drifts. He pushed it aside as he came closer, the noise becoming louder.

Then he saw her, under a kial tree. From under the snow was the sound of Angelik's beating heart. He knelt down and began pushing back snow, until her curls unraveled themselves, casting forth a golden radiance like sunlight he had forgotten. Then, the wind began to lash them in a burning dance of gold and ice.

He brushed away more snow until her face was revealed. Her skin was as white as the snow. The lines of separation were hard to see, but he knew it was her. Overwhelmed at the moment, Victor had to stop, hardly believing the reality of what was happening to him. He took off his coat and placed the child into it. He realized that the blanket was soaked with blood, and questions started to form in his mind. He caressed her face, and tried to awaken her. When he was certain that she was not going to wake, he wrapped the coat tightly around her and gathered her safely into his arms, hoping that this was no dream. He held her there a moment, absorbing his new reality. When his feelings allowed, he began the walk back to the castle. Through the stream of tears that started to fall, he smiled as he looked upon her face. This would definitely be a winter to remember.

VI

Alexandria

Sarkian Forest, south

Having traveled for weeks, Alexandria was exhausted. First, she had traveled to the borders of Chimrion, a warmer land to the south, and then to islands dotting the ocean all the way to Sark. Along the way, the forest roads turned to paths of frozen land. The vegetation changed from hardwood forests to snow covered evergreens. Following a long expanse of ice desert, she had finally come to Sark. There were thick, tangled trees growing in intertwining mazes high above her head. They were strange to behold, and it surprised her that vegetation could exist this far into the cold. She had never seen trees like these and wondered how they survived. She reached out to touch them. They felt warm and hard as stone, more like statues than trees. She was certain they were made of more than just wood. They seemed to be some combination of wood and rock, with the heat of fire burning inside of them.

Alexandria pressed on in the cold of Sark towards her destination. Her bright yellow hair stood out like a flag in the snow, whipping past three painted black scars that stretched vertically over her left eye, stretching from her forehead to her cheek. She peered out with vivid green eyes at the landscape around her. Gentle snow was falling now, but as she came closer to the village she could sense signs of heavier snow to come. She knew that it would be tough to continue. She and her unicorn, Vortex, had to reach the town before the blizzard came. The air had already become so cold that she shivered under her layers of clothes. Even the tiger pelt she wore was not enough to keep her warm.

There was already ice on the ground and the winds had been getting steadily stronger. It roared over the trees, and twisted its way through the branches, and into her eyes. Alexandria squinted as she pressed forward. Vortex was struggling, too. It had been a long journey for him as well, especially since he had become accustomed to the warmer weather of the southern land, Chimrion. She could sense the smells of a settlement some miles ahead, but it would be another night or so before they could reach it. They traveled in a haze of sameness and steady hoof beats on the ground, until suddenly, Alexandria's angelic senses started to pick up a soft, rustling sound that would have been inaudible to mortal ears. She sensed eyes upon them. Perhaps rogues lived around here, or perhaps it was one of the tribes inhabiting the wilderness. She gripped her staff firmly in her hand. She would be ready if circumstances called for action.

The trail that brought her out here became stronger as the weather worsened. She was sure she would be where her senses were leading her very soon. She would see to it that nothing stood between her and the duty that she had been called upon to perform. She was ready to silence the rushing sound of screaming that filled her head and the pains that became heavier and more acute as she came closer to her prey. Nothing, especially rogues, could keep her from her target. She urged Vortex forward, as she stared around cautiously with her yellow hair blowing across her painted face.

There was more rustling high above them, and the creaking of branches as the weight of bodies shifted in the trees. She could hear the slow, steady movement of several people above her. Then she sensed it before it happened... she stopped Vortex just as a man leapt down from the trees. He landed on his feet in front of her.

"Dismount the horse!" he demanded. "He belongs to the Scithronians now." The man wore a fur and his face was shielded by fabric covering all but his eyes.

Alexandria heard the command, but decided she must press on. So she ignored the man, maneuvered Vortex around him, and continued on her way.

There were now the sounds of more men, moving faster than the first, making their way out of the trees. She heard the slashing of whips, and one of the men yelled, "Give us your horse, or we'll take it from you!"

She dismounted, smiling as the first man came closer. He reached out for the animal in one moment, and in the next, he was lying on the ground with the point of Vortex's horn aimed at his throat. It was a very sharp point, and the unicorn snorted furiously and kicked up snow with its front hooves. Alexandria laughed loudly. The other men had stopped advancing.

She eyed the men cautiously, trying to think of the quickest way to take them out without killing them. Alexandria raised her staff in the air and with a voice that carried through the whole forest, yelled, "LUMVEREN SUMABILA!"

There was a musical sound, like the sound of faint bells ringing. Light radiated out from her hand, knocking the thieves to the ground and blowing the snow into new drifts. She listened to the sound of the spell as it dissipated. When the light faded, there was only the sound of wind and the silence of winter surrounding her. She mounted the unicorn again and turned to leave, kicking Vortex into a faster pace. She heard the men coming to and gaining their feet behind her.

"Wait!" she could hear them calling to her. "Come back!" one of them shouted. "Come back. I give you my word that we'll not harm you. If we would have known it was you, we would never have tried to rob you!"

Alexandria wanted to keep riding, but some part of her couldn't. These men had something she needed, she could sense it. What it was, she was unsure, but she knew it would be important. She made up her mind to stay. Turning back to the man running toward her, she stared at him, allowing her divine perception to seek out his intentions as he ran after her.

Her eyes no longer saw the ordinary, but she saw in strange pulsing shapes, and dancing colors. In a split second, she saw all that she needed. Green and yellow told her that he was honest, and full of a genuine hope. He was sincere, with no evil intent.

She waited for him to catch up. "What is it that you want?" She stared at him until the colors faded, and she beheld him through human eyes.

"I'm sorry if we... ah... surprised you, we mistook you for one of the hunters." The man pulled the cloth away from his face. "Clearly you're not one of them. Klarrisa warned us to look out for you. To be honest, I didn't believe her when she told me. We really would like you to come inside with us. We'll serve you a feast that has been waiting for you for some time."

"Do you know who I am?" she asked, staring down at him with her vivid, green eyes.

"You are Alexandria," he said, "one of our protectors. If it makes you feel any better, then you can consider the feast an apology for trying to steal your animal."

She dismounted and reached out to the man, pulling him closer to her by his collar. "How do you know me?" She whispered.

"If you are Alexandria, the sister of Celeste of Trealon, then you are royalty to us. Now, come inside, out of this awful weather so that we can explain."

Alexandria was taken aback at the sound of not only her name, but that of her sister Celeste, and her homeland, Trealon. It was a place that she had not seen for many hundreds of years. Whatever this man knew, Alexandria was curious to hear. She released his collar and nodded her head, ready to follow.

The man motioned for another one of his company to step forward. The second was blackened with what looked like soot. He held out his hand to the angel. "My name's Barrett!" he exclaimed, through the black cloth covering his face. "Can I take your... um..." he peered over at Vortex.

"My unicorn?" Alexandria finished for him.

"Yes, your unicorn," Barrett echoed.

"Well," responded Alexandria. "That depends on where you're taking him."

"To the west tunnels," he said. "That's where we keep our horses."

"Fine," said Alexandria as she handed over the worn leather reins. Vortex kicked for a moment, but then calmed down when Alexandria patted him. "I'll warn you now that he doesn't normally like people, so you better take care." She eyed him closely as he led the unicorn away.

She watched them until they disappeared into the trees of the forest, and then she turned back to the man in front of her. "I'm Khiel," he stated, bowing clumsily. He motioned for her to follow him into the denser, more tangled part of the forest, as he wrapped the cloth back over his face.

As they walked, snow began to fall rapidly in a twirling gust of wind. Alexandria followed Khiel without talking until he stopped at one tree that had a deep hollow at the base. The wind was blowing so loudly that Alexandria could just make out him yelling, "Here we are! Have a step down!" He clutched the ragged fur he wore tighter around him and motioned toward the tree.

Alexandria peered into the hollow and saw a hole with a ladder leading down. She turned back to Khiel, "You first!" she shouted.

He nodded and stepped under the shelter of the tree. She watched as he disappeared down the ladder. She followed him, and as she descended the ladder, an increasing heat wrapped around her. When she stepped off of the last rung, she spun around to see a small, but cozy hall, lit with candles and torches. The stone structure was built around the great roots of the strange trees.

Shabby, modest furniture had been placed around a long wooden table. Weapons and furs had been piled all around the room. Alexandria noticed tunnels leading to halls that she could not see. More thieves sat around the table talking, looking over maps and leather bound books.

"Welcome to the den of the Scithronians." Khiel smiled as he removed the cloth over his face, quickly shedding the fur. The angel noticed that one of his top front teeth was missing.

A woman's voice suddenly rang out from the other side of the room, "Khiel! What are you doing?"

Alexandria stepped back just in time to avoid the woman's dagger, which lodged itself into the black root of the kial behind the dark angel's head. As the woman ran towards them, Alexandria readied her staff, but there was no need to use it. Khiel stepped between them, holding the angry one back.

"Now wait, Valassa. Just wait," he demanded. Valassa furrowed her brow, peering through her wild black hair with narrowed eyes. "You wouldn't want to be harming one of our protectors, now would you?" he asked with a touch of warning in his voice. Khiel shot her an authoritative glance. Her expression changed quickly as she backed away, still keeping her eyes on Alexandria.

Khiel turned to look at Alexandria, and chuckling with nervousness, he said, "There is no trust here, amongst us thieves." He smiled a sideways grin. He motioned for the angel to follow them and added, "I apologize for my friend's hostility. She's a wild one, she is."

"So, where's the feast?" asked Alexandria, looking around, seeing nothing resembling food.

"Well," said Khiel. "We haven't actually cooked it yet, but now that you're here, it won't take us long to put something together. We've saved some of our best foods, hoping that we might find one of our protectors. Now we can feast to the hope that this kingdom will be restored one day."

"What do you mean by protectors, and why would you think that I should have anything to do with restoring a kingdom?" Alexandria asked, peering down at the man beside her.

"Well," said Khiel, "It's no secret what you are. We've met your kind before. It's in your nature to protect us.

45

You can't avoid it…and the Scithronians are grateful for that."
Alexandria did not reply. She looked into his soul,
understanding the love and adoration he had for the dark
angels he called protectors. Dark angels like herself and her
sister. She was surprised by this sentiment. Most races that
came upon dark angels misunderstood their true natures,
regarding them as monsters to be feared. Alexandria smiled at
the thief.

"Well, let's go see Klarissa; she will no doubt want a
meeting with you right away. She is expecting you already.
Come with me, and I'll take you to her." He motioned for her
to follow him. As they crossed the hall, Alexandria noticed
many curious and wary eyes observing her, but as soon as she
met their gaze, the thieves turned their stares elsewhere. She
heard Khiel chuckle once or twice as he shook his head.
Many of the thieves were the ones she had encountered earlier,
and they were not ready to cross her again. He led her down a
warm, dark tunnel. They stopped outside of a wooden door
and he said, "Klarissa is inside. She'll see you now and I'll
see what I can do about that feast that I promised you earlier."
Khiel bowed his head politely and then walked back the way
that they had come.

Alexandria opened the door and stepped inside the
room. A woman was seated on a modest bed that looked like
it had been fashioned from the wood of the tall black trees.
Warm gray and brown furs were spread upon it. The woman
was dressed in a simple outfit consisting of traveling breeches,
a tunic and riding boots, all in black. Her hair was fiery red
and cut off right above her neck. She appeared not to notice
Alexandria as she entered the room. Her eyes were closed, but
the angel continued to move towards her. When Alexandria
was standing awkwardly close, the woman opened her eyes.
They were white for a moment, and then returned to their
usual blue. She smiled a welcoming smile and she spoke in a
soft, but powerful voice.

"Please, have a seat." She motioned to a chair by the

bed. Alexandria shed the tiger pelt, revealing the clothing of a Chimrion knight beneath it.

"I apologize for those who tried to steal Vortex," Klarissa smiled up at the angel. "I don't think they believed me when I told them to watch out for you. We've been waiting for you for a long time, and many of my peers have lost faith in my prophecies."

"Why were you looking for me?" Alexandria asked. "Of what importance am I to you?"

"Well, we have been looking for you, because I have foreseen your coming to Sark for some weeks now. Your sister was our queen and so much more. Most of us owe her our lives. She was like a mother to many of us."

The two women were silent as Alexandria took-in what she was hearing. "So, where is she now?"

"We do not know. She is lost."

Alexandria's forehead wrinkled. "What do you mean by that? Lost?"

"I mean exactly what I said. She is somewhere that she cannot be found. She is lost. Not even the other dark angels know how to find her."

"The other dark angels?" Alexandria asked.

"Yes," she said. "Our king and one of his servants are also dark angels."

There was silence as Alexandria pondered the news she was taking in.

"Something big is about to happen," the seer continued. "My heart tells me that it is both good and bad. We have been looking for your coming. Another angel arrives tonight as well, an angel of light. She is going to the king's castle, and setting the events of change in order. Our kingdom has been crumbling these past seven years that love has left us, and now we have a chance for restoration, a chance to overthrow the hunters who have ruled us in terror."

A sneer of anger crossed the angel's lips. "I just so happen to be here to deal with a hunter."

Klarissa let out a relieved sigh. "Good. They have been doing terrible things to the tavern girls. We've found some of them..." Her thoughts trailed off as she remembered the gruesome scenes that the thieves had come across while out in the woods. Alexandria did not need to ask what the seer's thoughts were remembering. She already knew.

"We need you," Klarissa said.

Later that evening

Alexandria sat at a table in one of the larger tunnels. The feast was spread out before her, and the young thieves were crowded either at the long table or on the floor around it. Klarissa blessed the food and then looked at Alexandria as they started eating. "The elves helped us put this together. They help us when it is too dangerous to go out into the woods. We owe them a lot as well."

Alexandria enjoyed herself, even though she was slightly annoyed at her delay. She couldn't deny that she needed the rest and the food, but she could not offend these people who needed her. So she ate and learned all that she could of their culture. They were only thieves because they had to be. The hunters hated them. They had been loyal to the dark angels when the hunters had overthrown their rule.

They had only been children at the time, but they escaped the raid on the castle. The same night that they had been attacked, a rainstorm flooded the lands, and they were saved by the elves. Since then, the elves had been helping them. They had been tunneling under ground, afraid to go to the surface. The hunters kill any that they find.

When they had eaten and talked, Alexandria leaned back in her chair. "I can't stay here, Klarissa, you know that. I have someone to find and the sooner I find him, the better."

"I understand," the seer said, "but I thank you for honoring us tonight. You have given us all hope. It means a lot to us."

"I do what I can," the angel said.

"When you've dealt with the hunter, you will no doubt want to meet your sister's husband. I do ask that you let us go with you. Please," she begged, "Khiel and Valassa would be honored to travel with you to the castle. They might prove useful to you."

"I..." Alexandria started to protest, but couldn't when she realized the disappointment she would cause if she didn't let them go. "I would like that," she said.

Klarissa nodded. "Good, they will be ready whenever you are."

VII

Celeste's Grief

Shea, Kialo's castle

The psychics stared at the man that the other strange race had called their king. He was a short man, with wrinkled skin that was a dark, reddish brown color, and his eyes were a dark green. He had long, white hair, and he was adorned with what appeared to be deer antlers and leaves for a crown. He wore a long cloak of green, and he held a wooden staff in his hand with symbolic carvings cut deeply into the wood. He had a thick beard and mustache that were the same color as his hair. He smiled as they walked in, and stood with open arms to welcome them into his hall.

"Welcome, strangers. I am Kialo, the Great; king of Shea, master of earth elements. Tell me now why you have come to my land."

There was silence until David moved forward. "We come from a land named Tahln. We are selbdes. There was a man from our homeland called Shekley. He destroyed all of our forests, all of our creatures and he used all of our water. He has left us with nothing but a desert wasteland as a home. Worst of all, he has corrupted the people who live there, and forced them into his slavery, performing horrendous experiments to try and make them into one of his Mahldrusecs. He is being controlled by the Shadow, a thing of the void. He left Tahln, because he needed more resources for his purpose. We followed him to try and stop him when we discovered that he had a way of reaching other worlds. He wishes to destroy all things, and we believe that he is here to destroy your world. We followed him, and then a great power pulled us from Tahln and put us to sleep. When we awoke, we were here."

There was a deep silence as Kialo looked at them.

They stared back, anticipating what he would say. No one else in the room was speaking. Kialo mulled things over in his mind, and then he spoke to the team.

"There is no shadow in this land, for no such evil would be allowed, unless we gods allowed it, and we do not! However, you are here now, and it is not up to me to judge whether or not you lie. That is up to yourselves, for if you bring evil here, it will destroy you, and not me." Kialo surveyed the expressions on their faces, and then smiled warmly, as he saw their concern.

"Now, I wish to hear this tale in whole later, for it seems you have skipped over many roots and branches in the telling of it. First, though, let my elves escort you to some rooms, where you may bathe, and get new clothes. Then we will have an honorary feast for you tonight. You will then be introduced to the other gods of Shea, and perhaps they will also like to hear your tale brought together thoroughly."

"Do you have anything to add at the moment?" Kialo looked at his son, Amicus, who stood beside him with long golden hair. He shook his head.

"Very well then," he turned back to the strangers. "Would you kindly allow my elves to walk with you to your new rooms?" They nodded, and then fell in line with the tall graceful creatures that walked beside them.

When they left, Kialo turned to his son, the messenger of the gods. "My son, I need you to get your sister and round up the elven nobles. Tell them there are strangers in the land, and that I'm holding a feast to honor them tonight. I need their input, for it seems that any decision or aid to these creatures will be one that will require the consent of us all."

"Yes, father." Amicus replied, covering his head with his simple, brown hood, he strode quickly through the entrance hall and out the door.

Shea, mushroom gardens

The elves had all gathered in the mushroom gardens.

The water elves had come up the rivers and streams all the way from the ocean, and the sky elves had descended on their winged horses. The plains elves had come a great distance on their antlered steeds, and the earth elves stood waiting for the last of them to arrive, Arista of the moon elves. She had come quickly, but on foot, taking her longer, but now she came walking quickly into the gathering.

"Fausti, Arista, where is Arik, your brother?" Malah asked, as the young, black haired elf took her place in the circle.

"I am sorry, but he could not be here. He is on an urgent errand for Kristiniva, and he will not be back until the night. I stand here for both of us."

"Very well," Mondlif began. "We are all here then. Now listen to our tale. We sat taking in the beauty of the summer forest, when Sigh Reen, a water faerie of the summer stream, came to us. She told us that a creature had been crying in her stream that was not of this land. She said that there were many of them, and they were stealing fruit from the trees of the summer forest.

We saw the creatures, and we know not from where they came. We have never seen the likes of them. We don't know the land that they speak of, but they call it Tahln. We have never heard of this land. Now speak the truth, those who keep our borders, and say now if you have ever heard of this land or these people, for they have been sent to our King Kialo by this most sensible gnome of the mushroom forest." He motioned toward Noggle, who had been sitting quietly on a stump, smoking his pipe. "We, as the protectors of Shea's borders, must always be aware of who we let in and out of the borders. Our king and queen will no doubt want to know how they were allowed into the lands, but my kindred have never seen them. Speak now the truth so that we may stand together on whatever is decided."

There was silence all around, except the sounds of the forest. There was no reply to his words.

"Can no one explain how we, the guardians of the entrances to this land, missed an entire group making their way into our world? How did we miss them, and how do we explain our failure to our rulers?"

"We cannot," the voice of that was the latecomer, Arista. "We would have known if they would have come by our borders. There is no explanation. Our rulers will have to question the strangers themselves. I trust all of you, and I don't think we are at fault. I think a higher power sent them here.

The others agreed in their rightful turns. No one seemed to have any idea how they missed such a large group coming through their borders, but somehow, some way beyond their understanding, it had happened. Arista's explanation was the only possible one.

Shea, castle of Kristiniva

Stillness had fallen over the castle of the sky. Celeste had become quiet and distant from the goddess. She dared not speak of the feelings that coursed their way through her veins. It was good for Celeste that Kristiniva was at her husband's castle at the moment. He was the earth god of Shea, and although Celeste had never visited him, she believed him to be good spirited. No doubt he had to be kinder than his wife. She was colder to Celeste than all the winds of Sark.

Celeste paced the castle, wondering what had become of her daughter, and regretting now that she had sent her away. Her hope was starting to fade and she wasn't sure about the decision she had made. She feared so much for her daughter. She tried to reach out to her daughter's soul, but she could not find her anywhere. One of the only consoling thoughts that raced through her mind was the fact that no one was here to take away her emotions. There was no one standing over her shoulder, forbidding her from feeling the guilt that swelled inside her heart. What kind of a ruler would outlaw bad emotions? She understood that it was a land of innocence and that the leaders had done so to protect their subjects, but she felt there had to be a better way of holding onto their innocence.

Bitterness drummed inside her heart and twisted its way through her veins to her stomach, where she felt the grief of having no child as she felt the knotting of anxiety there. She missed her so much! She tossed her thoughts back and forth, trying to wonder whether or not Victor and Angelik would recognize one another.

The castle had fallen silent, except for the sound of wind filling the halls. She wondered where everyone else was. Normally, quirials, the sky dwellers, attendants to the queen, would be bustling through the castle, cleaning, weaving, singing and going about the business of keeping the castle in repair.

She walked over to one of the towering windows and peered out of the paned glass. She watched as the lands below faded away, as the castle moved slowly over them with a breeze. She pushed on the glass, and the window opened with ease. The cool wind ruffled her long black curls as it came through the window. She felt tears welling in her eyes, but she blinked them away.

Down below, she heard a small click and a sturdy gripping of the door handle. She knew then that Kristiniva had returned. It was a familiar sound, and it was followed by a series of sounds that she knew would come. The hinges creaked on the great golden doors, and a whistling filled the passageways, where the wind fluttered in. Light footsteps ensued. It always sounded as if the wind made the queen weightless. The brush of Kristiniva's robes rolled up the steps, and Celeste became aware of her scent. The goddess had a sweet, humid smell, today, like the mist after a summer rain. The footsteps became louder, and Celeste turned around just as the goddess appeared at the door.

"Are you feeling any better?" she asked with a bright smile illuminating her face. The angel only nodded her head.

She felt that if she were to make a sound, the tears that she had been holding in would come bursting out of her in a rapid stream.

The goddess sighed. A small burst of air came with it through the castle. "You will feel better in time. All things eventually turn out to be for the best in this land. You will soon see." Celeste felt betrayal in the bright smile aimed at her. How could this woman speak to her of her loss, when she had never felt anything like it?

The goddess came over and sat beside her. "My husband is holding a great feast tonight. There are guests that we must entertain. We must welcome them, and learn about them."

"This will be a night for you to enjoy. I am taking you to the feast as a guest of mine. Now for a while, I will be in a council with the other gods, and I hope that you will use that time to see all that Shea has to offer you. I hope that you will get to know the creatures that call this their home, and enjoy yourself. When I come out of the council, the feast will commence, and I will introduce you to my husband and my children. I will be delighted to share such a lovely evening with you. There will be music and dancing, and of course the finest performances that Shea has to offer. You have told me that you used to be a dancer. Wouldn't you like to come with me? Or do you prefer sulking around the castle, and disobeying my laws?"

"I will come with you," she paused in thought. "Tell me about these guests, and why your husband has decided to entertain them." She looked at the goddess with large, anxious eyes.

"I can't tell you about them, we gods do not even know about them. All I know is that they are not from Shea, so you wouldn't have heard of them...and they are not from Sark, either, so get that thought out of your mind." She fixed her eyes on Celeste's, but Celeste did not turn away.

"I only wonder..." Celeste said, covering up her hope

that they could point the way out. "I wasn't sure why Kialo felt the need to hold a feast in their honor."

"Well, they are called Selbdes. They look similar to humans, but they have abilities that far outweigh that of any human. Their minds hold unimaginable abilities. I am eager myself to know what it is that they plan to do here in Shea. I'm assuming that my husband has already figured that out, and it is cause for such a wonderful celebration. Now let us hurry, we must prepare for the feast. The quirials have been working very hard to create beautiful gowns for us to wear."

The dark angel stood in the hall of looking glasses. The sunset had lit the clear roof with a pink and orange glow. The light footsteps of the queen could be heard approaching.

She appeared, and around her stood some of the tall blue skinned elves, with flowing strands of white hair, the quirials.

"I've had some dresses woven for you!" exclaimed the queen as she walked across the room. The quirials had garments draped all over their arms as they followed the queen into the room.

"These are regal gowns. I have had them specially made for this occasion. The quirials have worked very hard to make some of their finest pieces just for you." Kristiniva's voice raced to Celeste's ear like a sturdy wind.

Celeste walked over to examine the gowns that the quirials had made for her. They were all made of shimmering, flowing fabrics. They all felt lightweight and delicate. She spotted one that was silver, and thought it too beautiful for one such as her to wear, so she went with the simplest of them all. It was a plain, white dress.

She stepped behind a small divide, and pulled off her old red robes. She managed to avoid the mirror's eye as she put on the new, lighter weight dress. It slipped down her body like a smooth rain. She faced the mirror, but tried not to look at herself. She only looked at the dress. The neckline was low, and draped across her chest; it was embroidered with beautiful designs and patterns made from small slivers of jewels, and glittering bits of crystals. When she moved, the shapes seemed to dance, and the thought came to her again of how the clean purity of the dress clashed with her own horrid appearance. It made the redness of her burnt skin stand out. She made the mistake of seeing her face for only a moment. It was horribly disfigured and scarred. She looked quickly away, and stepped out of the divide to reveal her self to the others.

"What about this one?" she asked, turning to Kristiniva and the quirials.

"Wonderful!" exclaimed Kristiniva, as the quirials attended her. She was putting on a ball gown with yards and yards of fabric. Hers had long, tight fitting sleeves, and a high collar, both of which were decorated with shining white feathers, and the same designs that decorated the neck of Celeste's dress ran all up and down the queen's dress. Feathers also decorated the bottom of the gown, and she had on white boots decorated with the glistening slivers of jewels. Her hair had been placed on top of her head in a bouquet of feathers, and a white jeweled crown.

"It's perfect, but there is something else." One of the quirials brought a coat to Celeste. She put it on. It matched her own dress, but there were feathers lining the sleeve around her wrist, and also lining the bottom and the neckline. The quirial smiled brightly at her and then motioned for two more to come help. When they were finished with her, her hair had been styled, and there was a halo of feathers crowning her head, and her black curls cascaded down her neck, but not her back as usual. It was a funny feeling for Celeste. She felt absurd. She looked over at Kristiniva, who beamed with satisfaction, and then the goddess motioned for them to leave.

"My carriage is ready, isn't it?" she asked the quirials attending her.

"Of course, my queen!" one of them exclaimed. "It is

ready and waiting, and will be drawn by your two finest Pegasi."

"Well, then, all is well, and we seem to be ready. Come along, Celeste. Remember, tonight you are my friend and not my servant."

Celeste followed, already wishing that the night would be over soon.

VIII

The Way of Vengeance

Sark, northern wilderness

Alexandria climbed up the snowy slopes of the mountain. She held onto the worn brown leather reins of Vortex, who carried Khiel and Valassa on his back. The snow didn't seem to bother them, but the cold was making them shiver beneath their furs. Alexandria shivered too, but it was not as much from the cold as what she was about to face. She pulled her tiger pelt around her, as she listened for the sound of the victim. There was someone this way who needed to be avenged, and she believed that the woman had already been dead for some time. There was a baby, too. The mother had been calling to her for weeks now, as she headed here from Chimrion. There was something that had happened here, but before she could get vengeance for these dead souls, she had to know why. She would have to relive this so that she could gain the power that it would take to defeat her adversary.

A dizzying weakness took over her. She was close now to the cottage where the woman had been murdered. She could feel her skin crawling at the spirits' wailing cries. She felt that her feet could not carry her any further. There was a heavy feeling, as if boulders had been strapped to her shoulders with iron chains. She glanced back at the thieves. Khiel was looking around, as if he thought he was being watched. Valassa was hunched down in her furs, looking around from the corners of her dark brown eyes, as if she expected an ambush at any moment. No doubt, this deed was so bad that even the mortals could sense the energies of the spirits keening as they came closer to the place where the woman had died.

"So you feel it too?" Alexandria asked turning to look at the two atop the unicorn, her yellow hair blowing around the edges of her face, under the orange and black tiger pelt. Her eyes shone bright and green like a cat's.

"Feel what?" Valassa asked, trying to hide her fear, even from herself.

Khiel just nodded his head. "You go on ahead, angel, Valassa and I will stay with the unicorn. I'll not lie to you. This business that you have on this mountain top makes me feel like I've got some sorta' storm fairies dancin' in my head." He reached into his coat, and pulled out a Kial twig, and his tinder box. He struck a light to the twig, and put it to his mouth. It smoked with a pleasant aroma. He held it out to Valassa. "Here," he said. "This will keep that funny feeling out of your head."

"What are you so scared of, Khiel?" Valassa tried to sound as if she were not afraid. Alexandria was both annoyed by this and at the same time she couldn't help but to admire the young girl's bravery. Khiel put the twig back into his mouth.

"No need for it to go to waste," he mumbled.

"I think, Valassa, that you better take comfort in whatever you can. It is cold out here, and I'm afraid that I will be a while, but not too long, I hope." Alexandria encouraged.

"Well, is there anything that we can help you with?" Valassa asked. "I like feeling useful." She watched for Alexandria's action, eager to go along. Alexandria managed a small smile. She didn't understand why Valassa would want to come, but the thought amused her. She could do nothing about it, though. It was Alexandria's work, and it was something that she had to do alone, even if she wanted Valassa to come.

"Actually, I was going to ask you to take care of Vortex for me." Vortex snorted at this comment, telling the angel that he knew how to take care of himself. "I know that Vortex will do the same for you two." She turned to leave. "Wait for me here!" she shouted behind her. I'll try not to be long. If I'm not back by morning, then go on to the town without me. I'll catch up later." Her voice sounded weaker as she got further away.

The two on the unicorn sat in the silence, lost in their own thoughts in the winter chill of the Sarkian Mountains, as they watched Alexandria vanish into the snow and the tangled mess of the Kial Thierens. Valassa dismounted and started walking.

"Hey!" yelled Khiel. "Where are you going?"

She turned defiantly to him. "I am going to follow her and be useful!"

"Y'know, you could be damning your soul for doing such a thing. Don't forget that she is an angel, and she is working. I think that you are making a mistake. She will only get angry at you. You best do what she says!"

"Have you forgotten who we are, Khiel? We are thieves! If I haven't already damned my soul, then I'm surprised, but you know, I think that she needs my help. Besides, what will she really do to me? She is a protector. If anything, she will scold me and send me back to you, and have you watch over me like you're my father." She turned to leave, not really caring what Khiel had to say about it.

"But Valassa..." Khiel waved her away with his hand. "Aaah, never mind. It's not like you listen any way. You never have."

Alexandria struggled through thigh deep snow, feeling the psychic weight strengthen as the woman's wailing became louder, and the heaviness pulled her further down. She no longer saw in the sense that a human saw, but instead, she saw in perfect clarity the place of souls. The woman's soul was there, in the place between worlds, hanging on until peace came. It was here that the landscape became red. It appeared to Alexandria as if the trees themselves were bleeding. It wasn't the throbbing fullness of life that the Kial Thierens normally pulsated with, but it was the putrid color of hate, of pure evil.

The trees were speaking to her, telling her that the crime committed here had been beyond their belief. The land itself was under a curse, and the only way to end it would be to seek vengeance. Alexandria could hear the woman's wailing so loudly that it shot pains through her temples. The snow here was blackened, and the soul's red pain covered it, slithering through it like lava. She spoke to the woman.

"I am vengeance. I have heard your wailing. I have come to collect your memories, your power. I have come to put you at peace. Speak now, Elise, and give me your power, and that of your wailing child." Her voice became louder, stronger, more determined as she spoke, trying to coax the spirit into showing herself.

Suddenly the wailing stopped, and Alexandria saw an apparition. She saw the pregnant woman coming to her from behind the Kial trees. She knew that it was as close to her own likeness as the spirit could make itself, but she remained almost transparent, wavering and silvery white, all but the swollen red tint to her belly, and the burning redness around her neck. The woman reached her hand out to the angel, and Alexandria could feel her pulling her towards a cottage. This had been her home. Alexandria opened the door, and then she was reliving the woman's death; all the emotions, all of the trauma, and all of the physical pain. She was soon inside the memory of Elise's death.

He was angrier than usual. She could tell from his expression.

"Please, don't be mad!" She had spoken the words, as a desperate plea before beginning the news, but he was apparently angered at the very thought of bad news. He grabbed her by the jaw with one hand, and pulled her close to his face. She was so close that she could feel his hot, stinking breath, see the pieces of old meat still clinging to the edge of his teeth and gums. She could feel the prickles from the hair on his beard. He seemed to love threatening her with his presence. It was what he usually did. His eyes were still wild from his day out on the hunt.

"What have you done this time?" He growled the words to her and shoved her away. She stumbled into a chair, but quickly straightened herself up.

"I...just...I wanted to tell you...to let you know..." she fumbled with her words. She felt like running away. He wouldn't understand...she could feel her face turning red from the pressure, the fear of what she was about to say.

"Spit it out, woman!" he yelled.

"I'm going to have our baby, and I'm...going to go find someone to help me," as she spoke the words, tears welled in her eyes. Something warned her that she should get away. She did not like that expression in his eyes. She should probably leave. Yes...she should leave now. He was more than angry. She could tell.

She turned and walked into the bedroom, clutching the kitchen knife hidden in the folds of her skirt. She didn't know if she would really need it, but she had to protect her child. She wanted to go faster, but it seemed that she could not go as fast as she wanted. She quickly shut the door and began to gather her things. She should have done this already, but now she knew that she did not have the time. She had already wounded him deeply, igniting his insanity. She knew it would happen one day, but hoped that it would not be today.

He came busting through the door, yelling, "What kind of help do you need that I can't give to you?" She should have put a lock on the door.

"I don't think you understand how much help I'm going to need! Women need help, sometimes. I don't even know how to hold a baby right. I don't know what to do. I need to go back to my mother, and just talk to her." She released the knife. Maybe he would listen to reason.

"NO!" he shouted. Then he added coldly, reaching out to grab her arm, "You're not leaving me here, and if you do, then you will be sorry. I'll make sure of it."

"I have to!" she exclaimed, and then she threw some more of her belongings into the sack she had readied by the bed.

There was a tense silence, and then he spoke, his voice was so cold she shivered at the sound of it.

"You know, my traps are empty. A few hours hanging in there and you'll beg to be back in here with me."

Her hands went over her face and new terror shot into her. How could he think of such a thing? It had to be an exaggeration. She had seen him do it to some of the tavern wenches, but surely, he wouldn't do it to her. She was his wife.

"You will do no such thing. Not to me and not to my baby!"

"So you don't think I'll do it?" he asked, walking closer to her.

"You won't." She challenged him with a dark look, reaching secretly for her knife.

"Never tell me what to do!"

Then suddenly it was as if she was just yelling words. Her anger and her fear were overpowering her. She was not thinking clearly.

"You will not harm this child, and you will not harm me while I carry this child, or so help me, I will kill you!" She thought she meant every word of what she said, until she felt the pain of his fist punching into her stomach. It was as if she could feel the child within her screaming, too. The punch left her doubled over on the floor. She heard her own voice trying to catch a breath and scream all at once.

"You?" he asked, "Kill me? Just how do you plan to do that? You can't even stand up to a punch. Kill me! Heh!" He sounded as if he were laughing at a joke, but there was nothing funny to Elise. She could feel the child's pain, and her own. She wanted to believe that everything was all right, but she knew that it was not. She knew that if she were to escape, then now was the time. Standing was hard. Each small movement hurt more, but she did manage to reach out, and pull him down to the floor, and drive the knife into him, but only enough to wound him slightly. It was either flee or die. It was her only chance to make it to her feet. She struggled forward. She dragged her feet, but managed to make it through the cabin, to the front door. She felt the cold and snow whipping past her face. She was going to make it.

Then there was a blinding pain in the back of her head, as she was hit with one of the chairs from the table. She pitched forward, arms and legs sprawled out into the snow. The snow, thank Saigolai, the snow was there. She hoped that it was enough to protect the baby from the impact. Then there were arms picking her up and throwing her. She landed on her back this time. Then she heard his voice, angrier than she ever had before.

"Don't ever threaten me again, harlot!" She felt his kick hit her hard in her womb. She was trying to get up, now crying uncontrollably. She was shaking, trying to get up onto her feet, but she could not.

"Is your mother going to help you now?" She heard his words, and panic seized her body. She could tell from his tone of voice that whatever was to happen next, she would not be able to escape. She was right. She felt herself struggling, she felt a rope wrap around her neck, and she felt the slow strangling burn as she was pulled through the snow. Trees passed overhead, and then she was being pulled upward. The rope's burn was unbearable, and her blood was racing.

The burn from the rope seemed to be inside of her, but there was nothing she could do. She couldn't breathe any longer, and the blind panic of this thought seemed to fuel the burning in her throat. He had strung her and her baby up as bait in one of his traps, and the life was slowly burning its way out of her. She was choking, and all she could do was absorb the pain and flail around as she tried to accept what was happening to her. The burning was in her breathing, filling her with fire from within. She stared down into the ground.

He would dig a whole below her and cover it with kial twigs, and then an animal would rip her apart, or be another of his victims, as it fell into the hole. The fear was there, but she could do nothing but accept it. The horror, the humiliation, the anger and the failure all seemed to wrap itself around her vision as it became blurred. She swung from side to side, with the fading images of her husband Markus, blood oozing from the knife wound on his chest, laughing at her.

Alexandria suddenly came to herself. She fell to the ground coughing and choking. She had just relived the death of Elise, and it had taken her to the trees where her body still swayed back and forth in the wind. It was frozen, so it was well preserved. The ghost that she had seen earlier was standing in front of her pointing up at the body.

"Yes," said Alexandria, through her coughs and wheezing. She clutched her throat and her stomach. Her ribs and lungs felt like they were being stretched until they would explode. "I will give you a funeral...Elise, and then...and then Saigolai will...will give me the power," she stopped to breathe, "to exact vengeance on Markus for you...and then...your soul will be at...peace!" The words did not sound strong when she said them. Her throat still ached from the burning of the rope.

When she had spoken the words, she laid in the snow, trying to rid herself of the pain. She concentrated, taking it in, understanding that this is what Elise had felt. Alexandria concentrated, until she turned the pain into energy. Power. She would use this against Markus. She would use this for Elise's revenge. When she felt no more pain, but power, she pulled herself up from the snow, and turned to go towards the cabin. She would see to it that Elise would have a proper funeral and not be left to the wolves.

The spirit stood motionless while she watched the angel pull out an axe, and head to the cabin. Alexandria intended to gather wood and make a funeral pyre to burn the body.

The angel opened the door to the cabin, and to her surprise, she saw Valassa standing by the table. Alexandria wasn't happy to see her here, when she was trying to work.

"What are you doing here?" she asked Valassa. Her voice sounded deep and strained.

"I'm here to help you!"

"I never said that I needed your help." Alexandria said, as she flipped the table on its side, and started breaking the legs off.

"What are you doing?" Valassa asked.

"I'm working." Alexandria returned very shortly.

She started to turn the girl away, but she couldn't. Something in her angelic instincts told her that the girl needed to help. "I am going to make a funeral pyre for the woman that is hanging in one of those trees out back. If you want to help me, then you can find dry wood. I am going to burn this cottage down, and then I am going to go find the hunter named Markus, and I am going to kill him. You can't help me with that part, so enjoy this while you can." She glanced at her while she headed for the door. Valassa's face was amusing to the angel. She could see the excitement tracing its way around the muscles in her face.

Valassa followed the angel, as she headed to the Kial tree. "Tell me Valassa, is there fire inside of these trees?" she asked.

"Yes," Valassa responded, "but to get it out without a light, you will have to dig deep into its roots."

Alexandria took a moment to think. She was not about to risk these two freezing in the cold, while she went about her business. "I know how you can be of the most help, Valassa. Go back to Khiel, and tell him that we need his tinder box, then help me gather the wood for the funeral pyre. I'm going to use the tinder box to catch the wood on fire and save as much of the tree as I can." Valassa did not waste any time trudging her way back to the unicorn where Khiel was.

By the time she came back, the funeral pyre was already built. Alexandria had gotten all of the wooden furniture from inside the house, and broken it apart, and then placed it unceremoniously together. She had already cut Elise down, and had laid her atop the wood. She was saying a prayer for this woman, and giving her a promise of vengeance. Valassa came up, followed by Khiel on Vortex.

"You mean that you've already done all that by yourself?" Valassa asked, astonished. "You must have worked really hard!"

Khiel reached his hand over her mouth. "Shhh..." He hushed her until the prayer was done, and then Alexandria turned around to face them.

"Yes, I have been working very hard; now give me the tinder box, so that I can light the fire."

Khiel dismounted the unicorn and walked over to the angel. When she had gotten the light struck, she looked back at the two thieves. "You may stay if you wish. A proper funeral would have enough mourners to matter. I believe that Elise would appreciate that even us three strangers care enough about her to take a moment to consider her life, and mourn her death." The angel's gaze turned to the flames. "She was abused by her husband, forgotten by her family, and she lived a life that was full of fear, and next to slavery, being the wife of Markus. She was not a wife by her choosing, but rather by force. He killed her when she became pregnant with his child." The Scithronians could feel the anger in Alexandria's face, as if she herself had lived the life of this woman, and in a way she had.

"Markus has done many such acts as this, but it is now time for vengeance to pay him a visit. Elise will be at peace now, and her soul will thaw on the fire, and when the warmth reaches it, she will take flight, and then Saigolai will see that she finds her peace."

They all looked on the fire, as the flames rose higher

into the winter sky of Sark. The winds tossed the flames wildly about, and the snow began to melt. Luckily, Alexandria was using her spells to keep the winds under control, so that the fire did not become too wild. She wanted it to be a peaceful fire, one that would bring warmth to the land, and it did. She could feel Elise's soul as it warmed with the feeling of release from her bondage, and she could feel the Earth as it felt the curse being lifted. With her angelic eyes, Alexandria saw the snow turn from red back to white, and the trees stopped throbbing with the fear of the curse; once again thumping with the fires of life.

IX

The Homecoming

Sark, castle of the king

Slatkin, Victor's servant, awoke feeling that as he slept, something had changed. There was a difference in the air, but he could not place what it was. This disturbed him, for if an angel of his rank could not place it, then its power must be phenomenal. He got out of bed cautiously, intently reading the signs all around him. He opened the shutters on his window, and felt the cold ice and snow as it fell on his slightly wrinkled face, and melted into his grey hair. Winter had come to Sark. The blizzard was a bad one, but that was not unusual for Sark...no there was something else...he felt for the vibrations of his friends, as he closed the shutters. Belle was in the kitchen...she was a little worried, but otherwise content, this was usual for her. Carmina was praying in her circle, her usual evening routine. Victor was...Victor's feelings were complete chaos. The feeling then became known to Slatkin. He did not know what this meant, but he was sure that whatever it was that Victor needed, it would require the help of his friends.

Slatkin dressed quickly, and headed down the three stone staircases to warn Belle. It was during his descent down the last staircase that Victor's chaos subsided, and Slatkin was able to foresee that Victor had found his daughter. There was a jump of surprise, and wonder in Slatkin's own heart. However, something was wrong with her. Slatkin could feel the cold of winter in her soul, and he knew that she had absorbed the Sarkian winter. Victor would need the support and help of his friends. If nothing else, he would need them to take some of the stress off him. This would be a test for him, and they would be there to see him through it.

He stopped by Carmina's room to explain to her what

was happening. A large, blue eye peered out of the crack in the door, as she looked out at him.

"Carmina, I have news that you may be interested in..." Slatkin began as she peered at him.

"Don't worry, Slatkin, I know all about the princess." She said with her high pitched, very soft voice, as she cut him off. "The kraelvins came to tell me very early this evening. Now my visions of the past three nights have come to my understanding. What shall I do to help the two of you prepare for such a joyous occasion?" she asked. Slatkin nodded. He should have realized that the birds would have visited with her already. Each night she had a ritual that called them to her, and they would come to bring her news from throughout Sark, and sometimes from beyond.

"It would be helpful if you could find the child some clothes to wear. She will no doubt need them if she has been out in this blizzard, as I fear that she has."

"I will get on it right away!" replied Carmina, as she quietly shut the door the rest of the way.

Slatkin then continued his way to the kitchens, where Belle was no doubt already beginning the preparations for what they referred to as breakfast, even though it was after nightfall when their meals started. He stopped at the bottom of the stairs. He could not bring himself to go any further, and it had nothing to do with Victor or the princess. Belle was sitting by the hearth reading that ancient cookbook of hers. She was still in her red night dress, and her black fur sloped gently across her back from one elbow to the other. Her red hair was not put up yet. It cascaded down her back in soft waving curls, until it came to rest in the chair, and about her lap, where the book sat. It seemed to do a dance there as it connected the book to her, curling itself around the pages. He stopped for a moment to take this in. It was not often that he could catch such a lovely image, and he wanted to remember it always. He also knew that he could not stand in the doorway forever, so he summoned the courage to enter, and begin to tell her the news.

"Good evening Belle," he greeted her as he entered through the archway at the bottom of the stairs. "How are you tonight?" He asked.

She marked her place in the book, and wrapped the black fur around her shoulders, as Slatkin noticed a slight blush on her cheeks. She smiled a shy smile as she looked back at him.

"Well, I'm fine, but Victor went out in a hurry first thing this evening. He said that he had something to do, and went out walking in the middle of this mess of weather."

"Not to worry, Belle, Victor can take care of himself," Slatkin reassured. "He had something very important to do. It is something that he will need our help with."

"And what would that be?" Belle asked.

"He has finally come to the end of a long search, my dear Belle. He has found our princess. Angelik."

Belle's dazzling green eyes lit up with astonishment as she heard the news. "Do you mean his daughter?" Slatkin nodded in response. "She's coming here? Now?" She asked in disbelief.

"Yes, Belle," answered the dark angel. "At this very moment, they are making their way home, and I would think that Victor will need all the help that he can get from us."

"I can't believe it. After so long, he has finally found his daughter." A shadow of confusion fell over her eyes as she said the words. "But what about Celeste? Where is our queen, and why is she not with the child?"

"I don't believe that we have the answers to those questions at this time. She may still be around, or she may not. Perhaps the child can begin to answer the questions that we all have. I, for one, would like to know where they have been for these seven years, and why they have been so well hidden that even a dark angel can not tap into the traces of their energy. I have that and many other questions, but unfortunately, no time to ponder them now. The child has

72

been in the blizzard, and would be dead if not for her immortality. We have to immediately find a room for her. She will need clothes, and a warm place to sleep, and of course, one of your hot meals. Don't you agree, Belle?"

"Oh, of course!" she exclaimed. "I've already been getting some water heated to start breakfast."

"I shall go get a room ready for the child somewhere near the hot spring."

"I could help if you want me to come with you."

"You know my mind too well, dear Belle. Are you sure that you are only mortal?" he asked, jokingly.

Belle giggled as they exited the room.

Slatkin was by Victor's side even before he opened the door. Victor was barely aware of his friends hovering about. When he pulled the coat away from Angelik, he thought his heart would collapse on itself. For a brief second, he thought that she was dead, but he still heard her heartbeat, though there were no other signs of life about her. She was cold and stiff, her skin had a blue tint to it, and she was covered in a thin layer of frost. However, her hair flowed freely, and remained the color of shining gold.

"Well, look at that, she's a beautiful child, isn't she?" Belle exclaimed as she knelt down to get a closer look.

"She looks like her mother." Carmina declared, with her big blue eyes.

"Yes, but we will have time to admire her beauty later. I believe that we should get her into the hot water." Slatkin said. "That is the only way that I believe the winter will leave her...if even then."

Victor could only find it in himself to nod his head. He was overwhelmed with so many emotions at once that he did not know what to say or do, and he was glad that his friends were thinking more clearly than he was.

With their help, Victor got the child into one of the rooms where there were steps leading up to a pool in which the hot spring ran. It was shallow and was often used for bathing. Victor delicately placed the child into the water, partly afraid that further harm would come to her if she were jarred too much. She sank to the bottom of the small pool like a weighted stone. Each of them tried to lift her above the water, so that she could breathe, but all their attempts to lift the child's head from the water failed. She was so stiff that they could not get her into any other position except the one that she was already in. So they left her there to thaw in the hot spring, but they all stared at her for a long moment.

"What if she is not immortal and she wakes up under the water?" Victor asked.

"Victor," Slatkin laughed slightly. "I think that you will find that your daughter is anything but mortal. It is not possible. She was born of two dark angels, and so she shall be an angel of light." Slatkin responded.

Belle put her arm about Victor in a comforting, motherly way, as she spoke. "I think that you are worrying too much, Victor. She will be fine, and when she wakes, you will have one of the things that you have been waiting for. You will have your daughter, to teach, to love, and to nurture..." Belle's tone was warm, as always.

"And if we are lucky, she will know where Celeste is," said Carmina.

They all nodded in agreement to Carmina's statement, hoping that the sorrows of the last seven years were about to be over.

Belle walked over to the hearth, where she was warming water in a kettle, and began to again busy herself with the meal that she was about to prepare. The others slowly left the room, except for Victor. He could not bring himself to leave the room...to leave his daughter. He had been wanting his family together for so long, and now that he had his daughter, he could not bare to leave her, for fear that she would be lost again if he took his eyes off of her. He wanted so badly for her to awaken, and answer all of his questions, but there was nothing to do except wait.

Later in the evening, the others had rejoined Victor at the hot spring. All was quiet until Slatkin spoke.

"So, what do you think of the blanket?" he asked, as he motioned in the direction of the blanket that lay covered in blood, along with the wet fur coat.

"I don't know," replied Victor. "I'm hoping that she can explain it once she wakes up...she doesn't seem to be hurt, but it is her blood!" he said.

"I think that it is just from her tears. She has been through a lot to get here." Slatkin replied.

Belle then crossed the room, and picked the blanket up. "Maybe you could..." she started, but then a small noise and a quick flash of blue caught the attention of everyone in the room as a small item fell from the folds in the blanket. Carmina was quick to cross the room, and pick the small item up. She held it up to her dark blue eyes, and saw a fascinating blue jewel. It was a light shade, and seemed to give off radiance like she had never seen in an ordinary jewel.

"What is this?" She asked.

Slatkin and Victor had already crossed the room to get a better view of the item. Victor took it in his hand as Carmina held it out to him.

"I don't know," responded Victor.

"I've never seen anything quite like this, and I have beheld many things with these old eyes." Slatkin stated.

Victor looked at the pool of water, where the young angel lay. "I wish she would wake up," he said, longing to have her awake, and hoping that she had the answers to the many puzzles that were starting to fill his mind.

Belle was alone in the room with the child now. Victor, after waiting by the side of the hot spring, had finally fallen asleep at the table, and no amount of stirring would wake him. Slatkin had gone to get a bed ready for the child, whenever she did come to, and Carmina had gone to try to find clothes for her to wear.

Belle sang softly to herself, as she ground up her dried herbs, and dropped them into a steaming pot of water that heated over the fire in the hearth. She was not aware that the child was awake and sitting up in the pool of water.

Angelik looked around the room, as confusion took over her mind. She didn't know where she was, or what she was doing here. She tried to remember where she had been, but she could only remember having breakfast with her mother, and there had been a flash of lightning...and then...only visions of snow and ice, and a song of winter that seemed to shape the images in her mind, and make her feel as if she was spinning in circles. She rubbed her eyes, and stood up to get out of the hotspring. She had on a wet thin dress that was tattered by the wind and the ice, but the room was hot...she didn't know the woman by the fire, and she wondered what the woman was doing. There was someone sleeping at a table in the corner of the room...a man. His head rested in his left arm upon the tabletop. There was something about the man that seemed important, but she could not place it.

Carefully, she stepped down the grey stone steps leading down from the pool, and walked over to the lady. Suddenly, the woman gave a quick yelp of surprise, and jumped back. She grabbed her chest and took a deep breath when she saw that it was the child.

"You gave me quite a scare!" she seemed to be searching for words as she grabbed her chest and tried to recover from the shakiness of being startled. "I'm Belle. I hope that you are alright. We've been worried about you, my dear. Let's get you dried off, and into some clothes, and then I will wake your father. He is going to be so glad to see you...after all this time."

Angelik looked over at the man sleeping at the table, and saw that even though he slept, his expression was troubled. "Is that my father?" she asked Belle.

"Yes, dear, I'll try to wake him, as soon as we get you

some clothes. Now, come stand by the hearth and get dry, and I will go get the clothes. Hopefully, Carmina has found some. We haven't had a child in the castle for years." She bustled quickly out of the room, and the child did as she had asked, and stood by the fire. It was hot, but pleasant feeling to her skin. She could smell the herbs cooking in the pot, but did not recall ever smelling anything quite so pleasant. She leaned closer to the pot to take in the scent of it, savoring the fragrance. She turned to her father, and then something happened that she did not expect.

All sound left the room, and there was a pulsing feeling, a loud inhale and exhale of breath that seemed to coincide with the rise and fall of his breathing as he slept. All darkness and light seemed to shift, and suddenly every tiny detail in the room sprang upon her at once. The event was so jarring that she fell to the stone floor, and then as suddenly as it had come to her, everything turned back to the way it had been before. She was aware of other sounds now. She could hear the voices of two women, and a man, and some sort of birds chattering loudly above her...there was the trickle of the hot spring and the crackling of the fire, and then there was the boiling of the herbs in the pot, and a loud rush of wind, somewhere beyond the walls that she was in. She could hear footsteps, and then the click of the door handle as the two women came into the room. One she recognized as the same lady that had just been in the room before. She was a stocky lady with long red hair, and sparkling green eyes. The other was young, slender, and awkwardly tall, with long, straight black hair and large dark eyes of blue.

"This is Carmina. She has looked all over the castle for some clothes for you to wear." Belle said to her. "They're a little old, but I think that they are in good condition. Come child, pick one out," she said, as the two ladies held up dresses for her to see.

Each one seemed pleasing to Angelik, but she chose a white one. It had a high collar, and red embroidery about the sleeves, neck and waist. She slipped the dress on. It was only a little big. She took a moment to admire it. It was beautiful, and warm. She smiled at the ladies, and then looked across to the table in the corner.

"So that is Victor, my father?" She asked.

"Yes," Belle said. "He's been looking for you for so many years. Perhaps you should speak to him dear. He would probably wake up if you asked him to, though I'll warn you that he is quite a deep sleeper."

She walked over to him, and as she reached out to wake him, his eyes opened. There was a moment of awkward silence, as he came out of sleep, and realized that the person he was staring in the face was his daughter.

"You're awake," he stated. There was a dry, tired sound to his voice.

"Yes, and now you are, too." she responded, smiling a little.

"Are you well?" he asked. As she looked at her father, Angelik could tell what he was feeling inside. She felt the fear and the anxiety, and the sudden surprise of finding her. There were trails of grief that had been there for many years.

"I am alright, but I feel that you are not," she said as he looked back at her with questioning eyes.

"What do you mean?" he asked.

"You are worried for me, and you don't need to be. I am alright," she reassured as her smile lengthened, "and now you will be, too," she said to him.

He grabbed her quickly, and embraced her. She felt the relief washing throughout his emotions. There were tears filling his eyes, as he tried to put into words what he felt.

"I have searched, and I have waited, and you were lost to me for so long..." there was a pause as he tried to put into words all that he felt. "I'm so glad you're here with me."

She let him embrace her. Then, she wiped away the red tears from his eyes, remembering very distantly, as if it had been a dream, that she had done the same thing to another. Her thoughts were confused and she quickly shook it off.

When Victor could stand to take his eyes from her, he spoke. "Are you hungry? Is there anything that you want to eat?" he asked.

Angelik had not thought of it before, but now that Victor asked her she realized that she was indeed very hungry. The breakfast with her mother had seemed ages ago, and the memory was starting to fade.

She nodded her head in reply to his question.

"Oh, wonderful!" exclaimed Belle. "You know it is time that we all had a little bit of breakfast. You've been asleep for quite some time. When we brought you in here, we thought you would never wake up. You slept all last night, and all through the day, and now it is dusk again, and you are waking, as you should."

Belle spoke as she pulled some dishes from a rolling cart, and placed them to the table. Carmina pulled one of the chairs close to Victor for Angelik to sit in. The child smiled at Carmina and sat down. Then, looking at her father, she saw that a look of mixed joy and sadness was on his face.

"What is wrong?" she asked him.

"I will speak of it after we have eaten." He looked away as a door opened, and Slatkin walked in.

"Not going to have breakfast without me, are you?" He asked, jokingly.

"Of course not!" Belle exclaimed, seriously.

"Have you met the new princess?" asked Carmina.

Slatkin looked over to where the child sat. "No, but I had planned on doing so at breakfast. Good morning, Princess Angelik!" he pronounced, as he sat down at the table, and held out his hand for her to take. She awkwardly held out hers. Slatkin placed a gentle kiss on her fingers. "I am honored, my princess," he said.

"This is Slatkin," Victor said to his daughter. "He is my personal attendant and best friend."

"I have been waiting seven years for this honor. I hope that you will let me sit beside you. Is that alright?" he asked. Angelik only nodded her head in reply.

Belle and Carmina soon joined them, and Angelik got her first taste of Sarkian food. As she ate breakfast, she began to realize that there was parts of her that had yearned to be here all of her life, yet she did not know it until she was here. This was her true home. She felt it inside her. It was a feeling unlike any other, yet she did not understand where her mother was. She was more like a dream now, and emotions of her were strong, but the memories of her began to fade. She meant to ask her father about it as soon as she had eaten.

X

The Tavern

Sark, the Howling Wolf Tavern

The tavern had not been hard to find. Most of Sark was gathered there, and the sweet smell of burning Kial twigs and a variety of foods cooking could be smelled halfway up the King's Mountain. The three travelers had arrived at their destination under a cloudy starless sky. Alexandria had been quick to see the fatigue of the two young Scithronians, and had ordered a meal for them.

They sat at a small table by the door eating the food ravenously, Valassa more so than Khiel, who was content at smoking the kial twigs, and drinking kial brew. They looked around cautiously as they ate. Saltook, owner of the Howling Wolf Tavern and Inn, made all of his guests leave their weapons at the door. The Scithronians were wary about their weapons being left, and Valassa had warned Saltook that if anything happened to her weapons, then she would hold him accountable for them. Alexandria was not concerned. With her skills and gifts, there was no reason to fear. She sat by the bar, waiting to speak to Saltook. He was an elderly looking man with a black and grey hair, and a matching salt and pepper colored beard and mustache. He was rather busy at the moment, and had told her to hold on five times already as he bustled about getting things ready for various guests. The winter seemed to be his busy time of the year. The hunters would come to town, and take a break from their hunt. The weather would not permit them hunting in the winter, so Saltook had to see that they all got rooms.

Suddenly, there was a crashing sound and it seemed to drown out all the other noise in the tavern as curious eyes glanced around to see what had made the noise. Alexandria watched as an entire tray of food splattered all over the floor.

81

A plate lay in shattered pieces. She continued to look on the scene with interest, noticing the distress felt by the woman who had been holding the tray. The bar maid was panicking, but more so than one would normally panic over such of a thing. She nervously leaned down to start cleaning the mess. A group of men sat at the table where the lady was. Alexandria knew already that there was trouble brewing by the looks on their faces. She got up, and headed in the direction of the table, keeping her eyes on the scene.

"Clean it up, ya clumsy wench!" One of the men growled. The woman did not look at them, but busied herself with cleaning up the mess as quickly as she could, though her hands trembled as she did so. She reached closer to the table for a broken piece of a plate. One of the smaller men with a brown fur on stomped his foot on her hand causing the woman to shriek in pain. Alexandria could see that he had spikes on the bottom of his shoes, and the woman's hand was bleeding where the spikes had dug through. With his other foot, he kicked the broken dish across the floor.

Alexandria searched for a mark on the men, but none of them held hers, though she wished that they did. She could not kill them, but she could not let them continue this. She was nearing the table, when two hands were on her shoulders, trying to hold her back. Khiel and Valassa pleaded in whispers for her not to fight, fearing what the hunters would do.

"There are too many," exclaimed Khiel.

"Wait until we can take them one at a time," pleaded Valassa.

Alexandria shook them off. "I can handle it. You two go eat the meals I ordered you, and leave me to this." She turned back to the scene. The hunter had released the woman's hand from the spikes of his boot, but now he had her by the hair. Her face was turned up to his, a look of pure terror in her eyes, while blood poured from the punctures in her hands.

"Do you have a name, wench?" he asked through his teeth.

"Bas..." she sobbed as she tried to speak. "Bas...i...lla."

"Well, Basilla, we don't like your clumsiness..."

A young boy had entered the main hall from the kitchens, Alexandria assumed that he had come to help clean up the mess, and now he walked over to the man.

"Leave her alone...sir!" His tone was commanding. The table roared with laughter.

"What are you going to do about it?" One of the others asked.

"I will warn you...the wolves get hungry in winter, and Saltook asked me to tell you that he would rather you do your hunting on something bigger, like a wolf, and leave him his barmaids. I am also sent to tell you that the inn is full, and there will be no rooms for you here tonight. Find your lodgings elsewhere."

The hunter's face turned serious. "Saltook said that, did he?"

"Yes." The boy looked at the hunter, and his commanding stature did not change. He seemed to be the only one in the tavern that did not fear them.

The hunter sat back to turn this over in his mind, and then he thrust the woman away from him. She fell to the floor, clutching her bloodied hand with her apron. The boy was quick to help her to her feet. "She's not worth a dog's hide, anyway!" The hunter exclaimed, as he glared at the girl with cruel, cold eyes. "Bitch!" He cried out loudly, as he spat at her. The woman did not respond, but went with the boy into the door leading to the kitchens. There was laughter and approval from the other hunters at the table.

Alexandria approached them, and leaned in towards the leader. "Got a problem with the service here?" She asked, as she seated herself in an empty chair that she pulled up beside him.

"What's it to you?" he asked, in response.

"Oh, I think it's more to me than you could ever know," she said with a cold stare, eyeing the men closely.

Alexandria laughed a deep laugh, thinking to herself all the things that she could read in his soul. "Do you boys make a habit out of hurting the tavern maids, or is it her in particular that you have a problem with?"

"All of them that are dogs!"

"So, you only have a problem with the dogs...hmmm...from what your soul reveals, I can see that you run into more than your share of dogs." Her voice was a cold deep growl when she spoke to them. "Let's start with the bitch, as you boys call her...you were hoping that your buddy didn't kill her, or take her for his own, because you have been eying her for a while. Then there's the family that you robbed yesterday, so that you could pay for your room at the inn...and then, oh yes, your friend Markus lost a horse...one that you killed, because you didn't want him to get your prey...and all that in just a week."

The hunters looked terrified as she said this, and yet they didn't want anyone to see their terror, in fact, they did not want to admit to themselves that they were terrified. They knew what she was, and they hated her kind.

They all stood up, ready to lash out with the only thing that they knew how to do. They attacked.

She ducked the first one that came at her, and threw a punch back at the hunter's stomach. He fell over with his hands cradling his stomach. He had obviously not expected her to punch so hard.

She heard the heavy swinging of an axe behind her. One of the others had sneaked one in the tavern, but Alexandria jumped onto the table as it swished by where she had just been sitting. He swung it sideways again, but it came to an abrupt stop as her feet came down hard on the side of it. She kicked with her left foot, as he stared at her with surprise, and then shock, as his teeth gave way from the force of her boot. He fell back clutching his jaw, blood streamed from in between his fingers.

Alexandria's attention was then turned towards the door. Four more had gone to recover their weapons, and they came running towards her from the direction of the door. All of the other customers were hiding in corners, or fleeing the tavern.

The dark angel ran along the table, and jumped off the end. She started to scream for Khiel to toss her axe, but then she spotted a barrel of Kial brew on top of the bar. She ran and leaped up to the top of the bar, and placed herself by the barrel. Sneaking in a sly smile at the hunters, she picked up the barrel. She lifted it above her head, and laughed as the hunters stopped in their tracks.

"This is to remind you of what happens when you come after the barmaids here!" She shouted, as she thrust the barrel towards them. The impact knocked three to the ground, but the fourth jumped out of its path. It was the one who had started all of the trouble with the barmaid.

He came after her. She waited for the right moment as he started to swing his axe, and then she leaped off of the bar, landing behind him, and then quickly, she placed a solid kick between his shoulder blades. The axe flew from his hands, and his body was flung into the bar. He slid to the floor. Alexandria walked over to see him.

She saw that he had a gash on his forehead, and blood oozed out of it slowly. She reached down, and grabbed him by his collar, and pulled him outside the tavern, to a kial tree. She shoved him up against the tree, and stared into his eyes, with her stare like a cat on the prowl.

"Now, I need to know something." She whispered to him. "You have a friend named Markus, and I need to know where he is."

His eyes were closed, and he seemed to be staring somewhere else at the moment.

She shook him, and he came to.

"I'm asking you nicely...where...is...Markus?" She asked. With each word, she thrust his body forcefully against the tree trunk.

The hunter tried to respond to her. "'ee's...out...." There was a bit of mumbling, and then she managed to get the word "stables" out of him.

"So the stables, well, that is a start," she said to herself.

She released him, and he fell into the snow at the bottom of the tree.

She turned to go fetch her unicorn. Someone would find him, that is, if they cared to find him, she thought to herself.

Then, there were footsteps behind her, and the voice of Valassa.

"That was great!" The young Scithronian shouted. "Can you teach me to fight like that?"

"No!" Alexandria demanded, as she mounted Vortex. "To fight like me...it's a curse, and I'm sure that I have lost our lodging for tonight." Quickly she pulled out a bag of gold, and tossed it to Khiel, who had just stepped up beside the girl. "Give that to the barkeep, and do what you can to get us a room. I'm going to finish my job." Alexandria did not give the Scithronians a chance to respond. She kicked off, and sped away through the snow.

Valassa reached for the bag, but Khiel jerked it away, and held it close to himself. "We're gonna do what she asked us to."

Valassa shot a cross look at him, "I just wanted to see it for a minute. I mean...she could probably buy Saltook's tavern with that much."

"Maybe...we'll see, huh?" Khiel said as he walked inside.

Valassa started to go inside, but walked over to the injured hunter.

"Even with your face full of blood, I still know who you are...you're Chase. I don't think I could forget you no

86

matter how hard I try. Thank goodness for her...maybe now you'll leave us all alone."

Chase felt anger rise inside him...how dare this girl speak to him...

"You..." he tried to speak, but he felt too lightheaded.

"Y'know,' said Valassa. "Normally, I would pick your pockets right now, but I don't want to touch anything you've had. I wish she would have killed you, because I won't. I don't want my blade to get tainted with your blood."

Valassa turned, and went to go find Khiel, glad to have that said.

Sark, town stables

As Alexandria neared the stables, she knew that she was close to the one that she hunted. Markus was here. She could feel the power that she had taken from Elise's pain pulsing through her veins like white hot electricity. She was close now, and nothing could stop her.

The stables were warm inside. Alexandria saw that Markus and two other hunters were perched in the rafters. They were no doubt awaiting their next victim, invisible to any mortal eye, and ready for a kill. They were hidden in the darkest shadows. Alexandria's eyes saw them, though, and much more. All of her senses were awake and alert, and she knew that if she waited, that they would come for her. She walked forward, pretending to search out a free stall in which Vortex could stay, all the while, watching their faces go from the stone cold stares of waiting to the excited, hungry gazes of hunters creeping up on their prey.

She could feel their movements, and she saw that they were silently creeping down from the ceiling. Using ropes made of Kial fibers, they descended quietly, like spiders creeping down on thin, black webs. The wind howled furiously outside, and snow was blown in around the doorway.

Their breathing was heavy, but controlled, and their hearts were pounding out their thrill. She waited until they were almost to her, and then she quickly turned to face them.

"Were you expecting me?" she asked them.

They were caught off guard, not expecting her to know that they were there.

"I just ran into some of your friends at the tavern." She walked towards them as she spoke, making sure to let them know that she was not afraid, and daring them to strike at her with their weapons. She winked her left eye, and one of the hunters stopped, his expression was wild, an artwork of frozen animation. She had paralyzed him with her spell.

"Just who are you?" The one to her right asked.

She was suddenly at his face, before his mind had time to see her come closer. Her hand was over his mouth.

"Shhh..." she whispered, and then he found that he could not speak. The mental shock of his sudden loss, made him panic. He stepped back, and looked at Markus for some sort of help.

"What's wrong with you?" Markus asked, still in the shadows at the far side of the room. Alexandria winked her right eye, and the voiceless man was frozen just like the other. Now it was only Markus left to deal with.

She stepped into the shadows, and felt the coldness envelop her as the light passed away behind her. Markus could see nothing but her eyes shining like a wild cat's and the few strands of yellow hair that blew around her face like a wild blinding fire.

"Who are you?" he asked.

"Oh, I think you know!" she declared, as she descended on her prey, her dagger pressed into his neck. "I am vengeance!" The power she felt from Elise's soul arose in her, and it was as if she was looking at him through Elise. "You are a killer! You have killed for the last time...your own wife and child...if you had the decency to call her a wife. She was an unwilling wife, and a slave to you. What do you have to say about this, killer?" She asked.

"What am I supposed to say? Do you want me to tell you that I regret it, or that I enjoyed it? Both are true." His voice was growling, and Alexandria drew upon her power, then she punched him in the stomach, and watched as he writhed around. He was feeling the same pain that she had felt. He was feeling Elise's pain.

All around him, he could hear the screaming of babies in pain, drowning out all other noise, and he felt the pains he had inflicted, not just on his wife and child, but upon all of the people he had tortured and killed.

Alexandria held him down through his struggle of pain. When his thrashing stopped, she pulled out her dagger and held it to his throat. She struck, sliding the blade ever so carefully under his skin. Blood welled out. She did not strike him hard enough to kill him, just enough to drain what she needed. She took a vial from her pocket letting the blood fill it. She sipped the tainted, dirty blood, and felt it as it purified through her throat. The energy was leaving her now, evaporating into the air. She took the Kial twine that the hunters had used to slide from the rafters, and she wrapped it around the hunter's feet. She pulled it until he swung back and forth, writhing again in his torment, and then she tied it around one of the hooks along the wall. He would stay here until he was found by someone else. He was not her concern any longer. She had collected the taint of his soul, and he would now be tormented until death came for him, as it had for Elise.

Alexandria did not glance back at him as she left. She grabbed Vortex by his reins, and walked him out into the falling snow and wind. She mounted him, much weaker than she had been coming here. All the power that she had gained was now gone. It was spent in its own purpose and now even though she could probably outfight most mortals, and cast very powerful spells, she was drained. She looked forward to sleep in a bed.

XI

Questions

Sark, the king's castle

Slatkin could feel the pains coming as he sat eating at the table. The pressure gnawed at his joints, making him appear as nothing more than an arthritic old man. He knew all too well the familiarity of the pains. They were a warning to him that there was work to be done. He would have to leave the table. Victor was looking at him, sympathetically. He understood more than anyone else in the room what Slatkin was going through, though he did not know all that his friend had to endure.

It was a painful transformation, one that stretched his bones and features into something resembling a wolf's. He would grow massive, leathery wings, in which he could hunt his prey from the sky. Once the change was complete, he could not turn back until the job was done.

Slatkin was one of the Orostiro, the angels whose power was greater than all the others. He was the angel of retribution. He dealt the dealers of pain more pain, and to those who deserved good, he was the bringer of great blessings. Give to each what is owed to them was what he lived by, but because he was once disobedient, he was cursed to turn into a terrifying beast before he could hunt.

Slatkin knew that his time was limited, and as much as he was enjoying his dinner, he knew that he had to abandon it, his friends, and his princess to answer his calling.

He stood up abruptly. "I apologize, my friends, but I must excuse myself," he said in his deep voice, and always polite manner. "Duty is..." he flinched back more pain in his fingertips, as he clutched his hand into a fist. "Duty is calling me. Enjoy your dinner. Perhaps I will get a chance to meet back with you all tonight." He turned, and walked swiftly from the room.

Victor turned to Angelik. "Slatkin does this often, but you should never take offence if he leaves in a hurry. He has work to do, like me, and like your mother had, and like you, no doubt will have. Do you know what he is?" he asked her.

She shook her head. "No, but I can feel it. I know that he is something like us, but not really. He is different."

"Yes, he is. There are others like him, but it is a rare thing to hear of one, much less to see it. He is known as an Orostiro. They are a higher class of angels. They are like us, but more powerful. He is also a great beast, and that is his fate, for he loved a mortal woman, which is forbidden for his kind. Because our master is merciful, and because it was love, rather than hate that made him disobedient, he was not banished, as so many of the Orostiro were. The mortal woman pleaded with Saigolai for her lover not to be banished, and because he listens when faithful mortals speak, he made it so that the woman would be close by the angel, though their love was still forbidden."

Angelik nodded her head. Much of what she had seen in his soul now made sense to her. "I see." she said, with understanding now coloring her words. She looked over at Belle and Carmina with a delicate smile. It was returned by Carmina, but Belle stared at her plate, not looking up. Carmina quickly offered to help Belle with the clean up.

Victor looked at his daughter. "Now, I have a lot of questions for you and some cannot wait. Please, tell me, is your mother safe?" He looked at her, waiting for a response.

Angelik tried to remember her mother, but nothing was there. She searched her mind...there were dreams. There was a woman's voice telling her to find her father, and there was snow whipping the words past her, giving her light in the darkness, but there was no solid memory of her mother. "So this is what is bothering you, father?"

"Yes, it bothers me. I have searched all of my lands,

91

and all those surrounding it for years, and there has been no trace of you or your mother. I have to find her!" He spoke with such determination, that Angelik wanted so much to tell him whatever he wanted to hear, but she could not. She did not remember her mother.

The child hung her head, and tried to recall something that would help, but there was nothing there. "I don't remember her...I'm sorry that I can't be of more help, but I really don't know where she could be."

She felt the deep disappointment in her father's soul, as she said this, but there was a bit of relief there as well. "So this," he walked across the room and picked up the blood soaked blanket. "This is not your mother's blood?" he asked.

"I don't think so, but then again, I don't remember seeing that blanket before."

Victor looked at the blanket with confusion, and then looked at his daughter. "This blanket was wrapped around you when I found you, so you must know where it came from." His voice was full of a restrained frustration.

Angelik tried to remember where the blanket had come from, but she could not recall seeing it before. "I'm sorry, father."

"Well, what about this? Have you seen this before? Have you seen this blue jewel?" He reached into his pocket and pulled out the jewel. "Tell me if you know anything about it," he pleaded, holding the jewel up for her. The blue light from the jewel illuminated the expression of desperation on Victor's face.

"I wish I knew where it came from, but I don't know."

"Angelik, do you remember anything? Tell me why you were in the woods. What has happened to you?"

"I was in the woods, because...I was coming to find you." Finally, here was an answer that she knew.

"Very good, now how did you know to come find me? How did you know about me?" he asked.

"You are my father, and when I left the basket, I was

very upset, and I knew that you would be able to help me," she said.

"Okay, what basket? Where have you been?" he asked, his desperation now turning to excitement.

"Well, I've been in the basket, and before I was dreaming under the tree, I was dreaming in the basket, and the blankets were filled with elf magic, so my dreams were all so very bright and lovely."

Victor thought for a moment, the creases in his forehead deepening. "Elf magic," he stated mainly to himself.

"Yes," said Angelik. "The elves weave the best dreams. You should have them weave for you, father."

"Elves," he said again, as he puzzled this over in his mind. Then he looked at Angelik. "So tell me," he said. "What was there before the basket?"

"Well..." she began, and then she looked at Victor. She smiled a wide delighted smile. "You are silly, father...before the basket!" Then she giggled, closing her eyes and hanging her head. "Silly," He heard her say again, when her giggles subsided. Then a few more slipped out. When she saw the seriousness of his gaze, she stopped. "I was just there, father. I don't know of a before. I really don't."

Once Slatkin was outside the door, the pains worsened. As he walked, he felt dizzy and distant. His head was aching, and everything around him seemed to swim in a blur. The growing of his bones had begun. The stretching of his arms and legs into the long, skeletal appendages that would end in beastly claws was one of the worst parts. The pain was unbearable, and he fell once he reached the stairs. His transformation would barely be remembered later. He passed out on the steps. When he came to, his arms and legs were strangely long for his body, long bony claws sprawled around him, and fur had started to grow all over him. It caused him to itch horribly, and his eyes watered and stung uncontrollably as his face contorted in pain. Soon, he would feel the stretching of the bones in his head, as he grew the face of the wolf. He struggled up the stairs, awkwardly crawling, until he reached a black iron door at the top of the stairs. There, he blacked out.

When he came around the second time, there came the gnawing pains in his back, as he grew his long, leathery wings. His clothes cast on the floor, tattered and ripped where he had fallen. Blood poured from the newly torn wounds on his back where new bones pushed their way through his tissue. There was hardly room to hold his massive size, wings and all. He now stood on two legs, twelve feet in height. He looked like a wolf, with long skinny bones for legs and feet that ended in long sharp claws. His black leathery wings were greater in their width than he was in height, stretching to more than fifteen feet. He walked over to the opening that was once a window and sniffed the cold wind. There was a scent there. It was a trace of his victim, and he was intent on finding him.

He stepped out of the large window, and perched for a moment on the balcony. This part, he actually thought was fun. He let himself drop, and then stretched his wings. Soon, he was gliding through the darkened, snowy sky, unseen to most. There were the dark trees beneath him, and the snowy, rocky slopes of the mountainside. He looked down to the small area interrupting the wilderness, where the settlement of the Sarkian village was filled with the smoke of fires in burning chimneys. He circled above the town, enjoying the moment of free flying. The cold wind ruffled his fur, and the wetness of the snow cooled his back, which was hot and sweating from the exertion of flapping the wings. When he had delayed long enough, he descended.

He landed silently outside of the Howling Wolf tavern. No one would be able to hear him, because although he was large in size, angels have such delicate movements that even at his size, they can be almost silent. Slatkin could feel a dark heaviness saturating the air all around him. He understood that his prey was already outside. He sniffed the air. There was tainted blood here. It was certain. He spotted a kial tree

94

nearby, and started toward it to hide himself better, but he stopped. Someone was coming. It was another angel, a woman no doubt, and she had his prey in her fist, as she slammed him up against the tree. She spoke to him, and he seemed barely conscious. When she was done speaking, he fell to the ground. Slatkin waited until the angel departed, but he sensed others around. After a few moments, another girl, a human, walked up to say something to his prey. She went inside after a brief moment. Then, Slatkin could hear sounds from the tavern and the howling wind.

When he was sure no one was looking, he carefully walked to the tree where Chase, the hunter, lay unconscious. From his first glance of the man lying on the ground, someone, probably the other angel, had already started his job for him. He grasped the unconscious man in his thin claws, and looked closely at him with his large, beastly eyes. The man was certainly injured, but not bad enough, he thought to himself. He walked quickly with his long stride to a clearing where he spread his shadowy wings, and took to the sky, building up his power for the night ahead of him with Chase the hunter, unconscious in his claws.

Sark, the Howling Wolf Tavern

Alexandria returned to the tavern, dreading to go inside, for she was sure that she would not have a place to stay for the night. She hoped that Khiel and Valassa were able to pay for whatever damage she may have caused. She rode up to the tavern on Vortex, and quickly dismounted, realizing that Khiel was standing by the doorway, smiling, with her bag of gold.

"What are you doing?" she asked as she turned to him.

"Well, I tried to give out all of your gold, but no one will take it. It seems that everyone is glad you gave those hunters a good beating. Here," he said, tossing the bag of gold to her. She reached out reflexively, catching it.

"Some thief you are!" she exclaimed, with a wide

smile. "You're not supposed to give the money back!" Khiel laughed aloud.

"Then toss it here!" he exclaimed. "I'll use it for somethin'."

"Good try," she said, "but it's too late for that."

"Well, have we got a room and a hot meal?" she asked, seriously.

"Yes, well, a room, but I'm sure he'll give you a hot meal, if you ask for it."

"So, how much was the room?" Alexandria inquired.

"Let's see, the room cost as much as a barrel of Kial brew, and the pride of some hunters." He motioned for her to come inside, and when she got close, he reached out to put his arm around her shoulder. They walked inside to the stares of all the guests, and Saltook. The barkeep walked over to her, and to her surprise, he bowed to her.

"Thank you!" he exclaimed. Then he stood, and spoke again. "We need more warriors like you. Thank you for making my tavern a safe place, if even for one night." She looked then into his soul, and saw that he was filled with joy. "Now your friends tried to give me the gold, but I won't take a bit of it. I'm giving you a room tonight, and any other night you wish to stay, for you have certainly freed us from the hunters and saved my daughter's life. Is there anything else that you require? I'll be happy to give you whatever you ask for."

"Actually, I could use a good, hot meal." She smiled at the innkeeper, who led her over to the bar.

"What would you like?" he asked her.

"Well, what would you recommend?"

"How about some nice, hot, roasted Valka beast and some stewed Kial root? That's a favorite here, and I'll even add in some soup. How about some good caib soup? That's also a favorite if you like seafood." Saltook talked excitedly, and seemed to want to impress the angel.

"If that is what you recommend, then I will gladly

accept it, and if my friends require anything, then I will gladly pay you for it."

"That may be necessary eventually, but for tonight it's all on me. You have saved my daughter's life, and for that I cannot thank you enough. Tonight, we are having a celebration!"

Sark, the king's castle

Angelik looked at her father. "I'm sorry I can't tell you more about my mother. I would like to know about her, but I don't."

"That's okay," said Victor. He reached out, taking her small hand in his. "Come with me and I will tell you all about her." Angelik followed her father's long strides through a series of halls, and then up a long straight staircase. They walked through several other rooms until they finally reached the one that he wanted. Several comfortable chairs were located around ornate looking tables. Shelves lined the walls, and one large window looked out over the ocean. Victor walked over and opened the shutters. Wind blew the curtains around, and the light angel felt exhilarated by the rushing of the air. She ran over to the window and looked out. The deep sound of the ocean filled the empty space of noise between howls of wind. Angelik took a deep breath, and she could smell a salty bitterness blowing in from the ocean. It was a good scent. She smiled, and then looked at her father.

"This is beautiful!" she exclaimed.

Victor smiled back at her. "Yes it is. Out there..." he gazed out over the ocean, "is where I met your mother. I was human at that time."

"She was beautiful, and unlike anyone else in the whole world. You share a lot of her features. You have her curly hair and her smile."

Angelik's smile grew. "Really?"

Victor nodded his head. "Your mother was a dancer and a singer."

"She could sing?" Angelik asked, because she enjoyed singing also.

Victor smiled at the memory of her voice. "Yes, she could. She never missed a step or a note. The first time I ever saw her, she was dancing with a group of gypsies on board a ship. Her voice was one of the most beautiful sounds in the world. Whenever she would sing, everyone around her became affected. It made them happier just to hear her voice. If there was an argument or someone who was upset or lonely heard her voice, their mood changed...everyone was different, better. All but the hunters."

"They are the ones who wronged your mother and me. They took her away, and lost her."

"How can she be lost?"

"You were lost too, remember...but I know she's out there somewhere.'

Angelik looked back out over the ocean, trying to remember anything about her, but she couldn't.

XII

Beast and Pray

Sark, the Howling Wolf Tavern

Alexandria ate the plate of food that Saltook placed before her. It was an interesting mix, the best of what Sark had to offer, which she was thankful for, but it was certainly not familiar. All the food was dark colored, and even the kial brew was almost black. She was used to the sparkling, light colored wines of Chimrion, and the red and white meats of the livestock and fowl. Everything here seemed to be black or very dark colored. She was always up for an adventure, though, so she had plunged her fork in, and swallowed it down. The taste was pleasant. While she ate, Khiel and Valassa sat close by. Khiel was smoking a kial twig, and Valassa had helped herself to more kial brew. Alexandria turned to look at the young bar maid that she had saved. She was bringing them more food.

"I want to thank you for saving my life," she said, as she seated herself at the bar next to Alexandria. "You have no idea of my gratitude. If there is anything that I can do for you, then I will do it if I can."

"Think nothing of it," replied Alexandria. "I was only trying to help. I do not expect payment for doing what is right, and as for your gratitude, I know more than you might think." She looked down at the woman's bandaged hands. "So how is it?"

"Very painful, but it will heal." she replied.

"Let me have a look." the angel said.

The barmaid reluctantly pulled the bandages away from the punctures.

"It still looks bad," said Alexandria, 'but I might be able to mend it." She reached out for the woman's hand, and cradled it in her own. Intertwining her fingers into Basilla's shaking palms, she closed her eyes. She spoke whispered words that no one but herself could hear, and when she opened her eyes, Basilla was staring at her hand, shocked. Alexandria had healed it completely. Alexandria pulled a cloth from around her waist, and wiped the blood away. There was no trace of a scar. It was as if the wound had never happened.

"How did you do that?" she asked, staring at the angel.

"I have many gifts. All are to be used for the well-being of mankind...the ones that deserve it, anyway," she responded.

"Father, look!" Basilla held up her hand for the barkeep to see. The boy who had saved her earlier looked on too, as he was pouring Valassa more Kial brew.

"That is amazing!" the boy said.

"Yes, indeed," responded Saltook. "I hope you'll be staying here a while!" he exclaimed, with a smile at Alexandria.

"Actually, I will be moving on tomorrow, but I can see what you are all thinking. The hunters will be angry, and they will be coming back. I can only tell you that I will do what I can. I can put protective spells on the tavern, and I can bless the land that the tavern is on. It will then be holy ground, and the hunters will not be able to come upon it unless their intentions are for good. I also think that you will need extra protection. Valassa..." she patted her on the back, "will be glad to guard your tavern while Khiel," she grabbed his shoulder, "goes back to his tribe to rally a guard for the tavern."

"However, this alone will not be enough. They are going to need some help. They will need lodgings for two at a time, for no one should be alone on a watch, and they may need a hot meal. Only what you can spare each night. They have their own weapons, and with my spells they will not need much from you. Can you do that for me, Saltook?"

"Yes, anything that you can do to keep the hunters away will be greatly appreciated."

"Good," responded the yellow haired angel. Then she looked at Khiel and Valassa. "Can the Scithronians agree to this?"

"Yes," responded Valassa.

"Very well," said Alexandria. "It is agreed upon."

Sark, the king's castle

Victor watched his young daughter sleep. He smiled as he looked at her. His heart had not felt such overwhelming joy since he had first heard her heartbeat as an infant lying in her mother's womb.

All will be well soon. He thought to himself before blowing out the candle by her bedside. He laid the book that he had been reading to her on the table. Surely, she had to have some memory of her mother in her head, but it had just been pushed aside. He would help her to remember, and so would Belle. He took one last look at her as he closed the door to her bedroom, and then he made his way down the halls to the kitchens. Belle was just cleaning up from the night. She was putting her clean dishes away. He noticed the absence of Slatkin, who was always helping Belle. She had a tired look on her face, and some part of Victor felt awful for asking her to aid him. He decided that he would help her with her clean up. He wrung out one of the wet dish cloths, and started wiping down the table. Belle stopped what she was doing, and turned to look at Victor with hands on her hips.

"What is it, Victor, I know you, and there must be something that you need." She smiled jovially. Her red hair was put up in her kerchief, and her eyes warmed the tiredness on her face.

Victor smiled back at her. "Well," he started, "I'm sure that you are somewhat aware that Angelik has no recollection of the events of her life, no memory of her mother. I hate to ask you to do this, on top of all the other things that you do for me, but I was wondering if there is any way that you could conjure up some sort of memory potion, elixir, anything that may help her to remember?" He asked this with a pleading look on his somber face.

Belle smiled sincerely. "Victor, there is nothing that I wouldn't do for you. Of course I will help you," Belle almost laughed out loud thinking of how at times Victor seemed to her no more than a lost child which she would scold, or feel the need to redirect. "Don't worry about anything, Victor. I will do what I can, but if I cannot come up with something, then you may have to let time do what it can. She has been through something that may be bigger than what she is at this time. Her memories will come back with time, I'm almost certain of it. However, I will do what I can to speed the process. Have you tried doing anything else for her?" she asked.

"Well, I've told her stories of her mother, but nothing seems to have come back to her, and all that I can see is snow. There is nothing in her memories but fog, snow and wind. There is great shock and suffering, but I cannot see Celeste anywhere."

Victor stared at the table in deep contemplation. "The elves, though, that is my clue! I have seen them in her memory, and she has told me that they brought her here. I have seen them place the blue jewel in the basket with her. What it means, I still don't know, and I can not be sure of their intent. In all the dealings with all the other tribes of this land, the elves are the ones who have never wanted dealings with anyone else. They have kept to themselves, and made it a point to never cross any king, and to keep their own borders with peace in the forest. Now I may have to visit them. I want to know what they were doing with my daughter, and I only hope that they can lead me to my wife."

"Perhaps this will all come to a close soon," said Belle. I will do what I can in aiding you. Though, it will be tomorrow before I can start. I hope you don't mind, but I'm so exhausted." Victor noticed the small wrinkles forming on her face as she said this, and again he felt bad for asking her, but he knew that she was one of the only ones he knew that could help him do this.

"Belle, why don't you let me finish cleaning the kitchen tonight, so you can get to bed early?"

"No, I'm okay, Victor, this is what I am here for, and I will not have you taking my place here. Now, good evening! This will not take me long to do. I'll get to bed soon enough."

"Very well," he said. "I'll be upstairs if you need me."

Elsewhere in the castle

Slatkin stared at the man now huddled in the cage. He was pitiful to look at, but Slatkin was not feeling pity or mercy. Not at this moment, not for this man who had caused him so much anguish and physical pain. Lying, cheating and stealing were just the beginning of a record scarred onto his soul of unimaginable crimes of which only Slatkin could fully feel the anguish from. He had murdered. He had raped. He had tortured. Slatkin had felt it all. Every one of this man's victims had either gone into the beyond, or been relieved of their pains, so that Slatkin could store it in himself, and use it to bring this man his deserved retribution.

Slatkin would allow him the fitful rest of nightmares that plagued him in his sleep. He would even see to his wounds, but it would not be long before the man would have to endure what he had coming to him. Slatkin in many ways dreaded it, but it was what he had to do. There was no way around his binding laws. He had to see that this man was punished for his wrong doings, but yet allowed a second chance, as all of his victims were. Slatkin had all the time he needed. In his beastly form, he paced back and forth in front of the cage, until he became quite bored with the task, and then he lay on the floor, folding his nose and paws under his black leathery wings. There was plenty of time, he thought, and he would need his energy later. A nap was in order for this hour of the cold night.

Chase awoke from his strange and violent nightmares, with his swollen head pounding with pain. There was darkness all around him. He could barely see at all, though he could make out a window high up on the other side of the large space that he seemed to be in. His brain couldn't form where exactly he was. He had no recollection of going anywhere other than the Howling Wolf Tavern. He tried to replay in his head what had happened, and to make some sense out of the scrambled memories that drifted through his mind in no particular order. He could not come up with a solid conclusion at the moment.

He decided that he should get up to see where he was, but he found that he could not stand. He reached above him and felt the smoothness of iron bars. Puzzled, he followed them, and found that they joined more bars. Realization started flooding into him, and he felt more and more of the bars forming a box around him. Was there no way out of this? He was trapped. Then he began to come to some reasoning. He was probably at someone's house. He had gotten too drunk at the tavern, and they had put him into this cage to teach him a lesson about drunkenness. Then another thought occurred to him. What if this was no trick? What if he had gotten into some sort of trouble with someone? Who could it be? What had he done? His mind was racing, but at the moment he was too tired to do anything about it. He lay down on the floor. His plan was to wait for daylight. Maybe if he slept off this pain, then he would be able to think more clearly when the morning had come. He lay down to sleep, with more fitful nightmares filling his pounding head with more horrors.

Slatkin awoke to the dying light of day. He looked beside him at the cage where he had put Chase. A grin spread across his face. The hunter was awake. Slatkin unfolded his wings, stretching them across the open expanse of the room of cold grey stones. The hunter looked back at him with a mixed expression of anger, desperation and confusion.

"Good evening, Chase," Slatkin growled out. "Do you have any inclination as to why you, a mighty hunter, would be locked up in an iron cage?" His face came closer to the bars as he spoke. Chase could feel his hot breath on his face. He did not respond. Slatkin sat waiting for some reply, but it didn't come. The only thing he got from Chase was the same gaping expression. Slatkin rolled his eyes and began pacing back and forth. "Come now, Chase, surely you must know why a hunter such as yourself may now become the hunted. If not, allow me to show you." He stopped, staring down at the hunter for a moment, his red eyes glowing in the swelling darkness. He reached out with his wings, unfolding them over the cage until there was only darkness, and his red eyes. Chase could see nothing else.

The hunter was speechless. There really wasn't anything that he could think to say about any of this. Was he dreaming? He must be. Slatkin assured him with his growling voice that it wasn't a dream. He was, in fact, taking back all that Slatkin had built up for these many years.

The hunter felt it. He was a woman standing all alone, one of the Astrid warriors, a mighty tribe that inhabited the Sarkian wilderness. It was morning. She was making her gathering rounds as she walked about, checking the mighty Kial Thieren trees for any sign of cracking. She had to produce the firewood every morning, but it was always easier to get the fire started if she could use the fire inside of the tree to light it. There was a cracking of branches behind her.

Her reflexes sharpened, as she turned to see what the sound was. To the untrained eye, it would appear that it was only an animal rambling through the snow, but she saw that it was no animal. Instead, it was someone wearing the skin of an animal. She screamed a warning to her tribe. Chase could feel her readiness, her awareness of everything around her as he was suddenly seeing his life from his victim's perspective.

He shot one of his arrows. He felt it, as it hit her hard

and sharp in the leg. He felt the shock and pain as she tried to flee, and he felt the panic as she reached for her knife. Then he was pummeled with the jumbled emotions that she had felt, the anger, the desperation, the fight within her soul, as he dragged her away into one of the caves by the river.

He had heard her shouting at him that day, he had heard her screams. Not caring to understand her language, he had remembered it as an exciting feeling, a feeling that escalated his mood. Now he felt it as she had. She screamed as he tore the furs and clothes from her body, he felt her tears streaming down his own face, and all the feelings that came with them. There was helplessness, hopelessness, betrayal, fear and pain. She had whimpered beneath him. It was whimpering. He had felt it that day like a climactic release of emotion as he had moved over her, thrusting himself into her. She had felt something he never had. She had been whimpering, not from ecstasy as he had, but she had been whimpering from pain, and a betrayal of all she had held sacred.

She had so many emotions and thoughts running through her head that he couldn't understand them all. They flew through his mind as they had through her mind. He remembered that he had covered her up when he was done and tossed her his skin of water. He had planned to take her for a mate. He thought she would make an ideal mother. She was beautiful and strong. He had watched her for months. There had been others, but he had wanted her. There was something about the way she moved which had drawn him.

She couldn't leave with the arrow buried in her thigh, or so he had thought, but when he went out to gather firewood, she dragged herself out into the snow. He felt as she had felt, betrayed. Why would her gods render her useless to her people? She couldn't go home. She was shamed forever. Defeated, with nowhere to go and no strength in her body. She rummaged through her belongings, and pulled out her knife. She crawled, trying to stand, but couldn't. Then she reached the icy river, swollen in the thawing of the warm season. She said a prayer to her gods. It had been an apology. She didn't know what she had done to deserve such treatment, but she promised that she would no longer burden them with her life. She mustered all of her strength, and then with all the energy she had gathered, she thrust the dagger into her heart, and with her dying breaths, she managed to land in the raging river. Her dying thoughts were servitude to the goddess of the sea, Adrianna.

The hunter had remembered his own disappointment that day, and his anger. He didn't understand why she was gone when he had gotten back with the firewood. When he had come back to the tavern from that week's hunting, he had called on one of the whores, but she was not the woman that he had meant to be his, he still craved the flesh of the Astrid. He had felt anger towards himself and everything else. A deep seeded frustration that would not let up. He had pushed the whore off him, and when she had demanded payment anyway he had beat her until she was unrecognizable.

Slatkin now took him through what the whore had felt as she had been beaten. She had been trying to earn enough money to pay Saltook for a room for her two children to stay in. Her husband had died in one of the winter storms that had plagued them, and the house had been destroyed by fire when one of the children had been careless with their candles.

She had nowhere else to go. Saltook's tavern was the only place she knew to go. So she was selling her body to feed and house her family. She had felt panic and a strike to her self-esteem when she had been pushed away from Chase. She had to have money, so she demanded it angrily. She was unprepared for the fist across her face. She had slapped him back. It was simply a reflex. Shock swept through her, as she was unprepared for the following series of blows. Chase now felt what she had felt that day, all the pain that she had felt, and all of the pain Slatkin had carried these many years. Each blow stung him deeper, and he felt the life, the energy ebbing away from him. He could feel himself dying. He had tried to call for help, but he was choking on his own blood, as it swelled into his throat, and finally, all he could do was to accept his fate, and say a prayer for the children who had been left alone in the room down the hall. He prayed and prayed with dwindling hope as the crest of the wave of death fell upon him.

Slatkin stepped back and looked at Chase lying on the floor, whimpering as the women had. "So tell me, Chase, what are your thoughts? Have you had enough? There is more, if you want it." Slatkin could feel the change starting to take place in the hunter's soul.

The hunter could only look up at him with large, scared eyes. "What are you?" he managed to say, with quivering lips. Slatkin could make out the tears welling in the hunter's eyes.

"Who do you think I am?"

"You are some demon who has come to torture me," he said.

"No, Chase, I am no demon. Think harder." He smiled his wolfish smile, and continued. "I am retribution. Giving to each what is owed."

"You are torturing me, why have I just seen these things? Felt these things?" he asked. "Why are you doing this to me?" Slatkin sat beside the cage, towering over it.

"I give to each what is owed, hunter."

Chase crouched down in the cage, hanging his head. "Can't you see that I meant no harm? I meant to take her as my mate."

"That does not make it right, in my eyes or hers. Deep down, I think that you have some regrets about this. Though, you will not admit it. What of the other, the whore? She may have been doing wrong, but what you did was just as bad. How did it make you feel, Chase?" the beast asked.

Chase did not respond.

"Very well, Chase, I will leave you to ponder what you have taken in, what you have felt. I will also leave you with a gift. It is the rest of your retribution." When Slatkin had spoken the words, he caught the hunter's eye. Chase could not look away, and in a few moments, he was left with a waking nightmare, reliving all of his victims' pains from the most worthy opponent to the smallest animal murdered for sport.

Slatkin felt his pain leaving, but also his strength. He turned to the door, his wings receding into the bones of his back. He felt the shrinking of his body, the releasing of the weight of the fur and leathery skin. There was a feeling of freedom and weakness. He could barely walk as he stumbled out of the room and to his quarters. There was a fire burning bright for him, and his chair had been pulled close to it. He collapsed into it. A blanket suddenly covered the nakedness of his body. A weak, but meaningful smile spread across his lips.

"Thank you, Belle," he mumbled.

She smiled back. "As always, you're welcome." She responded, watching him fall into a peaceful sleep. A tear slid down her cheek as she picked up his feet and placed them on the footstool, wrapping them snuggly in the warmth of the blanket. She walked to a table set up in the far corner of the room, and picked up Slatkin's clothes that she had been stitching. She moved to the rug by his chair, and went back to work mending all the tears in the fabric, waiting patiently for him to awaken.

XIII

The Council of the Gods

Shea, Kialo's dining hall

Kialo sat, his white hair standing out against the dark features of his skin and garb. He greeted his son as he entered the room.

"Gazevi, Amicus," he greeted in the manner of the gods.

"Gazevi, father, and Fausti from your subjects." He bowed before his father, then took a seat beside him.

Amicus wore a brown robe, but he crowned himself with a simple hood, and nothing else. He prided himself on simplicity. He sat down, humbled in the presence of the earth god. Only the edges of his golden blonde hair could be seen until he pulled the hood back to reveal a young kind face with hazel eyes. The young god watched the door as his sister entered.

She was Adrianna, goddess of the sea, and she brought the essence of the ocean with her to the council. As she entered the room, it suddenly smelt salty. Her skin was the grey color of the ocean, and rough to the touch. Her hair flowed freely behind her. It was sea green, with bits of shells and seaweed woven into it. She had a crown of shells and barnacles, and she had garbed herself in sponges and coral. Her eyes were a light grey.

She did not greet the other two as she entered. She merely took a seat at the table, and waited patiently for her mother.

Kristiniva was the last to enter the room, adorned with her white dress designed with matching feathers atop her head. She entered the room, and waved her hand to the others in greeting. A breeze dispelled the ocean scent, and then she joined the others at the table with a smile.

"Gazevi," she announced. "So glad to see the family together at last," she smiled at her daughter. Her greeting was only returned with a blank stare.

"Father, tell us about them, the strangers," said Amicus. "Tell us all that you have discovered this day."

"Well, I have never been a man of many words, son, and so I thought it best to keep this as simple as I can." He sat back, and folded his hands over his plump belly. "It seems that our borders have not been maintained. These new strangers claim that they are from a land by the name of Tahln, but I have never heard of it. They say there is a man named Shekley, who brings the wrath of the Shadow along with him."

At this, there was a noise of surprise and fear from Kristiniva. "Yes, the Shadow." He continued, giving his wife a very serious and knowing look. "Now they claim that this Shekley was trying to go to a new land full of resources because he had destroyed everything in Tahln. He was going through a gateway, which he made from a machine. They followed him, and ended up here. They seem to be telling the truth, but the only thing that doesn't add up is the fact that he is not here. They did seem starved, and so they have been forgiven for stealing the fruit from the trees in the summer forest."

"Now the interesting thing is that they claim to be able to read thoughts and some of them can do extraordinary things with their minds, such as illusions and controlling thoughts of others. Some of them can move things and explode things. I've been keeping them in my holding cells until we make a decision on this."

"I don't see what is to be decided," said Kristiniva. "They are trespassing in the land, and they mean to do it harm. Any dealing with the Shadow, if that is the case, is nothing that I intend to get tangled in. I want nothing to do with it. Besides, how did they get in without the elves seeing them?" she asked. "They must have seen something, or been idle at their jobs. They are supposed to watch our borders, and defend them if necessary."

"I think, mother," Adrianna began, her voice was strange and full of the roar of the ocean depths, "that we should hear them out. Perhaps nothing is to be thought of the elves letting them in. If they were in need of healing, then that is all that they had to know. It is not up to us to judge why a person needs healing. We must offer it to them, and then release them back to their homes. I say the least we can do is to help them and offer them plenty of supplies before sending them on their way."

"I must say that I agree, at least to this," stated Kialo.

"Well, what is this *Shadow* they speak of?" Amicus asked.

There was silence among the gods.

Finally, Kialo sat up, folded his arms on the table and then leaned in to the others. "I don't like to speak of it, but I must say that it is something that terrifies me. I have heard of it long ago as a child. It was told to me by my great-grandfather. It goes all the way back to Selfirin and the dark god Nometheog. That is why he created this land. He had to make a stronghold of light, to keep the evil Nometheog back. The Shadow is this god. He is void of love, void of sympathy, empathy...he is the very essence of pain and loss, he devours everything he meets. Only the purest of light can dispel his evil. This Shadow is not a shadow like the shade from a tree, or the darkness of a night sky. It is the very seedling of all the dismay and chaos seen in all the other lands. If it is true, what these people say, then it would make sense that it has destroyed all of their resources. That is what it does. It is like a whirlwind, pulling all good things into the realm of nightmares."

"You speak of things that you should not, Kialo!" exclaimed Kristiniva.

"I only tell you this because I have heard of this Shadow before, and despite what you may think, it has the ability to penetrate our land of innocence. If nothing else, we are vulnerable. We are innocent, and we have made our people so. If we refuse to look it in the face, then it can weed its way in here, and destroy our land from its very foundation. Now the elves control our borders for a reason, or am I the only one who can remember this tale?

Long ago, Selfirin, the great god of light dispelled the shadow, back to its home in the void. He did that by making our land, a land of innocence, and pure light. We were made to be a force to keep the shadow back. He made it so that our borders would be defended, and so he created the elves from the light, though they would be the least lighthearted, for they would have the gift of opening and closing the spaces between worlds. Therefore, they would have to endure the darkness of other lands. He then built up our land to be impenetrable to the dark, but only as long as we kept our innocence and virtue. Now the fact that these creatures could come through our borders without our permission shows that they are creatures who defend the light, and therefore, I do not see them as liars."

"I remember the tale," began Kristiniva, very seriously, "but how do we stare something like this in the face without losing our innocence?" she asked.

"I think that we should find out where this Shadow, this Shekley is hiding. Perhaps he is in a neighboring land, one close to our portals. We should look, and if he is close by, we should ask that land for help," Amicus stated.

"First, let us consult the Selbdes themselves, and hear the story straight from them," stated Kristiniva.

"Very well," replied Kialo. "I will have my elves fetch them, and you will be able to question them yourself."

"Yes. I would still like to know how they got into the land without the elves' approval." Kristiniva stated.

"Why do you always blame the elves?" exclaimed Adrianna.

"I do not trust them all!"

"Well you have to...."

"That is enough ladies," proclaimed Kialo, standing and holding his hands in the air. "I will summon the Selbdes, and they can tell you all that they know."

He then shook the staff that he always kept by his side. There was a noise like the rustling of leaves. One of the tall, masked elves entered the room. He was a young male, with a mask of oak leaves and acorns. He had on a robe that although it was made of cloth, gave the illusion of being made of oak tree bark. When he entered the room, he walked over to Kialo, and bowed.

"Summon the leader of these strangers. We would like to speak to them."

"Of course, Great Kialo, it would please me to do this for you." He bowed, and left the room. In the next few moments, he returned with both David and Shiana. The gods watched them with interest.

"Good evening, I believe that is the terms you use, is it not?" Kialo asked them, as they walked through the doors, and made their way towards the table. There was a nod from Shiana. "Very well, have a seat, and we will begin eating shortly." He motioned toward some empty chairs at the ornate table that the gods sat at. The two Selbdes seated themselves.

"Now, I have summoned you here to tell your tales to these, the other gods of Shea. We are very interested in the tale of this Shekley and the Shadow that you claim has destroyed all the resources of Tahln. Please tell us in full, all that you know from the beginning so that we may decide if it is in our interest to help you heal, or help you in your endeavor to eradicate the Shadow. Please, let us hear it," he said with a kindly smile.

"I have a better idea," said David. "Why don't I show you all that I know?"

Once he spoke the words, he locked on to the minds of the gods. Then he pulled up memories of his brother that he projected into their thoughts. They were now remembering exactly what he had been through with his brother. Every scent, every noise, every feeling was now being broadcast into their mind as if they had lived it and not him.

The first memory was of him with his brother. They were young children. Shekley sat stacking blocks, obsessively lining each one exactly the way that he wanted.

"What are you building?" David asked.

"It's a city," said Shekley. "It's a city where I'm king."

"Cool, can I play?" asked David.

"Yeah, but you can't be the king." Shekley continued placing the blocks carefully.

"Okay," said David. Then something happened, and he understood exactly what Shekley was imagining. A look of amazement spread itself across Shekley's face.

The two boys could really see what they were imagining, as if it were there. David was bringing his brother's imagination to life. They played like this for hours, but when their mother called them, and David got distracted, the beautiful fantasy faded. The city had turned back into a pile of blocks. Their parents never believed it was real.

The memory flashed forward, and the two boys were older now, adolescents. Shekley sat cross-legged in the garage. He was tinkering with an old radio. Wires, tools and parts lay scattered on the concrete. He nervously fidgeted with a screwdriver, and he cut his eyes up at David when he saw him enter.

"Get out!" he said. Anger was surging through him, and David knew it. His thoughts were nothing but hatred.

"Shekley, I'm sorry for prying into your thoughts. I can't help it. You know I've tried to stop." David reached out reflexively, catching the screwdriver that Shekley had flung at him.

"Get out! Get out of my head!" Shekley shouted again, and then he flung himself at his brother, and both of them started hitting the other until their parents rushed to intervene, pulling them apart. Shekley spit at David.

"I hate you!" he yelled as blood rushed from his nose. David's forehead was red and swollen. He reached up to touch it. The memory moved forward again.

They were two teenagers sitting in the living room of their parent's house. Shekley was on the couch, and Xandra was beside him. She was her old self, the beautiful, dark skinned girl they had gone to school with. Their parents were cleaning up the dinner that they all had just eaten. David sat in a chair with his hand stretched out to Shiana, in the chair next to his. They held hands, their fingers intertwining. The tension in the room was unnerving. Shekley glared at David, and then he reached over to turn up the radio, a blaring static noise filled the air.

"So, Xandra, have you taken your military exam yet?" asked Shiana, trying to cut through the tense situation with small talk.

"I scored top of the class," she said, smiling. Shekley thought her smile was beautiful. His thoughts were of getting her alone now.

"Don't act like it's a surprise!" Shekley yelled. "Xandra's very intelligent. Besides, I know you're both trying to pry around in our brains."

"It's okay," said Xandra, pulling his hand into both of hers. "I think they're just trying to be nice." David could hear his brother's thoughts shift toward listening intently to her voice. He loved her voice.

"I'm glad to hear you did so well," said David. "We've all been worried about the exams. Shekley feels better knowing you passed. He loves it when you are happy."

Shekley reached out with his free hand to turn the static sound up louder. He was rolling his eyes back in annoyance. He was trying to keep David out of his head. It was hard for David to stay out, especially when his feelings were so strong, and his thoughts were so dominant. The radio helped them both, but it annoyed everyone else, especially their parents.

"Shekley," his Dad's voice came from the kitchen. "Turn it down."

Shekley glared at his brother from across the room. The volume dial on the radio seemed to turn down on its own. Shekley reached over and turned it back up.

"Shekley, I said turn it down," his father's voice came louder. A second time, the volume turned itself down.

"Would you stop it?" Shekley yelled standing up, and pulling Xandra with him. "Leave us alone," he yelled heading for the door. "What is in my head is nobody's business but mine."

"I'm not trying to be in there," David said.

"Stop lying, and turn the radio up!" Shekley shouted, close to David's face.

"I'm trying to keep you from getting grounded. You know that's what dad will do if you don't turn it down." David said through clenched teeth.

Shekley walked towards the door, and before their parents understood what had happened, Xandra and Shekley were already gone. David was left sitting guiltily with Shiana's hand in his. Her thoughts were trying to comfort him, but that was one time it didn't work.

Again, the memory moved forward. Shekley was weeping. David was trying to find him, but everytime he thought he was close he lost his brother's thoughts. He finally found him at the university. He was in the lab. The doors were locked. It was the middle of the night. David found the broken window Shekley had used and followed him upstairs. David's own heart broke as he realized what was happening. He stared through the glass panel, down at Shekley, weeping in torment. Xandra's body was laid out on the operating table, but she no longer looked like herself. Silver metal had bonded to her flesh and bone, and her mind was no longer her own. It was now controlled by whatever had possessed Shekley. The Shadow was not with him now, and he couldn't bring himself to realize what he had done. He couldn't remember what had happened while it had control of him, but the evidence of Xandra's slaying all pointed to him. The blood on his hands and clothes, the spatters of the hot metal splashed across his skin. He wept as his hands moved over her face and body. David felt tears roll down his own face as he listened to his brother's thoughts. *Who did this? Was this me? How could I do it to you? No, it wasn't me. It couldn't have been me.* He couldn't remember days of his life. They were blacked out from his memory, and he didn't know how she had died or where he had been. The last memory he could recall was five days old. They had been together then. He was trying to imagine her as she had looked before, but all he could see was the way she looked now, and it made him angry. David tried to pull it up for him, to give him the image that he longed for, to comfort him, but there was something blocking him. The shadow was coming back. It kicked him out of his brother's mind. When Shekley looked up at the glass, David felt a chill run down his body. His brother's eyes were not the way they should be. There was no color and no white, only blackness looking up at him. Then he spoke, but it didn't sound like him. It wasn't him. "I bet you couldn't see this one coming!" he said. The voice had a strange echo to it. There was a loud cackling coming from him, but David knew it was not his brother laughing. "It's not wrong. She asked me to do it," he said, an unnatural grin spreading across his face. David turned to run. He didn't know why, but what had just happened scared him like nothing else ever had.

The memory changed again. The world had changed. David was looking at a newspaper. The picture on the front was familiar. It was the city the two boys had played in so long ago as children. Only it was not the way they had originally imagined it. The city was dark, made of black metal, and even the skies were black. David turned the page. There was a picture of him with a wanted sign above it. There was a large bounty on his head. Shekley would do anything to get his revenge. He believed that David killed Xandra, and that his own experiments had resurrected her.

A series of flashes passed through their thoughts. It was the violence of the Shadow. People being pulled from their homes, slaughtered. Scenes of the Selbdes trying to stand up to the Mahldrusecs, but more and more it seemed that there was nothing to be done. The humans and Selbdes alike were being killed or captured. David couldn't bear to bring every detail forward. He didn't like to remember these, but he had to show them what the Shadow had done.

The memory changed a last time, and the gods witnessed David trying to heal Michael. Then there was the call from Shiana to come into the city and finally, the strange fog as the psychics were transported to Shea.

"What is this?" Kristiniva asked, trying to shake the memories away. "I see that your powers consist of making nightmares."

"That was no nightmare, dear wife," said Kialo. "I believe with every bit of my being that what he has just shown us is indeed real. It is the very thing that they need help with, and it is the same Shadow that Selfirin intended us to stand up to. We are meant to stand up to this Shadow, to stare it in the face, and to send it back to the abyss where it belongs."

The Selbdes sat quietly, waiting for the gods to discuss the matter.

"I agree," said Adrianna. "I think that in order to maintain our innocence, we must keep the light that makes our land be what it is. We must help them vanquish this Shadow, and as for how to do that, I'm not sure, but we will need the assistance of all the creatures that call Shea their home. We must be a land that works together. Our light will be brighter that way. So, we must start getting organized, and getting ready for whatever storm that we must weather."

"Mother, I'm sorry to inform you," began Amicus, "but if we do not go after it then it will come after us. You have seen a vision just now in your mind, and I think that we face choice. We can do nothing, and see our beautiful land turned into such an image, or we can do something about it now, and maintain the light and the purity."

"Very well, if I am the only one against it, then I will do what you three wish, but I hope you know that we are ill prepared. We have much to do if we are to be warmongering. Our subjects know nothing about war. They know nothing about violence. They have never seen a weapon meant for killing. Only ourselves and the elves even know about such things. I will do what I can, but convincing our subjects will be a lot harder, I think, than what all of you believe."

XIV

Arik

Shea, Kialo's palace

Celeste was alone, yet surrounded by drunken revelers. She sat at one of the ornate wooden tables placed in the courtyard of the earth god's castle. She waited for Kristiniva, and entertained herself by looking at the various creatures that danced and frolicked all around her. There was music playing like she had never heard before. Food was laid out on top of each table spread with a white cloth. Lanterns hanging in the trees and a bright silver moon brought light streaming down all throughout the gardens. White canopies were strung high above their heads, and the cloth from it swung in a breeze that was warm, and scented with the smell of the Shean summer. It was a sweet scent permeated with various mixtures of flowers.

The gods had yet to make an appearance, but from the bits of conversation that floated her way, she could hear that the other Sheans were not concerned about the strangers. She turned her head, when she heard a loud sizzling sound behind her. She turned to see a group of Party Sprites dancing about a keg. One of them was jumping on top of it, and every time his feet hit the wood, it turned a different color. The ones around it seem to be sending sparks flying all about it. Sprites were such colorful and vibrant creatures, that it made Celeste smile without thinking about it. When she did, she immediately stopped. The nerves in her face sent rivers of pain running all over her body. She turned away, and looked down at her lap.

There was a voice across the table from her. "I wouldn't try the ale, not after the Sprites have spiked it. Trust me, you won't remember anything for days." Celeste looked up to see a dark haired elf with a familiar face. It was the same one who had taken her daughter.

"It's you!" She exclaimed. "How is she? Did she...?"

"Shh...!" The elf put a finger over his lips. "She's okay." He said calmly. "How are you?"

Celeste understood that this was to be a quiet conversation so she leaned over to him. "I'm..." there was so much she wanted to say. Regret, worry, depression, she wanted to pour her heart out, but the tears started. The nerves in her mouth had forgotten how to quiver, and so she hung her head and turned away, trying to blink her tears into oblivion, but they just kept coming, each with its own sting.

"Here, sweet angel," The elf said as he passed her a white handkerchief. "Dab away all those stains of red. Your daughter is in Sark, as we promised, and the gods are too busy talking to miss our escape at the moment. Walk with me, and perhaps we can talk a little more in depth about your situation." The elf stood up, and Celeste followed, welcoming the fact that Kristiniva was busy.

It was a while before either of them spoke again. Celeste was busy wiping the tears away, and the elf walked patiently beside her, leading her into sections of the castle that became more remote as they walked, yet still exposed to the night air. Finally, he stopped outside of a door.

"Here's a room for us to talk in." He looked around, and then pulled out a key to unlock the door. "I doubt anyone will bother us here." He opened the door silently, and held out his arm to lead her in. In a quick moment, he had the door locked, and an oil lamp lit. Celeste looked around to find that they were in a room with a stone floor, and stone walls, with no windows. There was a couch, with a small wooden table in front of it, a chair by a fireplace, and a writing table on the opposite side of the room. "Have a seat, and make yourself at home. No need to fear prying ears or minds while in here." He said, while he knelt in front of the hearth to start a fire. "I assure you, lady, that this room is protected. This is where I stay while I'm here, and I don't stay anywhere that is not enchanted with protective spells."

"Thank you for your help," Celeste began. "I have tried my best to stay positive these last few days, but my mind is racing, and my heart is heavy, for I have already lost so much. I am afraid that I have doomed my daughter to a terrible fate. I feel like I'm a bad mother."

The elf settled him self into a chair. "I don't believe so. I think that you are doing what you believe to be the right thing, and if you, being an angel, believe that it is right, then I trust your judgment more than that of others."

"We can make mistakes, too. We are not perfect, and I'm worried about her." She looked at Arik, with pleading eyes. "Tell me of her father, what did he say? Will he make the journey here to find me?"

Arik was silent for a moment, contemplating what to say next. She entrusted him with so much, and he hated to tell her the truth, but he owed it to her, even though she would probably not understand why the elves had done what they had to her daughter.

"Well," he began awkwardly, with knots forming in his stomach, "We never saw her father. We left her in the forest, though I assure you, my lady, that she was protected with the strongest magic that we could send with her."

Celeste just stared for a moment. She didn't know what to say to this. Was this elf playing a game with her, or did he really leave her daughter all alone? Now her fears and hopes swelled in her mind. There was no way that she could possibly get home without Victor coming to find her.

"Did she know her way home?" She asked, but before she could get an answer, she was forming more questions, "Why would you leave her all alone? She's never been to Sark, and she might not be able to find her way!" Celeste found herself straining her voice between the choking back of tears and the yelling. She found that her words and her thoughts were jumbling themselves over each other, and it was hard to tell one from the other. "I don't know what to do now!

That was my last chance, and I was so sure that the dream was telling me to send her home... I was so sure. Oh, how could I be so...so ...I just feel like I've abandoned her...Oh, Saigolai! Saigolai, where are you?" She hung her head and wept into the tissue. She rocked back and forth. There was so much trying to come out of her at once, that she didn't know what to do with it all.

Arik let her cry until there were no more tears left inside of her. He knelt beside her, taking her hands in his.

"Does it feel good to let out all of the bad things that Kristiniva has tried to keep inside of you?" Arik asked her quietly as he sat down beside her.

Finally, Celeste looked up with the left side of her face in a twisted half smile half cry. "Yes, and no," she said. "I know that she is trying to help me, and heal me, but there is a part of me that makes me think she is trying to take something from me."

"Well, it seems like a reasonable idea to only express good things, but I know as well as you that sometimes we must release the bad to make room for the good, especially for creatures like you and I. Elves, as I'm sure you know, are the only Shean creatures that have access to the gateways to Sark. I prefer it there. At least there, I feel freedom. I have the freedom there to fall in love, to get angry, to feel grief. Here, there is no anger or grief, or at least that is what Kristiniva would have us believe. There is also no love. It was not always so."

"Really?" Celeste asked. "What changed it?"

"The current gods. They believe that the way to maintain innocence is to never feel bad emotions, and so they have done all that they could to rid this land of its negativity, even going so far as to outlaw it. Though, you still feel it, don't you?"

Celeste nodded her head. "All the time."

"So do I" said Arik. "So do all Sheans, but they can't admit it, or they would be breaking the law. I however,

124

believe that there is no way to maintain innocence. You cannot bless creatures to have a mind, and not have them use it. As long as there is intelligence, there will be no innocence, but you cannot take away the intelligence without destroying us."

"You say that these are not the first Shean gods. I thought that gods were immortal, so how is that possible?"

"There is no such thing as immortality here. All the previous gods have died. Some live again, but all of them die. There is only one constant thing in this land, and that is change. With the coming of each new god, the world gets reshaped to fit their imaginings. Laws and rules change. In fact it wasn't until seven years ago that dark emotions were outlawed, and I'm sure you'll be interested to know seven years ago, Kristiniva put her laws into effect to govern those who worship her in Sark. Anyone she saves must serve her for five years.

"So she made the law to keep me here." The realization now dawned on Celeste.

Arik nodded his head. "I'm afraid so angel, and not to cut the wound deeper, but I must tell you that she could have healed you in less than one month. You could have been back in your home soon after you left."

"Why would she do that to me?" Celeste asked. There was a hurt look on her face.

"I will tell you. You have something that she wants. It is something that she has never felt before, and she can't get enough of it to fill her up. Can you think of what it could be? It is the very thing that she is trying to drain from you."

"My love," Celeste barely whispered the words.

Arik nodded. "She has felt compassion and pity for the dying, but she herself had never felt love or been loved until you arrived. You brought with you something that she had never fathomed, and she is trying to drain you of your power. She cannot get enough of it."

Celeste understood so much of it now, and so many

things started to make sense to her. "You say that nothing is immortal, but love is. There is no end to it. She cannot drain it all!"

"I know," said Arik. "She will keep you here forever if she can get away with it. I agree with her that it is a wonderful power, but it is not for her to wield. She would abuse it, and perhaps not understand it. That is one of the reasons that the elves have vowed to help you. We know that in order to be handled the right way it must be you that does it."

"You are right." Said Celeste, "but how does that help me, how am I going to get home?"

"Well, I think that we should try to wait for your plan to work. However, I have some things that I'm working on that could possibly get you home sooner. I have no doubts that your daughter will find her way home, but I have worries that she will not be able to find her way back here. It is very hard to find Shea once you leave it, unless of course, you know the way already, which she won't. I can assure you that." Arik finished off his wine, and then looked at Celeste very seriously. I hope that you are not angry with us, but we put protective spells on the basket. We did it to save her. One of those is a very potent memory fog. I doubt she remembers much before waking up."

"Why would you do that?" Celeste asked, jumping to her feet. "Why? You knew that she needed to remember the way back!"

"We have our reasons, all of them with her protection in mind. There are many creatures who would relish the idea of stealing her powers, too. Many who would think to capture her, as you have been captured. She is a light angel of innocence, and therefore, the most vulnerable of you all! Innocence itself is forever vulnerable, naive, ignorant! She must be protected, but so must this land. While we are willing to aid you in your plan to get home, we still have a job, and that is to protect this land, and while I may disagree with many of its laws, I am loyal to my reason for existence. There are laws of the universe that I'm too weak to stand up to, and giving away the location of this land is one of them. We exist here for a reason, and I'm not about to directly or indirectly lead strangers here unless there is a reason, and it is always within the law that we wipe the memory of this place from their minds."

"I understand what you are telling me," Celeste said, as she paced back and forth, "but if she can't remember anything, then how will she find her way back? How will she lead her father here?"

"Well, she'll remember us, and we've given her a clue, as long as she or your husband follow it, they will be able to find you."

Celeste tried to think about what Arik was telling her, but her head was buzzing from all the information she had received, and her eyes felt scratchy and more swollen than usual from all the tears.

"I'm just so tired..." she said.

"I understand," said Arik. "Here, I may have something that will lift your spirits, and perhaps your vitality." He walked over to the writing desk, and pulled open a drawer. Celeste could hardly see in the flickering firelight what it was that he had pulled out, but when he showed it to her, it was a small bottle of what appeared to be writing ink, but when he opened it, there was a silvery sparkle shining from inside the bottle.

"What is it?" She asked.

"It is something that we elves like to call endless dust."

"What does it do?" Celeste asked.

"Let me see your arm, and I will show you." Arik said, reaching for the sleeve of her coat. Celeste jerked away.

"Trust me, please!" He said sincerely. She could see from the look in his eyes that he wanted to help.

Celeste took a deep breath, and with a lot of reluctance, she managed to pull off the coat lined with

127

feathers. She removed it slowly, and carefully, so as not to irritate the skin on her arms. When it fell to the ground, she looked at Arik expecting to see some sort of judgment on his face, but there was only sorrow.

"I know it hurts", he said, looking at the burns that traced their way down her side.

She nodded her head. "I'm lucky to have the movement of my arm again. When the wound was new, my arm had fused with my side..." her thought trailed off with those words.

Arik pitied the angel, and he hoped that he could offer her some hope. "I pray that this will help. If it does, then you can have this bottle." He held it out, and gently shook it over her forearm. There was a soothing feeling, as it fell over her skin, and then Celeste was amazed as the wound began to heal itself. When the healing was done, her forearm from her wrist to halfway her elbow had been healed. She managed a small noise reminiscent of a laugh as she rubbed the now smooth white skin with her hand. She looked at Arik, pleading with her eyes. Excitement was overwhelming her.

"Do it again!" She demanded. "This time, fix my face."

"In time, angel," began Arik, "It would be my greatest wish to heal you now, but if Kristiniva knew that I was helping you with this, then terrible things could happen to me. It must be our secret. This is powerful stuff, and she doesn't want you to heal, remember. So my advice would be to use only a small amount once a week. I know that is slow, but it is faster than her healing. My second bit of advice would be to only use it in places that will be covered by your clothing. As much as you would want to heal your face, now is not the time."

"I understand," Celeste agreed as thoughts of healing tonight faded with a great disappointment, his words made sense, and she was thankful for even this small bit of relief. "Thank you so much!" She explained. "I wish I could repay you for this somehow."

"You will think of something in time, I'm sure, but really, think nothing of it, I am glad to help you in any way that I can." Arik explained to her.

"Now, wouldn't you like to enjoy this reverie tonight?" He asked.

"Oh, not really," she said, "I don't exactly feel like I fit in."

"Well, you don't. But that shouldn't stop you. If anything, the Sheans are fascinated by you."

"I can't. You understand, don't you?"

"I understand. Well, you are more than welcome to rest here," said Arik. "I, however, would love to dance under the trees with the full moon shining, and dine until I can hold no more. If you leave, do not worry about putting out the fire or the lamp, and do not lock the door. It will lock itself. However, I warn you to take all that is yours, because you cannot get back in without the key."

"Thank you," said Celeste.

"Anything that I can do to help you is well worth my time. You are welcome." He responded, and with that he gave her one last smile, and put the bottle of endless dust on the table, and then made his way out the door into the warm summer night.

Celeste lay down on the couch with her thoughts racing through her mind, and spinning in circles, until they spiraled into dreams as she fell into a sleep of enchantments.

XV

The Earth God's Holding Cells

Celeste awakened from her short nap and found that the fire had gone out. She could still see with her eyes that were accustomed to the darkness, and rightfully so. She stared at the bottle of endless dust, still in a state of disbelief. She reached out, clasping it firmly in her hand. Discovering a pocket in her coat, Celeste stashed the bottle away. She stood and opened the door, letting herself out into the warm Shean night. She stared around her, but there was no one. When she turned to see if the door was locked, it was no longer there. Nothing seemed to surprise her, though. She assumed it was part of the enchantments. She walked away, still clutching the bottle of endless dust inside her coat pocket. She had no destination in mind. She only wished to get away from the festivities and find the new strangers. She needed to speak to them. Arik was sincere, she could tell, but she knew that she had to talk to the strangers for herself. She had to know the way home, so that she could form a plan of her own.

She wandered around marble columns and white canopied ceilings, through full, lush, aromatic gardens. She stepped through stuffy, damp smelling caves, and dry, stuffy rooms encased in wood and stone. She walked until she was far away from where she began. Then as if she had been summoned there through her angelic senses, she could hear the echoing sounds of someone's voice. It was coming to her as if through a cave. She was in a garden with a cliff as one of its walls, and the stone walls and columns of the castle were the other three. It was a courtyard. She was silent and still as she listened. For a moment there was nothing, and then she heard it again. It was like laughter. She followed the sound to a well covered with vines. There was a fountain carved as a statue of a young woman clothed in a robe. She was pouring water into the well. Celeste peered into the well, and saw that the waterfall from the fountain almost hid a ladder made to be camouflaged into the color of the well's stones. She smiled, thankful for her keen senses. She reached out to the ladder with her left foot, taking a hold on the statue's arms. The water that splashed over her was icy cold. She placed her second leg on the ladder, a rung below the first, and then she grabbed the ladder first with one hand and then another. The water splashed over her like a flood, but she held her breath and felt her way to the bottom. She looked around, wiping water from her face, and squeezing it from her hair. The water at the bottom was only knee deep, and there was a tunnel leading to a light, where she heard more voices. She was certain that this was where she wanted to be right now.

She squeezed some of the water from her dress, and held it above her knees, and she began following the tunnel. There were beautiful vines and flowers lining the rocks, which shimmered with a light of their own. She took a moment to marvel at the beauty, but only a moment. She would not be delayed from her task at hand. She splashed further into the cave and then she stepped up onto dry grassy land. High above her, she could see the sky poked through several holes in the top of the rocks. She looked around. There were walkways made in stones that led to several different passages. The main entrance was lit with a warm, orange glow coming from the flames of torches and oil lamps. She listened, and heard the voices ahead of her. So she followed them.

She was surrounded by darkness, but slowly coming up to the sounds of the voices. The voice of a man was becoming more defined. He spoke in a calm baritone. "Well, if anyone can convince them it's Shiana, we shouldn't force them. No one should be forced into war, and if anyone can understand that, it would be us..." the voice trailed off, and Celeste caught on to the sadness in the meaning behind it.

She listened as a second voice now spoke. "I know,

but I do hope that she can be persuasive. I mean, Shekley may already be on his way. I would rather that these people be prepared. If he comes upon this land, with no defenses in place, it will only be a matter of hours before they are wiped out. We should know that, too."

There was a drawn out silence. Celeste continued forward, coming up to a wooden door. There was a window of sorts at the top, and it was open, but she noticed that it had been covered with a patterned design of wood. She peered inside. A group of people lay about on cushions and beds. Some of them in the corner were seated on pillows, and eating from baskets of food placed on a blanket. One of them looked up, and took notice of her.

He was a short man with choppy brown hair. He was clothed like all the others. It was apparent that the Sheans had clothed them in simple white robes. She could tell the man coming towards her was muscular, built for fighting. He had dark brown eyes, filled with sadness.

"Hey, who's there?" hasked. He walked to the door, and she came eye to eye with him. She looked at his soul. Redness, the color of pain, ran over the deep creases of gold. Such a valiant fighter he must be! She brought herself back, remembering her purpose for finding them.

Celeste looked at him, water dripping from her wet hair. "I'm..." she could not tell him who she was, if word got out that she had spoken to them, she would be guaranteed a life of servitude to the queen. "I'm...someone who wishes to speak with you. Will you speak with me?"

"I understand you!" he exclaimed. "How is that?" The others now became quiet as they all looked on.

"I can communicate to all creatures. It is a gift of mine." She smiled, bearing the stinging in her face. She could see pain ebbed deep into this man's aura. She could see the suffering and the tragedy that had befallen him. There were horrors from his past that were far worse than anything that this land had seen since its forming. She took a moment to gather her thoughts.

"You are strangers to this land, correct?" she asked. Her eyes shimmered deep green as she spoke.

"Yes, and what a world this is!" he exclaimed. "It is truly a gem of all realms."

Celeste nodded her head. "Yes," she responded. "There are others still, though, that are more suitable for some races. Where is it that you came from?" she asked.

"We come from Tahln. It was once a very prosperous land, but it was darkened, and stripped of all beauty and prosperity in the war."

"War? What war?" The angel listened intently.

"We have been at war for many years with the man called Shekley. He is intent on dominating the world under the rule of the Shadow. He is filled with hate and his thirst for revenge has decimated all of our land, all of our resources. We followed him here, and we think that your people may be in danger."

Celeste sorted through this information in her mind. "So, how did you get here?"

"We followed Shekley, and we ended up here. We don't know how he managed to do it, and we have no way of knowing until we get into his facility and override his machines."

A frown curled at the corner of Celeste's mouth as she took in the information. He was telling her nothing. There was no way home. Yet, he offered so much to her. There was Shekley, something called the Shadow, and a war that was possibly endangering the people of this land. She thought to herself that maybe there was a reason that she had been placed here after all. Perhaps these people needed her. Maybe they needed her love more than any Sarkian. She smiled with a new meaning.

"I want you to know that I hope that you and all your people will remain safe. I will help you in any way that I can. I am sorry for the hardships that have befallen you. I am not a ruler of this land, but I do have some power over the queen. We will do all that we can to aid in abolishing your pain and suffering. I will ask the gods to help you."

"Thank you, lady! Thank you!" the man exclaimed.

"You are welcome, but may I ask your name? Who am I speaking on behalf of when I go to the queen?"

"My name is Michael," the man said. "Do you know when David and Shiana will be speaking with your leaders?"

Celeste nodded her head. "I think they must be doing it now." She smiled at the man, quickly and jerkily, so that her face contorted in pain again. "So, why is it that all of you are in this room? Why are you not partaking in the events tonight?"

"We have been asked to stay in here. It is much safer if we do. We agreed to it. We don't want to endanger the citizens of this land. If Shekley were to find out that we are here, he would kill you all and do as much damage as he could."

"How awful!" Celeste exclaimed. "I do hope that you all get the care that you need." Celeste smiled before turning to leave.

Michael watched as Celeste walked away. There was a strange feeling that took hold of him while she was standing at the door. It was indescribable, and as she walked away, he felt a deep longing to follow, but he turned to the others instead. All the others had smiles on their face when he turned around.

"Did any of you..." he searched for the words he wanted to say carefully... "Did any of you feel...something...something different when she was at the door?"

There was some nodding and agreeing in the room. "It feels like love, like a home," someone said.

"Yes, like love..." he said, as he stared out the door.

The dark angel was headed back towards the well,

134

when she spotted Arik sitting under one of the gas lanterns.

"Arik, what are you doing here?" she asked.

"I should ask you the same thing. You are keeping out of trouble, I hope."

"Well, probably not, knowing me. I have just offered my help to the strangers. I am going to go to Kristiniva on their behalf, and ask that she do all she can to aid them."

Arik glared at the angel. "You did what?" he asked with exasperation.

"I offered them my help, and I am going to ask Kristiniva to aid them."

Arik shook his head. "I hope you are not serious. Celeste, what are you doing? You cannot save everyone in the universe. Keep your goal in mind. You have to get home. You have no business aiding anyone unless it is your own people in Sark."

"I'm sorry, Arik, if you disagree with me, but I believe that these people have seen great suffering, and I feel that as a dark angel of love, I must help them. These people are in need of that. They have suffered, and I wish to see it ended."

Arik smiled. "Love is not always wise," he said, "but it is forgiving." He stood up. "Come with me, Celeste, I want you to come speak to my sister. I have told her about you, and she wishes to meet you. She is aiding us, even if she seems loyal to the queen at times. She has her reasons, though."

"Okay," said Celeste. "Lead and I shall follow."

"It's this way." He led Celeste down one of the darker tunnels. "So, do you realize where you just were?" He asked her as they walked.

"I was in a cave at the bottom of a well," she responded.

"Not exactly, angel. You were in Kialo's holding cells. That is where he keeps his prisoners. You see, even the Sheans who have outlawed any bad behavior and negative thoughts have prisons. Kristiniva keeps her prisoners close by to watch every move they make, where she can listen to every whisper from their lips. Kialo has holding cells. Adrianna imprisons outlaws in a kelp pool surrounding her throne room. You must be wary, angel. The gods rarely abide by their own laws, and they will annihilate you if they get the chance."

"You've made that clear to me. I know to watch my step now."

"Good, you'd do well to remember. I know that you must have used your senses to look into that man's soul. I don't need to know what you saw. It is none of my business. However, I must tell you that the enchantments in the holding cells are some of the strongest in the land, other than those at the borders. You know that they are not being held there against their will."

"Yes, they told me they believed that they are in the safest place, one that will not endanger the people of the land. It is a place where their enemy will not find them.

"This may be true, or it may not be," said Arik. "I think the gods are terrified, and so they have made sure to put them where they will be the least threat to them."

"Why are the gods scared of them?" Celeste asked.

"They are capable of things, very dark things."

"What do you mean? Dark magic?"

"No, it is a gift. Like...your gifts, but they are not angels. They are humans with abnormally advanced minds. What they can do is different in each one. Some of them can manipulate the actions of others. Some can change their physical appearance. Some of them can even explode things or destroy things just by thinking about it. Now, to be fair, not all of the gifts are dark. Some of them are quite extraordinary, and they mirror the gifts of the gods. They can heal others, or interpret other languages. Some can make flowers grow, or reproduce an object just by thinking it. It is amazing, but threatening at the same time. I'm not sure what to think of it."

There was silence for a while, and Celeste began to wonder if they would ever reach the end of the tunnel, but they soon came to a stairway, and as they ascended, Arik continued his thoughts.

"You went there, I'm sure with good intentions, thinking that you would not be discovered. Now you leave, with evidence to put you in there. You have promised to speak to Kristiniva on their behalf. How will she know that you weren't there if you speak to her about them?"

Celeste looked up at Arik with astonishment and realization. Her gut suddenly felt like a great knot of twisted branches.

"What have I done?" she asked.

"I can warn you, but the enchantments may still get you. I think, though, that you have been saved by your own angelic grace. Kristiniva may believe your intentions this time, since you are the angel of love, and it was love and sympathy for these creatures that tricked you into promising them help. In the future, though, I will warn you again, you must be careful. If enchantments are strong enough to manipulate the advanced minds of these creatures, then surely no one can stand up to it."

They walked on in silence for a bit longer, and then they came to a wooden door with an iron knocker and iron hinges. "We need to get you dry. How did you get so wet, anyway?" Arik asked.

"I came in by the well."

Arik smiled. "Ah, yes indeed, I must tell you that there is a way to turn the water off before you go down the ladder, and then back on once you get to the bottom."

"I shall have to be more careful!" Celeste laughed, before following the elf through the door.

XVI

The Meeting

Sark, the Howling Wolf Tavern

Alexandria had come to her room late. The dawn was breaking in a pink line at the bottom of a grey cloud as she was just getting to her room. When she opened the door, she was surprised to see the young boy who had stood up to the hunters cleaning the room for her.

"Oh, I'm sorry!" he explained. "I was supposed to be out of here before you arrived. Saltook wanted it to look nice."

"Really, it's fine," the angel said, "as long as the bed has clean sheets."

He laughed then. "They're clean, don't worry. I made sure of it. Besides, this is not one of the rooms that we usually rent out...you know, to that kind. It's Basilla's room."

He smiled at the look of alarm on Alexandria's face.

"I can't take her room!" she explained.

"Oh, no, really, don't worry about it. Trust me!" he exclaimed. "It's really not a problem."

Alexandria started to protest again, and then she caught a flash of his soul colors. "Oh, I see."

"See what?" He asked, turning to look at her.

"I see why you and she wanted to give me this room. She's staying with you tonight."

He smiled a huge smile. "Saltook agreed to it."

Alexandria smiled as she saw again all the excitement and the love running through him. "I'm probably supposed to give you some advice, but from looking into you, I believe that you already have everything worked out. She's lucky, you know. Finding someone with honorable intentions is rare...and you're lucky. She's a good girl."

He nodded his head. "I know. Believe me. Besides,

finding someone, you know, like me, is rare. That's why there are so few of us. We love to go around in packs, but the hunters make sure that we are as scattered as they can make us."

Alexandria now understood the strange patterns that she had seen in the souls of some of the citizens of Sark, including this boy. "So what kind of creature are you exactly? I mean, I know that you are not human, but I can't tell exactly what it is that you are."

"I'm a werewolf."

"Oh!" She smiled with understanding. "Well this is a first for me. Until tonight, I had not met any werewolves, though I have studied them. I hope you'll forgive my rudeness in asking, but there are some things which even my kind can't see."

"That's okay," he said. "I would probably ask too." He looked around the room. "I think that I'm done here, so I'll leave you to rest. If you need anything, there is a bell on the wall there, just ring it and I'll come." He walked to the door and started to leave, but then turned back to the angel. "By the way, thank you again. I'm forever faithful to you now. I mean you saved Basilla's life, and probably mine...and you saved so much more. If I can ever repay you, just let me know, and I'll come if I can. My name is Lazaris."

"Thank you, but I do not seek payment for anything. I just do what I am here to do. I am thankful for your appreciation, though."

He gave Alexandria another grin before exiting the room. When he was gone, Alexandria closed and locked the door tightly. She undressed down to her under clothes. She looked forward to resting in a warm, clean bed. When she finally lay down in the bed, it was only a matter of seconds before she was resting peacefully in a long awaited, warm sleep.

Alexandria awoke quickly, packed up, and headed

downstairs to have breakfast with Khiel and Valassa before she left. They sat at the table. Alexandria looked at them seriously. "I'll be going to the castle by myself. I can find it from here on my own. These people here need you more than I do. One of you should go back to Klarissa to explain about the arrangements. The other needs to stay here in case my enchantments don't hold.

"I'll go back to Klarissa!" exclaimed Khiel.

"Good!" Valassa shouted more loudly than what she should have, then lowering her voice she said. "I am the best fighter, after all."

Khiel rolled his eyes as he tried not to laugh and turned away.

Alexandria smiled. "Well, I'm glad that we're all in agreement." She reached to her waist and pulled out her satchel of gold. "Here," she said, handing Khiel a hand full, and then Valassa another handful. "This is just in case you need it. I may not be back for a while. I have that feeling that it'll be a while."

She stood up to leave. "Khiel, you be extra careful when traveling alone, and make sure that whoever comes back here understands that they need to travel in pairs. Okay?"

"I will," he responded. "You be careful yourself."

"Really, Khiel!" Valassa exclaimed. "I'm sure she can handle it."

He waved her comment away, and they bid farewell. Alexandria turned to wave at Saltook, and then she walked out into the cold, snowy evening.

Alexandria could feel her sister's presence dimly as she neared the castle she had been eyeing the whole journey up the mountain. She knew there was a need for her to be here. She dismounted Vortex as they came to the dilapidated gate that lay broken and in disrepair. A massive pile of wreckage littered the castle ground. She could see that the stones had not been maintained. There were signs of kial thieren trees and vines poking holes through the stonework of the walls. She sniffed the night air, full of a crisp snowy aroma, and the bitterness of the cold salty sea. She could smell, too, a fire burning close by and...a spice perhaps? Maybe an herb, she told herself, as she pulled Vortex closer to the castle. She walked up the stoned pathway leading to the castle, noticing the trees now growing through what used to be fountains and benches. She led the unicorn past them to the main entrance.

The angel gazed upward at the large grey, castle and turned to Vortex, "Well, Vortex, it's worth a try, even though I know I will not find her here." She turned and pounded on the large door painted with a fading hue of red. There was not an answer. She put her ear to the door and listened for any signs of life that may be thriving within. There was hardly any sound at all, and then she heard the thumping of quick footsteps coming closer.

Slowly, the large door creaked open, and she was looking at what appeared to be an old, rather worn out looking man. However, she recognized him for what he really was, and her heart leaped. It was such a rare thing to see one of his kind. She smiled politely. "I would introduce myself, but given your status, I assume you already know," she said to him.

The Orostiro nodded his head. "Yes, indeed! I could feel your presence days ago, but I didn't know why you were here, until now. Please, come inside, and we will talk."

Alexandria patted Vortex's nose. The unicorn nodded understanding and trotted towards the stables. Slatkin motioned the dark angel inside. Alexandria followed him through the doorway, a long hall and then through several more doors, before finally reaching the kitchens. Victor, Angelik, Belle and Carmina all sat around the long table by the fire. Slatkin led Alexandria through the entryway and motioned for her to have a seat at the table. All eyes in the room were suddenly on her. She hesitated for a moment, looking around at everyone in the room, taking note of who and what it was that they were. She walked over to Victor.

There was a look of revelation on his face.

"You know me?" she asked him. "I think I know you."

Victor returned the stare. "I think so," he said. Belle looked at Alexandria, confused about what was going on. Victor stood up and embraced the yellow haired woman standing by his chair. "You are always welcome here, though I'm sorry to say that Celeste is not here to greet you. She's is lost."

"I already know," she responded. "I came to see if there is anything that I can do to help you, and I bring news from your people."

"My people?" Victor asked.

"They are alive, and want you back in power. They are terrified of the hunters, and what they might do if they are caught aiding you."

"Well," Belle finally said. "That's all wonderful, but a little introduction would be helpful for some of us."

"I apologize," Alexandria said, "I am Alexandria of Chimrion, Celeste's sister."

"Well!" Belle exclaimed, quite speechless otherwise.

"Oh," said Carmina, as if she had just placed the missing piece of a puzzle together. "Perhaps you would join us, and the mystery of my signs may be revealed."

Alexandria took a seat at the table and turned to Angelik. "You..." she stated... "You are the other one that Klarissa spoke about. It was you that arrived here the same night as I did. You have enchantments about you, you know. Deep enchantments. You will not easily be cured of this magic. It may take years."

"What enchantments?" Victor asked.

"Well, I don't know exactly, but I am trained in the magic arts, and I can recognize the workings of others. It does not take much knowledge to see that sorcery hangs heavy about her. The root of the enchantment may be hard to trace considering the power behind the spells."

"Well," Belle started. "We know that she has had her memory wiped, and that she has absorbed some of the winter into her. She is an angel of light, and no doubt, she is magical just in that aspect alone. I have been working on a potion of sorts to help her memory. She is starting to remember some things, but mostly in dreams, so she isn't sure if they are real or not."

"We have a clue about where she may have been," said Victor. "She remembers waking up in a basket woven by the elves, and then there's this." He reached into his coat pocket, and pulled out the blue stone. He handed it to Alexandria. "Do you know what it is?" he questioned.

Alexandria peered at the blue stone. The light from it cascaded onto her face, she turned it around, trying to remember if she had ever seen anything like it, but she hadn't even read about anything as intriguing as this small blue jewel. She looked at Victor with a defeated glance. "I'm sorry, Victor. I have never seen anything like this!" she exclaimed. "I can assure you that it has great power, though. I can feel it, as well as see it. I think that if we could find the elves, then maybe they could tell us what this means."

"My thoughts precisely," said Victor. "I have never had dealings with them. They are one of the only Sarkian groups that keep to themselves, and do not try to fight with their neighbors, but I think that the time has come for me to meet with them."

"I agree," Alexandria responded. "I've studied them and recently met some. They are rumoured to have very potent dream spells, as well as amnesic power. Their presence alone is dreamlike."

"I will go with you to meet with them."

"I will be going, too, Victor. There is a foreboding gloom hanging about it the air. You may need me," Slatkin stated.

Victor smiled as he mulled things over in his mind. "That sounds good. I think that we should leave as soon as possible, tomorrow night, as a matter of fact. I think that we should try and pack as soon as we have all had our meal."

"Wait now! Wait just a minute," protested Belle quietly. "This is all happening so quickly. She's only just arrived. Are you sure you want to leave so soon?" There was a stunned look still on her face. "I mean, I haven't even gotten the child's memory potion prepared. Victor, are you sure about this?"

"Yes, Belle, I feel it in the air. If I don't do something now, then I may not be able to later. I can't explain it, but there is this sense of urgency I feel. It's like something big is about to happen."

Belle nodded. "Well then. If you need me, I think I'll start packing you some food to take with you." She glanced quickly at Slatkin before leaving the room. She exited the room with more haste than she normally would have. Slatkin peered down at the table, and Alexandria felt waves of worry pour through him.

"Can I come?" Angelik asked.

"Of course," said Victor. "I wouldn't let you go anywhere else except with me." She smiled as he said the words, and clapped her hands together.

"Good!" she exclaimed, smiling at her father.

XVII

The Servants of the Shadow

Sark, northeastern wilderness

Shekley had left with Xandra to find willing servants of the Shadow. He had journeyed through the barren lands and to the top of the Sarkian Mountains, not thinking of food or rest. He simply did as the Shadow bid him. The Shadow would not let him die as long as he was useful. He had come into the forests of black trees that ran throughout Sark, but he hardly had a chance to see the wilderness that surrounded him. His vision was clouded in a dark mist, as it so often was whenever the Shadow possessed him. Xandra stepped steadily beside him. She was aware of what had happened to them both, yet she was powerless to stop it. It was like a constant nagging in the back of her mind.

"You must find a way to stop it!" the voice told her. "You must find a way to stop it, because you love him." The voice was always there, but Xandra could not grasp the free will of her own mind. She could not understand why, but there was nothing she could do to help him. She could only do what he asked and hope that someone somewhere would come to their aid, and rid them of this lunacy.

Sark, outside of the Howling Wolf Tavern

Haz gathered himself up clutching his swollen, now almost completely toothless mouth. He knew the bruising would go away, but to be beaten in a tavern brawl by a woman was something that would harm him the rest of his life. He did not know how he had ended up outside the tavern, bleeding in the snow, but he knew he would have to find Markus. That woman had been looking for him, and if she intended to kill him, then he was certain that she would.

She was stronger than any other opponent he had

encountered, and she was set in her intentions. He stood up shakily, his vision blurring to the whiteness of the Sarkian day. He assessed that he had been knocked out for hours. He wandered around the side of the building. There were no signs of his friends. He tried whistling for his horse, but there was no movement from his lips, or any part of his mouth. There was pain throughout his neck, and it stabbed into his head unlike anything he had felt before. He figured that his jaw must be broken. His thoughts were hazy as he looked for his horse. He didn't see it, so he pulled himself up and staggered to Saltook's tavern stables. When he arrived, he found that it was still where he had left it. There was a bit of parchment bound to its neck by a leather strap. He didn't know what the words on it said, as he had never learned how to read. He pulled it off and tucked it into his coat. Perhaps he could find a person along the way who could read. He saddled up his horse and headed for the town stables, where he intended to find Markus, and warn him about the woman, all the while pushing aside a need to pass out.

He rode weakly down the alley and then groggily dismounted, before walking in. He looked up to where he knew Markus would be, and found that he was too late. The woman had already been here. Markus swung from the rafters, blood dried around his neck. Haz wasn't sure what to do, so he walked back out to his horse.

"Serves him right, don't you think?" The voice of a fellow hunter cackled behind him.

Haz couldn't reply, so he turned to face him. The other hunter was Galan, the youngest of them all, the son of that whore Khali and the old man Volkhan.

"What in the hell happened to you?" Galan asked with surprise as he saw Haz's face.

Haz searched in his coat for the parchment. He pulled it out and handed it to Galan.

Galan read the letter aloud.

Dear hunter,

After the circumstances you were involved in at The Howling Wolf Tavern, we do not in any way regret to inform you that you, your friends, your animals, or any acquaintance thereof, are no longer welcome here. Consider last night free of charge, your payment will be made by staying away.

Seriously,

Saltook

Haz fingered the blade of his axe as Galan read. When he had finished the letter Galan turned to Haz with a sly grin on his lips that seemed to mildly mock the wounded hunter and give him encouragement at the same time. He handed the paper back. Haz put it back in his pocket.

"What happened there last night?"

Haz's only response was to mount his horse and grab his jaw.

"Well, come back to our home. My mother might be able to heal you."

Haz tried to nod his head, but found it painful and difficult. He followed Galan like a wounded dog, feeling the same inside as he appeared on the outside.

Sark, northwestern wilderness

Khabria was a huntress, and she sat now sharpening a valka bone into a blade. Her husband, Havink, was stitching a sheath for it. They smiled at their daughter, Kaila. She would have her own blade soon, a very important part of becoming a young huntress. She would be old enough soon to go out and make a kill. She could already dress all the animals and cook them properly.

"I have a funny feeling." the small girl stated. "I'm afraid!" she exclaimed, as she looked up at her mother and father.

"Well, then, whatever you're afraid of, you must stare

it in the eye, and stab it in the heart. That's the only way to conquer fear!" The hunter explained to his daughter.

The mother grinned, as her eyes met her husband's eyes. "Your father tells the truth," she said, keeping the gaze. "That is how I conquered him!" Their faces were serious, and then they both looked at the girl, before the mother turned her gaze to the Valka bone in her hand. She admired her craftsmanship. It was sharpened to a deadly edge. She held it out to the child.

"Go conquer your fear!" she demanded.

The child took the bone, hesitantly. The bone did not bother her, but the fear was still there. "I don't think I can kill it with a bone!"

"Go find your fear and kill it!" her father shouted. Then he lifted her into his arms and carried her to the door. He gave her a gentle push, and she felt herself sink into the snow.

"I don't know what it is, father! Wait!" She screamed, but the door was already closed. She turned to face the looming darkness. She wasn't afraid of the night, or the animals...that was why she had the knife. She knew she should not linger by the door, for surely her father would be checking that she was gone. So she started walking. Maybe she would find her fear before it found her. Either way, she gripped the Valka bone tightly in her right hand.

The small huntress still had a feeling of overbearing fear. She didn't know how long she had been walking in the snow, but it seemed the further she walked, the more afraid she became. She could feel the hair on the back of her neck rising. Her spine was cold and tingling. She knew that she was close to her fear. Then she saw movement.

It was a glittering, a flickering in the distance. She held her ground as it came closer. Then she saw Xandra, though to her it was impossible to fathom what she was, and then she noticed the man beside her. He appeared to be just that. He was simply a man, yet the feeling of fear was overwhelming when she saw him. Despite the cold, she felt sweat on her brow and between her hand and the Valka bone. The man smiled at her, but she did not see him clearly. He was a looming shadow in the darkness. "Child!" He exclaimed. His voice sounded funny, like he was from another place. "You must take me to your parents!" Something about his voice made her more afraid, but she didn't have the courage to look him in the eye, and stab him in the heart, so she simply ran. She was running home and knew that they were following her.

She ran all the way to her family's cabin. She stopped at the door and knocked, knowing that her parents would be answering the door soon. She turned around and saw the man and his creature walking in the distance, so she ducked away from the door and willingly fled her home to escape. She stopped when she thought she was safe, and crouched next to a kial tree in the snow. She heard the dogs barking and growling inside the cabin. She saw her parents open the door and the two scary people entered the house. She listened as the dogs began to whimper in fear.

The father opened the door, expecting to see his daughter, but instead he stared at the man and the strange creature beside him. Shekley smiled at the look on their faces, as he pushed his way inside, with Xandra behind him. "You are hunters! I need you," he said, staring down at Havink.

"I need you to come with me, now." He looked at the hunter, who saw the empty blackness in his eyes. The hunter gave a gasp of horror, and turned away. Perhaps it was a trick of the light. He looked again, to see if he might have been wrong, but saw the same image. Shekley's eyes were empty blackness throughout. The hunter pushed aside the feeling of sudden shock that weaved through him, and then looked Shekley directly in the dark emptiness of his eyes.

"What do you need?" The man asked. The woman

149

clutched a necklace of Valka bone that hung around her neck.

"I need a hunter!" he stated. "Follow me!"

"Has someone been attacked by something?"

Shekley just smiled a cold smile. "No," he answered shortly, "not yet."

"Get out!" yelled Khabria, the wife, making signs in the air to ward off evil. "I can feel the evil around you. Get out of my house!"

Shekley laughed.

"Do what she said and get out of our house." Havink demanded.

"Follow me!" Shekley was becoming agitated, or rather the Shadow was. These should be willing servants. Why could he not get through to them?

"You are not welcome in my home. Leave now," the lady hunter responded while walking toward them with amulets held out in front of her. She pushed him out the door. He landed sure footed in the snow. Xandra followed him without having to be pushed.

Shekley stared up at them from the snow. A deadly silence hung oppressive in the air. "You will regret not following me," he said, and then he turned to Xandra. "Let us leave them. If they will not follow, we can find someone who will."

Shekley and Xandra turned and left, though his cold stare did not leave them until he was out of sight.

The small child watched as they walked away and then ran back to the safety of her home. She didn't have to explain why she didn't kill her fear. Her parents already knew and they forgave her.

XVIII

The Gathering of the Hunters

Sark, northwestern wilderness, home of Volkhan

Haz and Galan had arrived at Galan's home, and to Haz's surprise, so had a lot of other hunters. Galan walked in first and Haz followed. Much to his embarrassment, the other hunters all had a comment as he came through the door. The most common was "What happened to you?" Galan stood up for him, though, and said, "Probably the same thing that happened to Markus!"

The others could not think of a comeback for this, and so they sat quietly in their corners. Galan pulled Haz over to a corner, where his mother, Khali, was healing some of the others. When she looked at Haz, she shook her head and motioned for him to sit down. She mumbled some words to her son, in the old Astrid language. Galan looked at Haz to interpret. "She'll get to you soon, but she wants to finish taking care of the others first. Haz rolled his eyes, and then sat down with the others on the warm bear furs that she had placed in the corner. One of the dogs walked up to him, sniffed his face, then walked over to Galan, who reached down and petted him with a smile spreading across his face. Another crawled forward to rest its head in Haz's lap. He normally would have kicked it away, but that movement would have caused him more pain. So he let it lay there. When Khali finally got to him, Haz sat patiently while the old whore did what she could for him. When she was done, it seemed that his whole head was bandaged. More and more hunters had started gathering. News had gotten out that Markus had been slain, as well as what the yellow haired woman had done, not only at the tavern, but at the town stables as well. No one had been able to find Chase, so they all assumed that he would either be found dead, or turn up when he thought all threats were gone.

Haz was glad that he couldn't speak at the moment. He was ashamed at having lost the fight. Someone would have to pay for his humiliation! With all the huntsmen gathered, she could not stand a chance, no matter how good she was. The other hunters were gathering and sharing tales. The more he listened, the more he became less ashamed. After all, he had survived her assault. Markus had not been so lucky. To his surprise, many of the others voiced their opinions that Haz and the others were fortunate, and they swore vengeance on this woman.

"If it is as we hear," Volkhan began, "then we have a much bigger problem than an ordinary woman. Think about it...she's one of the same creatures as that stubborn king that we got rid of. She must be here to plant herself on the throne and take his place. Why else would she be going for one of our best hunters? She knows things that only one of their kind would know...if what you men tell me is true. I think that we must strike quickly before she has the chance to gather a following."

There was nodding and agreement all around. Then there was silence for a while, as Khali started handing out food. She made sure that each hunter was well received, and they all got a bowl of her hot stew and their choice of fine cuts of Valka beast. Haz watched as she tended to the wounded and walked about singing in that funny language of hers. It was more of a chanting than singing, really, he thought to himself. It seemed that as she sang, it made him sleepier, and soon he was passed out on the pile of furs in the corner.

Haz was awakened by a knock at the door and the dogs barking and growling. The other hunters were all either sleeping or talking quietly in dark corners. The knock came a second time, but this time it was louder, and more like a banging. Khali opened the door and there was a horrible shriek from her as she turned to run. The dogs whimpered and ran to the far side of the room. Volkhan was quick to take her place at the door. He saw a man with a rather worn appearance dressed in funny clothes, and some sort of ...was it a woman or a creature standing behind him?

He started to turn them away, but something about the woman was intriguing enough for him to ask them their business. "What do you want?" he asked.

"I'm looking for hunters."

Shekley could feel the Shadow's excitement as it fed off the darkness brewing in the small cabin. Shekley smiled coldly.

"What do you need from the hunters?" Volkhan asked.

"I need you to follow me."

"It's urgent?" the hunter asked.

Shekley just stared.

"Come in, stranger. It's cold outside. My wife has been cooking and if you're looking for a hunter, I'm sure one of us would do. Come in and rest for a moment."

Volkhan opened the door wider to let Shekley in, eyeing Xandra's strange appearance with intrigue as she walked by. He turned to the others, kicking the ones who were sleeping. "Get up you lazy dogs, and make room for this man!" he yelled. They stirred and situated themselves so that there was room enough for the two visitors to sit down. They gawked at Xandra in amazement.

Galan started lighting candles, so that they could see better and his father motioned for Khali to bring them some food. She shook her head and cowered in her kitchen. "Get over here!" he demanded. She shook her head still.

"Excuse me. I'll only be a moment!" he exclaimed as he went into the kitchen. "What is your problem, woman? We have guests that need serving." She continued to shake her head. "What is wrong with you?" he asked, vehemently. "You know my rules here! You do what I say, when I say it! Now, I say get in there right now and serve the damn food!"

Tears were coming from her eyes as she shook her head, knowing what would come, but not willing to serve these people. Volkhan did not have much to say to her. He simply grabbed her by her hair, pulled her outside and then pushed her out into the snow. "Don't come back in until you're ready to obey!" he demanded. He came inside, locking the door, so that he could decide when she could come back.

He turned to Shekley. "I apologize. My wife is being disobedient, so I'll have to offer you some food. Would you like some of the stew that we have?"

Shekley's stomach growled. It had been days since he had eaten, but he shook his head. The Shadow smiled gleefully as he felt the lusting in Shekley for the food, and then even more joyfully as he was denied.

Volkhan seated himself opposite Shekley. "So now that we can all hear, explain to us what you need us for."

Shekley smiled. "Follow me, and I will trade weapons for furs."

"I could use a new axe," commented Volkhan, with a wide smile on his face.

"My weapons are better than all the axes you carry."

"Really?" Volkhan asked, a hint of doubt forming in his voice.

"It's true!" Xandra spoke for the first time to the hunters. "They are the best!"

"If that is true, then I'll have to see them indeed!"

"I can also heal injuries. If you follow me, I will show you how."

Haz was fully awake, listening to the conversation. He stood up, ready to volunteer, but he was unable to speak. He walked in front of Shekley, motioning towards his head.

"I can heal that," began Shekley "if you follow me." He could tell what Haz was thinking by the Shadow's intuition. "I'll make you into a hunter that will be more feared than anyone."

Haz walked over to the door, his mind made up. He

154

wanted his jaw to feel better, and he wanted vengeance. This man, it seemed, was able to offer him both things. He didn't care what the price was. He would find a way to work it out, or steal enough money to pay for it.

Shekley stood up, and as he did, more of the hunters came forward. The Shadow was delighted by this small victory. He could feel all of the greed, the anger and prideful causes from which these men drew upon to make their decisions. He was ecstatic at the thought of a new army. Shekley smiled excitedly as it was decided that they would hitch up their horses and dogs and follow him back to Trost. They did not ask where it was, or how far away it was. They were willing to follow him anywhere he led them.

Khali sat outside on the steps to the cabin. She feared Shekley. She could sense the evil coming from this man and his companion, and she did not want to be the one to deal with them. She sat, shivering, freezing and so she decided to start an old Astrid dance that she had learned as a young girl to send the evil away. As she did, her bare feet got colder and colder, and she had slowed to a crawling pace when the man started to leave. She watched as all the other hunters mounted their horses and dogsleds, and began to follow the the man back to wherever it was he had come from. She kept her eyes on them, until they had all gone. She saw her husband riding away with them, without a word to her and her son was right behind him. Her heart leapt in both joy and sadness. She could go back inside, but she did not know to where her family was riding, or when they would be back. She went inside and immediately started gathering furs for herself. She needed to warm her feet, which she hoped were not penetrated too far by the cold.

XIX

Arik's Home

Shea, moon elf tree, lower entrance

Celeste followed Arik through the door, and immediately a nostalgic smile crossed her lips. She smelt the sweet, burning kial thieren tree bark. Arik smiled.

"It makes the best torches," he commented.

"I know," she said as they continued their walk. Her tone held longing.

Arik motioned for Celeste to stay where she was and placed a finger over his lips. "Hold on," he whispered.

Celeste watched with interest as he peered through the window in a door ahead of them in the passage. There were doors to the left and right as well. When he turned around, she saw a worried look on his face. "Well, I didn't think they'd all be here, but it looks like you'll get to meet a lot of my kin. My sister is here. I'll have to put a spell over your mind, or else the other elves will read it, and know that we plan to help you. I've already put one over my mind, so I'll not be a problem. Just close your eyes," he said.

Celeste did as he asked and felt the silent spell taking hold, it didn't hurt, but her head felt tingly. The feeling made her giggle. "Try to be serious," he said.

"I am, but it tickles," she said.

"Okay, I'm done.

"Okay, just remember to tell no one of our plan," Arik said, as he took her hand to lead her through the door.

"I won't," she promised.

When they walked in, Celeste peered quickly around Arik's shoulder and saw many elves sitting in a large circle on the floor, with their legs crossed underneath them. Their gazes were centered on one in particular. They each shared

156

similar looks, having long, black hair and pale, white skin that seemed to glow almost a silvery color. The one that the others were watching stood up when she saw Arik enter. Her movements were quick, silent and graceful.

"Brother, I see you have returned," she said in a voice that matched her movements.

Arik nodded his head, and pulled Celeste out from behind him. "Yes, I have, and I have brought a guest." There was a shockwave that traveled through the room as the elves laid eyes upon the angel.

"You have brought her here?" his sister asked.

"Yes, after all, it is a night of merrymaking and good cheer. I thought that I would introduce her to my kin, and teach her about the elves," he said.

"Kristiniva knows that she is here?" His sister asked.

"Well, she did tell her that she wanted her to see all that she could of Shea, so I have brought her here to show her some of our customs, and teach her about our culture. Is that acceptable?" he asked.

"I suppose, as long as Kristiniva knows that she is here," his sister said reluctantly. "I wouldn't want to anger the queen, especially not after being blamed for letting those strangers pass. She walked over to Celeste. "You are as beautiful as I have heard. It is a shame what those hunters did to you!" Then she bowed to Celeste. "I am Arista, the princess of the moon elves, and you are welcome here. Forgive my suspicions, but my brother is known for his mischief."

Celeste wasn't sure what to say, so she simply said, "You are forgiven."

"Thank you!" replied Arista. "I see you are wet, may I offer you some dry clothes or perhaps a blanket?"

"A warm blanket would be nice," Celeste responded with a smile.

Arista motioned for another elf to tend to the task. The elf gracefully stood and left down a corridor.

"Come, let us sit," Arik said to Celeste. She followed him to the circle, and the two were seated.

"So, sister, why do the elves hold council when there are so many festivities tonight?" Arik asked.

She gave Arik a look that Celeste recognized as irritation. "Brother, you spend all your time in the dark lands. Tell me, what evil has been awakened there? What darkness stirs? We have sensed it. It is a hatred that brews in the barren lands. That cursed place east of the Sarkian Mountains."

Arik searched his own memories as Celeste became alarmed. "I haven't seen or heard anything unusual. There is always some evil in Sark."

She shook her head. "No, brother, this is different. It is as if a great shadow sits over the land now, moving its way slowly over the mountains and through the forests. We have sensed it, have you not? You have been there."

"Well, I've been here and there. The queen has had me preoccupied with tasks of both lands. I have not had much time for reading into the goings-on of Sark."

"Very well, I believe you, but I must now ask you the second reason that we have all gathered...the strangers. We have met with the other elven orders, and none of them seem to know how these Selbdes came to be here. None of us understand it. We have not left our borders unguarded, and yet they are here. How is it that they came here without us seeing them? And where is it that they came from? All the elves have been trying to speak to them, but the gods will not let us."

"I know nothing of it!" exclaimed Arik. "Only that the gods are holding a feast as they speak to the leaders."

The other elf returned with a warm blanket, which Celeste took gratefully. "Thank you," she said as she wrapped it around her.

Arista sat looking at all the elves in the room. "We will talk of this later. Let us be dismissed in order to entertain our visitor, or join the other revelers in the king's castle." She bowed her head to signal a dismissal, and the elves gathered around Celeste to see her or speak to her. The more of them she met, the more she began to be shown. They all wanted her to see something that they had made.

They began to play musical instruments of their own invention, and they began dancing. Arik begged Celeste to join in, and they all became delighted as they saw how quickly she caught on to the movements. She danced with a smile and surprisingly there was no pain. How it had happened, she did not know, but she was glad of it. The dance seemed to rejuvenate her with every movement, and the longer she smiled, the better she began to feel.

The music seemed healing too, it was lively, and yet some part of it seemed to relax her aches away. When the song was over, she found herself laughing. "That was wonderful!" she exclaimed to the elves.

"Let's do it again!" one of them exclaimed.

"No, no!" said Arik. "I have a better idea," he said. "How about we break open a bottle of our faerie wine?" he asked. A chorus of excited cheers exploded at this suggestion. "I'll be back!" The elf prince exclaimed. "...with faerie wine..." he said as an afterthought.

"Come, sit by our hearth, and warm yourself," another of the elves offered Celeste. "We hope that you enjoy faerie wine, for with it you will be transported through time and space as you listen to our tales of old. We will explain to you why we are the moon elves. You will learn of Luna and how she gave us light."

"You mean the light in your skin?" Celeste asked.

"Yes indeed, my lady, and that is why we must tell you about her. For you have not truly been introduced to her until you have been introduced by one of her children."

True to his word, Arik came back with a bottle of clear, shining liquid. "Now we can begin the storytelling!" he exclaimed.

The elves passed out tiny glasses. Celeste took hers graciously and sipped it down. The others did the same, and then the tale began, as the light from the fireplace glowed upon their faces. Celeste listened to the beginning of the tale.

> Now let me tell you of Luna the fair
> First bride of the night
> Bringer of the light, through the air
> Lady of the dark, elven hair
>
> She clothed herself in the palest of light
> To see Selfirin
> Fight to save his kin, elves of night
> To them all she brought full moonlight
>
> Her sister, the sea, reached up with her arms
> asking her to aid
> to help the raid, with open arms
> to drive the Shadow back with charms
>
> She gave them light as the Shadow came here
> She helped them to cope
> She gave them their hope, fought their fear
> For she loved Selfirin, so dear

As Arik spoke the words, Celeste felt herself moving through the night sky; she passed stars and darkness until she was in another place. Her skin tingled and then there was a numb feeling. She was dizzy and disoriented. The flames flickering in the fireplace shifted and then they disappeared. There was darkness all around and she could feel someone close to her, though she could not see them. Then suddenly, there was light, and she looked up to see the moon full and aglow in a silvery, night sky. She realized that there were others around her, and everyone began to glow as bright as the moon. As she started glowing, she realized that there were dark creatures moving in the shadows. Celeste could not see them clearly, but she was aware of them. She wasn't afraid however, because as she walked, they seemed to flee from her. In the distance, she saw an elf clothed like a warrior, wearing armor, and weighted down with weapons. He was kneeling, with a helmet in his hand, and a dark haired female elf was standing over him. His hand was in hers. Celeste figured her to be Luna, the first of the moon elves. She was a very beautiful creature, but the glow from her skin was so bright, it was hard to make out her exact features. She was clothed in a shimmering robe. Her hair stretched out black, and shining, twinkling as if with stars.

"I have given you a light, Selfirin," she said. Her voice was heavy with sadness, but she spoke with confidence and hope. "It is all that I have to give you. I hope it will help you and that you will use it well. It is my last gift to you, and you know then what this means. I am powerless, so I must return to my post. I will love you throughout time, Selfirin, and whenever you miss me, just gaze into the sky. I will wait for you there, on the moon."

"Lady," he said, "I have done so much for these people, I cannot stop fighting, creating. I must find a way to end Nometheog's hold over the world. If only things were different, I could go with you to the moon, but it is not to be. I will love you throughout time as well, and I thank you for your gift. It will help to drive the Shadow away. Your children are grateful." He stood as he said the words, and then the two kissed. The lady vanished and Celeste watched as the elven warrior ran out to meet his waiting army, all now glowing with the moonlight. Celeste was aware of a great battle taking place, though she herself could not see the enemy.

Swords, spears and axes flashed as the moonlight glistened off them. The wailing of dark creatures sounded throughout the forest. There were screams too, from the elves, some filled with terror, others pain. The Darkness fled at the light from the elves, though, and they began to drive it away, shrieking. Celeste felt that it was not the end of the whole story, but it was the end of this one. She felt the warm glow from her skin fading away, and then the numbness and the tingling. The flashing of weapons raised became the warm flickering of firelight and she was aware that she was back in the elves' home. Many of them were entranced by the wine, but some of them began coming out of it. Arik was somber, but aware.

"That was Luna, the giver of light and her lover, Selfirin. They were together before time, and so they are together again. Now he lights the sky of Shea as the day, and she lights it as the night."

"So," said Celeste, "she gave you moonlight as a weapon."

"It is all that she had," he responded. "Though, she had given him many other gifts before, but the moonlight was her strongest weapon, and it remains so today. It gives us our life, and so we must always thank her for that, well, the moon elves anyway. The other elves were given different weapons at different times."

"So, how many elven kinds are there?" Celeste asked.

"Many. There are moon elves, my kin. Then there are sun elves, which live high up in the sky near Kristiniva. You know them as the Quiriels. There are sylvan elves that inhabit the summer forest. Plains elves dwell across the lands and usually stay near Amicus. Then there are sea elves..." Arik's thoughts seemed to wander for a moment and then return. "Yes, there are sea elves, beautiful creatures they are. They live near Adrianna, the sea goddess. It is rumored that there were once other races as well, but they have not been seen for many, long years."

"I should very much like to meet the other elves one day." Celeste said.

Arik smiled. "You never know what is going to

162

happen in the future."

Celeste smiled back, feeling no pain as she did so. "Thank you for the tale, it was interesting. She was very beautiful. I could feel her hope, as she spoke to Selfirin, and I could feel their great sadness as they departed."

"Another way around the law," he smiled, as he held up his glass.

Celeste laughed, and held up her glass in response. Arik brought them together with the small ting of crystal tapping crystal.

XX

Disturbances in Shea

The night had grown late, and the elves had all gone back to the feast, or entertained themselves elsewhere. Arik and Celeste still sat by the hearth and were joined by Arista. Celeste was wrapped in the blanket. Her dress had finally dried, and she had shed her coat. Her hair had been taken down and her shoes lay in front of her by the hearth. Arista spoke to them quietly now. Celeste suspected so that the other elves wouldn't hear them.

"I know the queen keeps you here against your will and that is a bad thing! I add it to the atrocities that she has already spread through her kingdom." Her voice was soft and whispery.

"Whatever do you mean, dear sister?" Arik asked. She gave him a reproving look at the sarcasm in his tone.

"I'm trying to be serious, Arik!" she explained.

"So am I!" he retorted.

"As I was saying," she continued, "I wish there was something that I could do to help you, but it seems that the queen's hand is against us all. You are not the only one she keeps from happiness. Many are kept from things we love doing, or people that we love seeing..." her voice faltered here, and she sighed.

Arik looked surprised. "I had no idea you felt this way, sister. I thought that you were totally loyal to your queen and would do anything for her."

Arista shook her head, "No, brother. I fear her and I am obedient. Loyalty is something she hasn't earned. I am loyal only to myself."

"She doesn't understand what it is she does to us, or she would stop. I cannot convince her to give us what we

164

need. She is set in her ways and I am only a servant," Celeste said.

"You are a dark angel, a creature with a gift so powerful that it could change all worlds!" exclaimed Arista. "You serve no one except those you bring love to."

"So what do you think I could do?" Celeste asked.

Arista shook her head. "I do not know. I cannot fathom how you use that gift of yours, but I think that if you were to use it in this realm, it would help those of us who need it the most."

"It's not the same here as it is in Sark," commented Celeste.

"How so?" she asked.

"Well, for one, I cannot feel Saigolai, my master, here. Not like I did in Sark. I have tried to heal myself, but I end up giving myself a headache."

"Have you tried your gifts on anyone else? Have you tried to make anyone fall in love?" she asked, "or..." she added, "out of love?"

"Why would I want to make anyone fall out of love?" she asked.

"Well," began Arista, "perhaps there are two creatures who love each other dearly, but they cannot be together because one of them is in union with another. Could you help them not be in love?"

"I've never tried," said Celeste. "Most of the time I don't have to do anything, my presence alone usually affects people, but it can only affect them because of what they already feel."

"Oh," said Arista, with a disappointed sigh.

"I think," began Arik, "that the best way for you to help us all would be to go back where you belong. Even if it doesn't help us, then it will help you and sometimes, you have to help yourself...of course," he added, "I don't think that Kristiniva is content to let you go. She needs a bit of convincing."

"Don't be a fool, brother! Kristiniva loves Celeste and she will not ever let her go. I'm surprised she is even allowed here tonight," the princess said as she stood to leave the room.

She left quietly and gracefully. Arik and Celeste were silent until she was gone.

"So," he said smiling to Celeste, "Will you be ready at a moments' notice?"

She assumed that he was talking about his plan to get her home. "Of course!" she exclaimed, smiling.

Arik and Celeste walked back through the tunnels, and soon they stood in the courtyard with the fountain. "So what is your plan?" Celeste asked as they walked. Arik put a finger on his lips and glanced around, his dark purple eyes scanning the courtyard for any hidden creatures.

"Not here!" He warned, "Just be ready when the time comes…for anything to happen!"

"Yes, I will, and I thank you again."

"You're welcome, and now, we must part ways. There's a lovely Quiriel waiting for me back at the party, and you don't want Kristiniva to see the two of us together anyway. She'll think we're conspiring," he said with a mischievous grin.

Celeste laughed as he headed back to the party. With a wink of his eye, he left, moving with long quick paced steps. She waited a little while and then she wandered back. She saw Arik speaking with what she assumed was a sea elf. Her skin, unlike the moon elves, shone with a silver sheen, but it seemed to be the actual color instead of a light source. She had long, bluish green hair, and she was smiling as they spoke. A Quiriel was close by, laughing with them. Celeste noticed that his sister, Arista, was with a sea elf in the corner, and she caught on to their attraction right away, although she noticed that they were trying to be discreet. She felt a hand on her shoulder and a noise similar to the hissing of sea foam. When she turned around, there was a woman whose appearance was striking, as if she was made of the ocean itself. It could only be Adrianna, the sea goddess.

"So, you are the one my mother wants to keep?" Her voice hissed as she spoke.

"I'm sorry," said Celeste, taken aback.

"You are my mother's pet, the one from whom she gets her ideas." The goddess stared at Celeste with dark blue eyes, too dark to read emotion in. Her grey face was cold and spiritless. Celeste could only stare back. Adrianna leaned closer to Celeste, sniffing her, and then she reached her cold hands out to her face, slithered them down her neck and then down her shoulders, causing Celeste's white coat to fall to her elbows. Celeste backed away, not sure what she should do, and then the goddess came close to her ear, whispering.

"I can feel it now, your power! I know why she doesn't want to let you go. She is intoxicated by your gift. She wishes to control it, to have it course through her own veins, but it is too strong for her to wield...we must end her desire. She lies to you, you know. She could have healed you, yet she keeps you here as a servant. She must let go of you soon. You have been here too long. It is unnatural for one with your power and your duties to be kept from your work. I fall with Arik, so remember that if you ever need help."

When she was done speaking, she backed away and peered around the room and turned her back to Celeste. Her voice had changed now, and instead of a foamy hiss, it was a roaring deep sound. "My mother will soon pay for what she has done to us all." She turned away as suddenly as she had arrived, and Celeste watched her watery movements as she made her way to a gathering of centaurs.

Celeste pulled the coat back over her arms and tried to make her way to the corner of the room. She heard Kristiniva's voice calling out to her as she walked. The goddess found her way to the angel through the crowd, and took her hand.

"My dear Celeste, how has your evening been? Are you enjoying all of the festivities?"

Celeste only nodded her head in reply. "Well, I am sorry to say that they will be short lived. Unfortunately, these creatures are going to do more damage to this land than anything that we've seen, at least in my lifetime." Celeste listened to the words from the queen, feeling the anxiety, the fear that came with them. "All of our laws are becoming twisted and confusing, even for the rulers. I fear the worst."

"Kristiniva?" Celeste asked. "What have they done?"

Kristiniva's face was stiff and concerned. The breeze had vanished, and left a heavy, humid feeling in the air. The bright moon was being dimmed by clouds creeping across the sky. "My son is about to explain it and perhaps you will learn a lot, but they have done what I have feared from the start. They have brought ruin to our way of our life. For now, our innocent land must become something different. We have to start fighting, we must learn of war and we have to remember Nometheog, a deep power of the abyss."

Celeste knew of what Kristiniva spoke. She had felt it before, and it was imbedded in her mind as something that she had to be able to counter. "How is it that they got here?"

"They were following Nometheog, but somehow, they passed and the Shadow god did not. Now it is up to us to locate him and try to eradicate the evil before it destroys our world, or any world."

Celeste thought about all that she had learned this evening. It was a lot to take in, but things were starting to make sense. She felt the emotions the gods had been keeping from their subjects coming back. She knew that it was time to leave. Her intuition was coming back to her. The angel's land, her people, needed her love, for it was Sark in which the Shadow had entered. The realization came to her. She remembered what Arik had been telling her, what she had learned from the Selbdes themselves, her strange encounter with the sea goddess, and now, Kristiniva's sudden submission to her negativity. She knew that her land was in greater peril than this one.

While she had been thinking, the sky had begun to lighten, though slowly, with dawn. Thunder rolled in the distance. The sunrise could not be seen for the dark cloud. When the light came, Amicus, the messenger god, was standing on one of the balconies high on the palace walls. He tapped the staff he held, and there was silence among all the Sheans. Celeste felt that even if she wanted to speak, she could not. Her voice had been taken from her, as had everyone else's. Amicus stood looking out at the crowd, still hidden mostly under the simple brown robe. His face could not be seen, but his voice could be heard as clearly as if he were standing beside the angel.

"Citizens of Shea," he began, "Kialo thanks you for attending this wonderful night of feasting. Many of you have heard rumors about strangers crossing into our lands. It is true." He paused, letting the Sheans take in what he had said.

"We gods understand that it was not the elves who allowed this to happen, but a greater power. There are many things at work now in the universe which are changing, many forces that are gaining strength.

The great Shadow god, Nometheog, has gained power, and he seeks to destroy all. These creatures were allowed to enter our land by the great power of the light, for they are good, and they wish for nothing but to gain allies in their attempt to defeat the Shadow.

Our land was made by Selfirin as a stronghold against the Shadow's darkness. We must act now, in order to counter it before it grows too strong. We will go to war. We will find the darkness, and we will drive back the force of the void, as Selfirin and Luna did in the beginning. You will each have a part to play. The elves will be our instructors, for they remember the before time, when the darkness was pierced.

When you see these new creatures, we urge you to observe them, to learn from them and to let them help you as we prepare to defend our way of life. I dismiss you now to ready yourselves for war." He waved his staff in the air and immediately, the voices of the crowd returned. The young god turned and vanished through a doorway leading into his father's castle.

"Did you hear that Celeste?" asked Kristiniva. "It is the Shadow and we have to fight it! My people know nothing of fighting! They know nothing of warfare, and yet that is what is coming."

Celeste looked at Kristiniva in the eyes, trying to comfort the goddess. "Your people will be ready. They are only as strong as you make them. I think that you have reason for concern right now, but you have to be strong for them. What about your people in Sark, the Astrid tribe? They worship you, they give you offerings, and yet they are fighters, aren't they?" Celeste asked. "Why not ask for their assistance in this matter?"

Celeste knew that the goddess expected this to be another way for Celeste to escape, but she also knew that this was a valuable piece of advice. The Astrids would do anything for their gods and goddesses. Kristiniva waved it off as they began the walk back to the carriage.

"We shall see, Celeste, we shall see." The goddess walked quickly, holding the angels hand in her own. "We have a lot to do and not much time," she said, pulling her by her hand and to the carriage.

Shea, the holding cells

David and Shiana bowed to the elves who had escorted them to the holding cells, and then they closed the wooden door and turned to face their team mates.

"Well," said David, "We've convinced them to help us."

There were sighs of relief and whispers of hope spreading through the room. Michael walked up to his leaders. "That's great news!" he exclaimed, "but how did you do it?"

"He had to show them...everything." said Shiana. "There was a strange thing that happened, too," she continued, "They have heard of the Shadow before. They told us that this whole land was created for the purpose of fighting the evil of the Shadow, and they say that it has been defeated before."

"How is that possible?"

"They must not have done a very good job!"

The two responses came simultaneously from Kim and Sassy.

"Obviously the Shadow's power is extraordinary, but I had no idea that it was so...timeless," added Michael.

"I think a higher power sent us here," said David. "It feels right that we have asked them for help. I might be wrong, but the fact is, they defeated it before, so we stand a chance of helping them destroy it again. We are doing the right thing by keeping them on our side." David spoke decisively and then walked across the room to rest on one of the white cushions the Sheans had left.

Shea, evening, outside the holding cells

Later that day, Shiana stepped outside and found David sitting by the door under one of the gas lanterns. His head was hanging down and he was absorbed in his thoughts. She saw into his mind. He had missed his brother so much, and the heaviness of being so helpless against the Shadow weighed on his shoulders.

"David," Shiana spoke his name. He shook his head, and then he looked up to see her.

"I can't imagine what it's like for him...having that thing inside! As fearful as it makes us, as powerful as we are...we can't fight it, so I know he doesn't stand a chance. That's the only reason he gives in to it. That man that we're chasing...it's not him. That isn't my brother. It may look like him, but it's not! I used to be able to read his thoughts, see his plans, as awful as they were, forming in his mind, but they got darker and blurred. I haven't been able to see into his mind for a while now. When I try, it's like the bad reception on one of those old radios. A lot of high pitched squealing and static...and then there are times like now...when there's nothing, and I can't help but wonder if there's anything left of him. I can't hear him, I can't see him. I just cannot connect."

Shiana sat down and leaned against him, trying to give him some comfort. "I'm going to help you get your brother back. I promised you that a long time ago, and I'm sticking to it."

"But what if there is nothing to get back?" he asked.

"David," she said, pulling his hand into hers, "We have to keep hoping and believing. That is what keeps us going. We have to fight for those we love and believe that one day it will be worthwhile. Don't feed the darkness with your thoughts. Together, I know that we will be able to help him. We have to." Her expression was compassionate, but determined. David nodded his head.

"I hope you're right," he said, as he wrapped his arm around her, and then he turned his thoughts to her. This is why he loved her. Her hope always brought him out of the darkest places.

XXI

A Favor to Ask

Sark, castle of the king

Carmina awakened before anyone else in the castle. She dressed and began the routine that she did every evening. She opened the windows, feeling the deep, Sarkian cold settling in as darkness fell over the land. The wind blew her straight black hair away from her face, and out behind her. She pulled candles from the walls and lit them by her window in a circle on the floor. The flames flickered wildly in the wind.

She situated herself in the middle of the circle and waited. Right on time, as they did every night, the kraelvins flew into her room. The large, black feathered birds were friends of hers, willing to give her news from other lands and realms.

Because she was a dark nephilim, one who was bred from a dark angel, and a human father, she could understand the talk of all the birds. They came to her often, and tonight there were many of them. Night Talon, the one who spoke to her most often, fluttered in through the windowsill.

"Good evening, Night Talon, my friend, what news do you bring with you?" Carmina held out her arm for Night Talon to land on.

The bird briefly perched on her arm, blinking its large black eyes, and then it looked at her, hopped down onto the floor as if doing a dance, and began a song.

"We come, we come, we come with news!
Something terrible stirs and brews.
The wastelands, they have opened up.
With darkness the hunters sup.
We come, we come, with news to hear!

173

You shall all soon be filled with fear.
Through forest paths do hunters tread.
With evil now do they break bread.
So careful when you tread those paths,
'Lest blood is drawn for your baths.
A new order comes closer now!
If only you could figure how.
We come with news, if you can bear!
The world's sewed seam shall split and tear.
We come, we come, we come with news!"

When the dance was over, the bird became very still and Carmina stroked its sleek black feathers. "You are so good to warn me," she said gently, "But this does not sound good. My friends are leaving tonight, and if the hunters are out, then I fear for them. I shall have to warn them! Thank you again, my good friends."

The kraelvins all nodded their heads and made cackling sounds. They plucked dried berries from the feeders that Carmina had placed by her window before they fluttered away. Carmina blew out the candles and placed them back where they had been, all but one. She held it in her hands, and hurried to pass the warning along to her friends.

When she came to Victor's rooms, she was surprised to see that the doors were already open. Everyone was up, except for Slatkin, who seemed to be missing. She walked up to Victor and touched his arm. He turned to look at her. "You must be careful when you leave tonight!" she exclaimed. "I have just had a warning," she said, "and although I do not understand it all, I know that there are hunters about tonight in the forests. Please be careful!" she pleaded.

Alexandria nodded her head. "No worries there, I know how to handle them."

"They are out for blood, and it seems to be all of them."

"Well," said Alexandria, "It's probably my blood they

174

want. I made it no secret what I did to them."

"Please be careful, it is not a safe night to be out" Carmina warned again.

Victor glanced at his daughter. "You will still go with us. You need to get your memories back, and this is a good way to do it. I'll not let anything happen to you." Angelik looked up at her father and beamed.

Slatkin silently entered the room and beckoned Belle out into the hallway. They now walked away from the others. "So what is it?" Belle asked.

"I have a favor to ask of you," he said, avoiding her eyes. He looked straight ahead as he walked. Belle followed.

They walked through Slatkin's rooms and to the prison, stopping outside of the door. They were silent as they went in, and then he turned to her. "No one is as good hearted as you. I know you have a lot that you are doing, so do not feel obligated to take on this task. If you don't want to do it, then I will have Carmina work on it."

"I'm not that busy, Slatkin. You know that all you have to do is ask, and I'm there for you." She hung her head, and Slatkin could feel her blushing.

"You can say no to this. Trust me," he was serious and intense. "It will not be very easy." Belle looked at him quizzically, trying to read his expression.

"Really, what is it now?" she asked. "You have stirred my curiosity."

"I need you to, well, just come have a look." He motioned to the locked door of the prison. Belle knew the room well and she always dreaded to see what would be inside. He twisted the key in the lock, and then pushed in the heavy iron door.

When Slatkin opened it, there was a large room with small narrow windows high up, close to the ceiling, but it was empty except for a cage in the middle, where a man lay inside, sleeping from his appearance. Belle edged forward slowly, her skirts rustling with each movement as she crossed the stone floor. She stopped when she came close to the cage. She looked at the man. He wore a fur hat and had light colored brown hair. She covered her nose and mouth as she looked at him. He had a horrible stench about him, and his arm had been branded, so she confirmed that it was a hunter. He carried their black sign, an arrow piercing the Valka beast. The artistry on it was detailed and lovely in a dark way. Slatkin watched her as she looked in the cage. He could tell that she was scared, but he said nothing. He only watched as she knelt down by the cage, examining the marking on the man's arm. When she stood up, he noticed that some of her red hair had freed itself from the black kerchief she wore tied around her head. Slatkin gave her a moment to take in the scene, hoping it didn't disturb her too badly. She edged away, one hand on her chest, the other over her mouth. When she had gotten a good look, she turned back and walked over to Slatkin.

"What would you have me do with him?" she asked, pulling her hand away from her mouth, as she overcame the shock.

"It is a task that requires a bit of teaching and the spreading of that glow that shines about you. I need you to release him."

"But why can't you do that?" she asked.

"It is complicated, and as I said, you have a certain presence that I do not have, a very gentle spirit." He was silent for a moment, trying to avoid staring at her directly. "He is no threat to you, I promise." He held out his hand to take hers, and as he touched her hand he felt a surge of desire, a deep longing for her that he always felt at her touch. He fought it off and taking a deep breath, he looked her in the eyes. The look gave her reassurance. "You know that I would not ask you to do this if it were dangerous. I would not ever purposefully harm you, you know that."

She looked back at him and nodded her head. "I know

that, Slatkin."

"I need you to free him, and to teach him how to be a good person."

"That's all?" she asked.

"Yes," Slatkin smiled as he could feel the release of the weight on her shoulders. "That's all."

Belle laughed. The sound echoed in the large stone room, and it increased the feelings that her hand in his had awakened. "You were so serious, I thought you were going to make me...well I don't know what I thought you would have me do, but it seems funny to me now." She laughed again and Slatkin could see her with his divine perception. Her soul had always been the most beautiful he had ever seen, glowing with bright light and colors that had no name. It never failed to intrigue him. At the moment, her glow was radiating all around the room, lighting even the deepest shadows. "I promise you, Slatkin, I will teach him to be good."

Slatkin was very serious, it would not be as easy as she thought, but her laughter made him smile. He turned his gaze away from her, and sighed heavily as he led her out of the room. When he released her hand, the longing did not subside. "I will leave you the keys," he said, "here on the table." He locked the door, and laid his key ring, full of large metal keys on the table by the iron door. "It will be there whenever you are ready."

When he looked at her, she still smiled. Belle's glow was making it difficult for him to be near her.

"So, you're all packed?" she asked.

He nodded his head. The thought of leaving her sent a wave of despair crashing through him. He wanted to remember her smile always, to burn it into the images of his mind. He watched her light as she turned to walk away. "Thank you, Belle," he said.

"Really, I don't mind the task at all," she said, her back to him.

"I meant for the smile."

177

She stopped and turned to look at him. "You're welcome for that too," she said. Her voice struggled to get the words past her blushing. Her eyes met his, lingered there for longer than they should have, and then she turned away. He could feel the burning in her soul as well, the painful desire they had to endure each day, at every look and touch that passed between them.

He walked closer to her. The longing for her was painful. He wanted to take her now, to press his lips against hers and feel her fiery kiss, share the glow from her soul as it wrapped around him, but he could not. Only once had he let that happen, but never again. The consequences were too much for him to bear. He was still being punished for the last time.

She didn't have to be a dark angel to feel what she knew he felt, the connection between them, the ache of banished passions.

"Slatkin," she said, "I don't want you to hurt." She closed her eyes, afraid to open them, afraid she would not be able to control herself or him. "You know..." she had started to remind him of the rules to which he was bound, but she stopped talking. Her heart fluttered loudly in her chest. He was so close to her now she could feel him with her eyes closed. She reached her hands out, to push him away, but instead she ran her hands down his chest and wrapped her arms around his waist. He reached his hand out to her, caressing her face. The black kerchief fell to the floor, as he ran his fingers through her red hair. It felt like a flame striking against his cold palm. His lips lingered close to hers, but he would not kiss them. She turned her face away. "Stop it now," she said, her voice reduced to a whisper, "before you harm yourself." Her mouth spoke the words, but he could feel her soul. She begged for the kiss, she wanted it more than anything else. She wanted the touch of death to come from him.

The colors in her soul started shifting and changing,

darker ones now emerged. He pulled his hands away as quickly as if he had been shocked. He had wanted the bright image to keep forever in his mind, something to help him while he was away, but as always, it disappeared before he could fully grasp it.

Belle reluctantly pulled her arms away. He saw her soul as it became distressed. Her glow faded, and he felt it in himself as well, a darkness, a gloom that was apocalyptic for them. He backed away. He had not meant to hurt her. Never had he meant to hurt her.

"I just wanted to get a lasting impression of you before I leave." She could hear the defiance and frustration in his tone. "I don't know when we'll return. Is that so wrong?"

"No, but what do I know? I'm an earth-witch."

He saw her now with his mortal vision.

She shut her eyes and fought back all that she felt for him, holding back tears.

"I'm sorry," he apologized, with a stinging in his eyes. He could feel his fear taking control of him rather than his desire. "I'm out of line. I will leave you alone." He turned away from her, intending to leave her be.

"It's okay," she said, as she reached out to him, pulling him back by his arm. He turned to face her. "Really, it's okay. I know exactly what you mean, about the lasting image." She reached up, and wiped away the red line that had traced its way down his cheek. "Now," she said, "That's better, perfect, in fact." Her touch was soft and powerful. Slatkin was calmed as her palm met his face.

It amazed him still that she could smile as she said the words. His angelic sight came back and he watched the glow come back to her as if her smile alone was enough to bring it to life. It made him glad. He knew that she could not go long without the light from her soul. "I might understand why I am being punished, but you should find love Belle. You deserve it, more than anyone. Live your life."

He pulled himself away and walked over to collect his

bags. "I have to join the others now," he said, collecting himself and acting as if the situation they had just faced did not take place.

Belle reached down for her kerchief, tying it on her head. "Yes, I have work also. I promised Victor that I would find some warm furs for all of you. And even though you probably won't need them, I will feel better if you have them, just in case." she said, heading for the door.

Slatkin smiled. Her worrying amused him. "If it will make you feel better." He said loudly as the bottom of her skirts slid out the door.

"It will!" He heard her yell back.

Victor was now in his black studded leather armor and chain mail. He took Carmina's warning seriously and if it were true, he would be ready for a fight. He reached into the black trunk at the foot of his bed, and pulled out his sword and leather scabbard. He unsheathed it for a moment. It was sharpened to a fine point. He returned it, deciding that if the warning was true, he may need it. He tossed it on to the bed and then he pulled out his hunting knife. There were more weapons, but he thought that these two would serve him the best. He closed the trunk and then belted his weapons. There were footsteps outside the door, then Slatkin entered. Victor could tell he was disturbed by something.

"What's wrong, Slatkin?" Victor asked.

"I'm ready to leave!" he said, in a growling tone, still trying to be reserved.

Victor walked over and shut the door. "What's wrong?" he asked again.

"I need to go before I harm Belle. I do not know how much longer I can be obedient in regards to our punishment. If it were mine alone to bear, I would carry it with all the other pains. It is too heavy for her." Victor just let him talk; it was rare that Slatkin discussed the punishment or the kiss that brought it on.

Slatkin's eyes were closed, and he leaned against the wall with his arms folded. He spoke in his slow steady voice, restraining his need to destroy something. "You know Belle's glow, it pulls me to her...I cannot stop it. I cannot stop loving her. To just look at her, to touch her, it should not be wrong, but it is. When I look at her it awakens emotions in me that I should not feel, and it awakens things in her that are forbidden. Her touch is dangerous to me and my kiss fatal to her." He swallowed deeply, and then continued talking in his slow, reserved tone. "It is against the binding laws for me to love her, yet I do, and I cannot make it stop!" Victor could hear the sadness and frustration as he spoke.

"Just now, I could have killed her! Her glow was so bright it filled the whole prison. I knew that I would not be able to touch her without feeling its pull. I know it's wrong, but I can't understand why. She feels the same wanting as me. When I looked into her soul, I was afraid. She was begging for me to do it. To kiss her, and end her life."

"That's what it took to make me pull away, a reminder of what would happen. I scared myself...torn between saving her and giving her what she wanted. Now I just want to leave before I do something terrible. I sealed our fate long ago with a kiss and I must learn from that mistake. I do not want to harm her any more, yet I might, out of a wish for her happiness. That is why we need to leave. It would probably be easier on us both if I never came back."

There was silence and Victor knew that nothing else would come from the Orostiro. He didn't know any advice to give. He understood the situation, and he felt guilty for being able to love. "I'm sorry Slatkin, you know I am," Victor said. His tone was quiet and sympathetic. "If you want to go ahead, you can get the horses ready and we'll join you in just a few minutes. You won't have to look at her again, just keep your eyes on the path ahead." There was a silence as Slatkin gathered himself up, and then he pulled himself away from the wall and out the door.

"Yes, I will go saddle up the horses," he said calmly.

Belle had packed all their bags with food and had stuffed an extra blanket into Angelik's bag. Carmina had rechecked everything on a list that she had made and had gone back to get Angelik's toy, which had not been packed. When everything had been checked and rechecked, the angels all sat on their steeds, ready to start the journey to the elven tree. Victor had on his usual coat, with an extra grey wolf fur. He was checking the old reins that were on the pack horse. Angelik sat atop the black horse, Dexon, her father's steed, wrapped warmly in a white bear fur coat. Alexandria had on a new tiger pelt, this one though was white and much warmer than the brightly colored one she had worn before. She was standing in front of Vortex, patting him on the nose and speaking softly to him. Slatkin wore a thick black Valka fur and he had already mounted his horse, ready to go. Carmina walked out to give them each a hug and see them off. Belle stood at the door waving, *strangely silent and distant,* thought Victor, *for Belle.*

Slatkin tried to look straight ahead, but he couldn't. He kept his eye on the door and Belle's bittersweet smile as they rode away. Only when the door closed, did he turn his head to the road before him.

XXII

Evingh

When she watched them all ride away, Belle turned to go gather her healing herbs and anything else she might need for the man in the cage. She gathered them all in a sack and made her way up to Slatkin's quarters. She picked up the keys and headed into the prison, stalling only for a moment as she prepared herself. She pushed hard on the heavy iron door and it slowly opened. The man was sitting up now, so she assumed that he was awake. She walked to the cage, gripping the keys firmly in her fist. Kneeling down, she laid the sack on the floor beside her. She examined the ring of keys trying to match the correct one to the lock. She kept her eye on the hunter as she did so. He had a distant look on his face as if he was still dreaming, but awake.

It took her several tries, but she finally found the black iron key that fit the lock. She turned it and swung the door open. It made a squealing sound. The hunter only shifted his head a little. He showed no sign that he was aware of her presence. The stench coming from him was awful.

"Come with me and I'll fix you up," Belle said from just outside the cage. The man showed no signs of moving, so she crawled inside and reached out to him. He did not respond. She wondered what Slatkin could have done to him to make him this way. She grabbed his hand and tried to pull. "Come on now, come with me," she begged. He didn't move, or speak. He just kept staring. "I'm not giving up on you, now come on!" She grabbed his other hand, and pulled him forward. He jerked back, startled.

"It's okay," she said, "I'm here to heal your wounds. Really it's okay, come with me and I'll have you mended in no time. I can't carry you, so you're going to have to help me, come on now!" she exclaimed, backing away. The hunter was

183

still expressionless, but he crawled forward and stood when he had exited the cage. Belle grabbed her bag and then took his hand. "That's better," she said, as she led him out of the room. She paused to lock the heavy iron door before she headed into the other rooms. She guided him towards a bathing room.

Once in the room, she started pulling off his clothes and throwing them in a heap on the floor. She led him to a tub, which she filled with hot water from over the fire.

"Get in," she pleaded. "I can't heal you until you're clean." Chase stepped in and sat down. He jumped a little when the hot water met his skin and then settled back into the water. Belle grabbed some of her Baika vine and sprinkled it into the water. The smell was strong, a clean, mint aroma. She pulled out one of her cloths and a large bar of soap, and began to wash him. She had healed many before him, so there was no embarrassment on her part. From his expression, the hunter wasn't aware that he was being bathed by a red headed earth-witch. The silence in the castle was deep. Belle had more time than she wanted to ponder her day. Her thoughts would not turn away from Slatkin.

"I don't know what he did to you, but I'm sure he did what he was supposed to do. Sometimes, he forgets that he is an angel, though. He has lived too long with humans and sometimes acts as humans would...I wonder what you did to deserve this..." she was quiet, and then she started humming. There was a knock at her door. It could only be Carmina.

"Come in, dear," she said.

Carmina walked in and took in the scene. "What's this?" she asked.

"Well, Slatkin asked me to take care of this man, and so, I'm giving him a bath, a good one. He certainly needs it!" She exclaimed.

"Oh!" Carmina exclaimed. "I was just wondering where you were. You know, it is the quietest that I've ever known the castle to be...even quieter than those first nights after the burning. I didn't mean to disturb you."

"It's all right, dear!" Belle exclaimed. "After all, this man certainly isn't much for conversation. I don't even think that he realizes he is here. He has such a blank expression on his face. I don't know how I got him to follow me here, but I did."

"Well, I'll help you!" Carmina walked over, picked up the large pot filled with water, poured more in the tub, and then filled it back up, setting it over the fire. She looked at the hunter. "I think that he must be reliving something in his mind, something traumatic."

"How do you know?" Belle asked.

"Well, I've been warned by the kraelvins. He will not be an easy man to help, but I will do what I can to aid him, if you will let me."

Belle smiled. "Well, thank you, Carmina," she said. "If you want to find him some clothes, then go ahead." She pointed to the pile lying on the floor. "I'm going to burn those outside. The stench is going to be awful!" Belle exclaimed.

"As soon as I've found him some new ones, I'll burn those for you."

"I would appreciate it," she said.

Carmina hastily left to find the hunter some clothes.

Belle turned back to him as she scrubbed. "I don't know your name, so I will give you one. For now, you are..." she looked at his face for a while, and then said, "You are Evingh!" She laughed after she said it. "It means young one, where I grew up, and you are very young. The more dirt I wash off you, the younger you look. You can't be more than twenty!"

After a while of deep silence, the doorknob turned, and Carmina walked in with a pile of clothes. "I think that I found some his size!" she exclaimed. She threw them over a chair, and started sorting through them. "I'm not sure, but I think some of these will fit!"

"Good," replied Belle. "Now we just have to coax him

out of the bath, and into the clothes. I also need to stitch the wound on his forehead. It's useless to clean it in the bath. He needs more than just soap for that. I'll have to get the infection all the way out. That's what's causing the rest of that foul odor and his fever."

"He has a fever, too?" Carmina asked.

"Yes, so I've got my work cut out for me."

"Well, I'm here to help you, Belle," Carmina said. "Here," she said, as she walked over to a cabinet to pull out a towel.

Belle looked at the hunter Chase, who she now called Evingh. "Now, let's stand you up, get you dried off and into some clothes!" she exclaimed. The hunter made no movement, and both women grabbed his arms and pulled him up.

"Come now, you have to step out of the tub!" Belle exclaimed. "Come on!"

"Yes, we must get you dry, and into some warm clothes before you freeze in here!" Carmina said as the two women pulled at him. After a few moments, he stepped out of the tub. They grabbed towels to dry him, and then they began the task of dressing him. They had him in warm black clothes woven from the kial fibers and extra socks with some boots that Carmina had also found.

Belle dried his hair. Carmina trimmed his hair and beard while Belle went about cleaning the wound on his forehead. At times, Belle thought she saw something like an expression on his face, but then it would leave him. She worked mixing her ointment and salve, then dipping her rag in the ointment, she gently scrubbed the wound. She couldn't help but wrinkle her face as liquids and blood oozed out. She could smell the infection as it ran from the gash. She cleaned it until there was nothing but blood running, and then she stitched it shut and wrapped a bandage sprinkled with ground cairag flowers around his head.

"There," she said when she was done. "Now you will

186

be feeling better, and I'll put the ointment on three times a day to help it heal," she said. Carmina looked at it approvingly.

"You know," she said, "You are a great healer."

"Thank you, dear," Belle replied with a smile.

"You know, I don't think he's much older than you," Belle said, looking at the man with his newly cut hair and clean face.

"Well, I'll be eighteen in the spring, so maybe. We really don't have any way of knowing until he starts talking."

"Yes," Belle responded, "and hopefully that will be soon. I don't even know his name, and so for now I will call him Evingh."

"Evingh?"

"Yes, it means young one where I grew up."

Carmina looked at him. "Well, maybe..." she said, looking at him.

"Come dear," said Belle as she pulled on the hunter's hands. "We need to feed him, I don't know when his last meal was, but he will never get better if he doesn't eat."

"Maybe we should eat too; it is already three hours into the night."

"Yes dear, we will all have our first meal together," she said to Carmina. She turned to the hunter. "Come Evingh, I know you must be hungry."

At the sound of his new name, the hunter looked at Belle. Though he was still distant, he stood, ready to be led.

"I'll clean up all this mess," said Carmina. "Just let me know when it's ready!" she said.

"Thank you, I will do that!" exclaimed Belle as she led Evingh from the room.

Belle hummed as she went about the task of preparing a meal for the three of them. She was very glad that Evingh was looking better. She had been worried earlier that she would not be able to live up to her promise to Slatkin, which she thought, would have been much more than she could bear.

When she looked over at him, he was still staring, but seemed to be moving his head more and expressions had begun to come back to his face. She peeled back the thick coating on the kial roots and dumped them into her stew. She ground leaves from the evergreen heith bush as she sat at the table and then she heard someone else humming her tune. It was Evingh. She stopped and listened for a while, he smiled as he hummed it.

She smiled back. "I see you hear some things," she said to him. "That is good. Maybe I can teach you many good things. Your voice is deep, and if you like music, then perhaps after you have eaten we will listen to some. Carmina plays a beautiful harp, and I'm sure that we could teach you some tunes you can hum with that nice voice of yours, if you'd like."

She smiled and went back to her work, thinking to herself that she would teach him anything in which he would be interested. She wanted to teach Evingh the good things of the world, if for no other reason because Slatkin had asked her to do it. She did not want to promise someone something, especially Slatkin, only to break her word.

Carmina now joined them for their meal and they ate mostly in silence. Every few minutes Evingh would hum Belle's song. The two women would giggle with delight every time. Carmina looked at Belle. "I think that he is starting to come around. Maybe you and I can teach him."

"Oh yes, dear, we'll teach him many good things," said Belle, with a confidence in her voice. "I told him that after we eat, you may play some songs on your harp. Then he can learn the tunes, and hum all he wants."

"That will be nice," Carmina commented.

Belle smiled. "Yes, and if I know he can see, I will teach him how to read and write."

"Well!" exclaimed Carmina "We will teach him everything!"

XXIII

The Ride of the Hunters

Sark

"Stop!" Shekley ordered, "There's something I have to do here." He had been riding one of the dogsleds, but now the hunter halted the animals, so Shekley could step off. Xandra had been running ahead of them, quicker than the animals, and she seemed to not be tired at all. This alone was enough to astound the hunters.

They had neared the cabin that Shekley had visited earlier in the night. All their attention was turned to him. "They are not like the rest of you!" he shouted, motioning to the cabin. He turned to Volkhan and put his arm around him. He pulled him near his mouth and whispered, "You remember Khabria, don't you? She's here. Remember how it felt to have a woman that you didn't have to fight with? One that gave you all the pleasures you could want? Remember too, how she left you for that ungrateful betrayer, Havink? How did that make you feel? What did it make you want to do?"

As he spoke, Volkhan became resentful, remembering his hatred for that woman and the man she slept with now. His breathing was heavy and his face turned red with anger.

"Remember how it felt when you tried to kill her, and she bested you? She left you wounded in the snow until your friends found you. They laughed at you. Remember...what did you feel? Now is your chance to watch my weapon do what you could not do, but first, tell the others what they deserve."

"They deserve no less than how I was treated!" he shouted. "Khabria is the queen of all the dog sluts, and that bastard lover of hers deserves nothing more than death!" he

189

yelled. "They are both betrayers, and I want them dead!" he shouted, emotions exploding. "They are betrayers! And we all know," he said, "I will not be betrayed."

Shekley looked Volkhan in the eye. "Sit, and enjoy your demonstration!" Shekley turned to Xandra. "When you are ready, kill the hunters in this cabin." His voice had turned to a whispery hiss as he spoke to her. "I want them dead, I want them bleeding, I want a show of your skills for these hunters, so that my army will be the best. Go now!"

Xandra despised Shekley when he was in this mood, but what else could she do? She headed for the door and kicked it. It came crashing down and she heard the people inside. She wanted to apologize for what she was about to do, but she could not figure out how. The hunter came at her swinging an axe in his hand. She caught it with one hand, grabbed him by his neck with her other hand and flung him out of the door. He slid across ice and snow. Shekley was laughing with glee.

Xandra stepped to the doorway and stopped. The hunters stared in amazement as her right hand shifted to form a long sharp implement of impalement. She shoved it through the man's lungs, and with a twisting movement she held him up for them all to see. He writhed on the end of her hand in a silent fight for his life, and then she flung him away. He hit the side of the cabin and fell into the snow, dead. The forest erupted in shouting and approval from the hunters.

Xandra's hand changed back, blood now covering half her arm. Then she stepped back inside the cabin. She could see in the dark, and her eyes turned green with night vision. She walked through the house searching. There had been two more here. "Go, go, go!" she heard a voice. It was coming through a door. She kicked the door down, splintering the wood on her first kick, and with a shove, it gave way. There was a woman pointing a large white sword at her.

"You are not welcome here!" she shouted. "Get away from me!" she swung the sword, but it was no good. Xandra grabbed her hand, causing the sword to fall to the floor. She seized the woman by the neck and pulled her outside, throwing her into the snow. The woman got up coughing, but stood to face Xandra. Xandra admired the woman's bravery, it reminded her of something, but she could not place it. Nonetheless, she had a job to perform. Her other arm changed to something that the hunters had never seen. It was a large, metal gun. She pointed it at the woman. The huntress stared at her down the barrel and with a loud boom; the splattering of blood, flesh and bone, the woman's body fell dead. The hunters exploded with shouts and cheers. She went back for the child. It was apparent the child had jumped out the window. She jumped out after her and ran past several trees, until she was hit from behind. She turned to see the little girl still standing in the position that she had thrown the knife in. The knife lay on the snow, where it had bounced off the Mahldrusec. Xandra walked forward, picked her up by her throat and carried her over to Shekley.

"She tried to escape!" Xandra said, throwing her down, pushing her into the snow, and holding her in place with her foot. The child was screaming and crying, wriggling under the weight of Xandra's boot, as she noticed the dead bodies of her parents lying next to the cabin. "I said to kill her!" he shouted.

"No, wait!" Galan dismounted and ran over to her. He never hurt children, especially ones that had his father's blood running through them. He couldn't help himself from intervening,

From the look on Shekley's face, he knew he had made a mistake and he hoped to cover it up quickly.

"Uh, I mean, she is a child, and therefore...therefore, she can be taught any way you choose to teach her. She could be useful to you, in the future." He looked at Shekley, waiting for a response.

Shekley peered at the child, with a smile spreading across his face. "I do not trust this man, yet what he says is true," the Shadow spoke to Shekley, "and even if you do not teach her, you could always use her in your tests. Her blood could be very useful to you, why spill it here?"

"Yes, she may be useful!" Shekley turned to the others. "I'm taking this child as a prisoner. I will use her blood in my testing." He reached down, as Xandra lifted her leg and he grabbed the girl by her shirt, shoving her towards the closest hunter on a horse. "You have rope, tie her up!"

The hunter grabbed her wriggling body and tied her to the horse, so that she could not move. She screamed and struggled. Galan gave the other hunter a grateful look and tried to catch his sister's eye to reassure her, but she was tied so that he could not see her face. Once she was on the horse they mounted up, and set off once again, following Xandra through the lands of Sark towards the wastelands. Xandra was feeling glad the task was over, and she was spared killing the child. She ran now, ahead of the horses, guiding them to the barren lands.

Galan kept glancing at the girl, Kaila. He hoped that she would recognize that he had tried to save her, but she was tied over the horse, belly thrown over its back and she would not look up. He noticed that she continued to squirm, trying to free herself from the ropes, so much so, that she had started to bleed in several places where the rope had slid against her skin, cutting into her with its burn. He looked away, and saw his father giving him an approving look.

He felt anger then towards his father, he knew what he was thinking just by the look on his face. His father was a sick bastard and Galan freely told him so at the cost of many beatings, but his father knew no other way to be. That is how his mother had always described it to him, though she spoke, or sang rather, in Astrid, because she knew that Volkhan did not understand her native tongue. He flashed his father the mean, angry look he had practiced so many times, showing Volkhan that he had plans for the girl later. He realized that if his true intentions were discovered, he would surely not be giving him the same look. He would beat him until he was unrecognizable, and yell at him for hours about how he was too much like his mother. Which, he admitted to himself was probably true. He thought about his mother and he hoped that she was alright, back at the cold dark cabin all alone. After going for some time, the dark sky started to change to a pale grey. There was a pink line on the horizon; a sign that more snow was coming. He was tired of riding and hoped that the party would soon stop, but they kept riding, on through the wilderness, over the mountains, and to the east.

The hunters were getting tired, but Xandra pressed them on. Shekley was beyond tired, but he could not let himself feel it. The hunters started falling asleep on their mounts. The Shadow cackled in Shekley's ear, and it said to him, "We must let these men rest, so they will maintain their confidence in you." The Shadow sounded annoyed to Shekley, but he was relieved.

"Stop," he shouted. At his words, Xandra stopped and turned to face the riders. The horses were now breathing heavily and shivering in the early morning hours. The dogs were panting heavily and lying down as soon as they were able to stop. The hunters dismounted and began stripping kial bark from trees to make a fire. Shekley stood and observed with interest. He had not realized that the trees held fire in them, but as he leaned against one, he could feel the heat coming from inside it. He wondered what the Shadow thought, but it was not with him at the moment.

The hunters had a fire already and they began pulling food from their packs to cook. Shekley had none, so he watched. His hunger pains were starting to make him feel sick, so he slumped down between two roots of the tree. The warmth was soothing to him. He soon fell into a slumber in which he fitfully dreamed the dream that he had every night.

His goddess was there. She was the most beautiful thing he had ever seen, reflecting the sun from every angle. She was metallic and more beautiful than any human. She sang a song that was so beautiful that it made him forget his pain. She had great metal wings, which emitted a gentle electrical humming as she danced in the air around him. Her warmth spread itself through him, giving him life.

Then the shadow came, replacing the warmth with coldness, and the light with darkness. It held the goddess from him. She had turned black, curled up in a dark crystal before his eyes. He reached out for her, but the shadow pulled her back. "We have an agreement," its cold voice said. "When I am done with you, I will consider giving her back, but for now, she is mine, to do with as I please. I will kill her if you are disobedient!" The thought of her light vanishing forever left Shekley with an indescribable feeling in his gut; it was a feeling of doom, filled with a sadness greater than he could fathom.

He awoke, abruptly. More snow had fallen since he fell asleep. Xandra was standing over him, on the newly fallen snow, with one of the hunters. The hunter had a large hunk of meat which he held out to Shekley.

"Eat some, it's Valka meat!" he growled. Shekley reached out weakly to take it from him.

"Never would I have thought it possible, but she has taken out one of the great Valka beasts. It usually takes at least three of us to kill such a creature, but she really...has some skill!" There was respect and jealousy in his tone.

"Earn his trust. Thank him!" The cold voice was back in Shekley's mind.

"Thank you," he said to the hunter as he took the meat in his hands, and began to ravenously devour it. He couldn't clearly remember the last time he had eaten. Xandra sat beside him, the sun shining off her in the afternoon sunlight, much like the goddess in his dreams. The cold voice in his mind cut off his thoughts of her.

"You will do well to remember that she is far from a goddess. Her willingness was useful, but her desire and determination are lacking. She has no real gifts or talents and her parts are old and outdated. We can do better."

Shekley finished eating the meat, hating the Shadow, and then he remembered something that the Shadow had said to him earlier, something about the craving of a woman's body. He stopped and looked at Xandra.

"What were you doing while I was sleeping?"

She turned to him and then spoke. "I was hunting the beast. I killed it and dragged it back here. Then I helped dress it, so that the hunters could cook it. I know you are hungry. You've not eaten for days. I was looking out for you."

"She speaks the truth!" Suddenly the Shadow was gone.

Shekley smiled, glad again that her voice was her own, and the Shadow was not here to torment him while he had some memory come back to him of other times. It was briefly lived though, as one of the hunters came back to him.

"Some of us will have to stay, or the meat will go to waste, not to mention the furs. We can get the highest amount of gold for Valka fur."

Shekley thought about it. "Fine then, do as you see fit. After all," he said, "I am not forcing you to follow me."

The hunter nodded his head, and in a few moments the hunters had sorted out among themselves who would stay, and who would go.

The girl would continue on with Shekley, though at the moment she had been tied to a tree. Hunters attempted to feed her, but she refused any food, even water. She would not look at their faces, and still struggled in her bonds.

"Who is that?" Shekley asked Xandra.

"That is the girl that you ordered me to kill, before you decided to take her as a prisoner." She had put up with his memory lapses for so many years that there was nothing odd about it to her.

"Oh!" he exclaimed. "And why did I order you to kill her?"

"Because her parents, whom I have already killed, were not like the other hunters, they refused your offer, and to demonstrate my skills."

"Oh," Shekley said, trying to grasp the memory, but there was a lot of jumbled confusion in his mind. He sat eating the Valka meat, in a state of confusion for some time. When the fire burned low, and the hunters had rested, the Shadow came into his mind again, and urged him to leave.

The following night, the hunters had made it as far as they were willing to go. Volkhan confronted Shekley. "You're not taking us into the waste lands are you?" he asked.

"If you mean the desert down the slope of this mountain, then yes!"

Volkhan looked down the slope. "We don't go there, it is cursed."

Shekley smiled. "Why would you say that?"

"It is. It's...unnatural. There's heat from the sun, it's dry, and no plants or animals can survive. They say that anyone who goes there is destined to die."

"Well, good thing you took up my offer then, isn't it?"

The hunter just stared at Shekley, who continued to smile. "I live there and I'm doing just fine!"

Volkhan turned to the others who sat atop their horses and sleds, waiting for some kind of signal.

"The man has a point. Let's go," and with that, the hunters continued down the last mountain, towards the great sea of sand that lay beyond.

XXIV

The Elves

Sark, Northern wilderness

The angels traveled in silence, listening, feeling the air around them. There was a heavy darkness spreading through the land. The kial thieren trees which normally seemed to pulsate with bright red fire were becoming dimmer and darker. The snow covered ground which stretched out silver before them was now a black mirror on which their horses stepped carefully across.

Victor was leading Dexon by the reins one-handed, the other clutched Angelik close to him. He was unsure of what he felt, but the power was immense and dreadful. It was not from the land itself, but it was something that had cursed the land.

The angels entered the territory of the elves. They knew it right away. The trees were strung with lanterns, and flowers which could not be found in any other territory of Sark grew here with ease. The kial trees grew smaller, but they were accompanied by trees that other Sarkians had never seen. The horses were soon stamping their hooves on moss covered stones, and small patches of grass, instead of snow.

"I can feel the magic," Alexandria whispered. "Be wary of where you tread. I do not trust this magic! It is full of forgetfulness and dreams." She glared from tree to tree with her green eyes and painted face, looking for signs of any elf.

"Where are they?" Angelik asked, staring around her in wonder.

"I don't know," responded Slatkin, "but I am certain that they will show themselves soon. We are not invited here, so they will confront us."

"Clever creatures you are," said a voice that came from

197

close by them.

"I am Victor, king of Sark, and I wish to speak to you!" Victor spoke with calm words, but inside he was feeling a great surge of emotions. He did not forget that these creatures had kept him from his family for so long. "Come out now, and I will do you no harm."

A female elf suddenly appeared hanging upside down, her knees folded over the branch of a small tree with light colored bark. Her hair hung almost to the ground, and her arms hung limply. "How exciting, that we have a visit from you!" she exclaimed. "But who are you really and what is it that you want?"

"I am Victor, the king of Sark!"

Childlike laughter filled the air. "Sark no longer has a king. He and his kin are lost. So who are you, really?" she asked.

"Sark will always have a king!" This voice came from another elf. It was Arik, who stood by a large holly tree.

He walked forward, "...and you, Felis... must be careful of how you greet guests in this land. Go now, I will speak to these visitors."

"But Arik..."

"Go!" he exclaimed more firmly. The elven girl swung herself down from the tree and smiled brightly before she ran away into the thickness of the forest.

Arik turned seriously to Victor. "I see that you got my stone." Victor stared at Arik, anger surging through him.

"Where is my wife?" He dismounted.

"She is waiting for you," Arik responded calmly.

Victor stepped forward, his hand on his sword.

"Wait!" Arik put up his hands. "Hear me out before you start threatening me. It isn't my fault that she's not home...far from it in fact." He spoke with a defensive tone.

"Take me to her!" he demanded.

"That's always been the plan. You can leave your animals, they'll get lost if they go any further. This is one of the doorways between Sark and Shea."

Victor felt the warm touch of Angelik's hand on his shoulder. "He's telling the truth, father. I know he is. I remember now. Shea. That's where I was."

Victor looked up at his daughter and reached up to help her off the horse. Slatkin and Alexandria dismounted.

Alexandria walked over to Arik. Her demeanor was intimidating. "Your magic is full of dreams, but I think that you are telling us the truth. I'll follow you, but I warn you, I am a powerful spellcaster. I will curse you if you try any of your magic on me."

Arik smiled. "You don't have to worry about that. I want you to remember how to get back. I'm supposed to put a memory charm on your mind as soon as you enter, but I'm not. I think that you'll understand why very soon. I promised Celeste that I would help her get back home. She had her own plan, but it was flawed, because she didn't know a way around the enchantments. I have helped her all along. She is bound here until Victor comes to get her.

She risked more than you could know by sending Angelik away. I put the stone in the basket with her. Without it, Victor would never have been able to see us in her memory. It is a powerful stone, a thing of the before-time. It was a gift to the sea elves. They gave it to me to help the child. It was the only way you would even have a chance to see your wife again," he said turning to Victor. "I will take you to her now, so that you can bring her home." He turned to walk away, and the angels followed.

Arik led them to the elven tree. They were now being led through a small room that seemed to be used for storage. Barrels and jar filled shelves lined the walls.

Arista was waiting for them. She bowed to the angels as greeting. "So, my brother has seen you into our land," she stated.

"Yes, and they must move quickly if things are to be

set right," Arik said. "We must speak in secrecy, for we risk our lives, or much worse by hosting you here." Arista folded her arms and listened intently.

"Yes," she agreed, "We risk our eternities. One of our rulers has your wife, and if she knew we were helping you...I don't want to think of the consequences."

Arik continued where his sister left off. "Yes," he agreed, "Kristiniva, the sky goddess of the Astrids, took pity on your wife as she burned in the hunter's fire seven years ago. That is why the great floods came, to vanquish the fire. Kristiniva herself was drawn to the power your wife wielded and wished to save her. She took Celeste back to her castle to heal her. When she discovered the way to drain her power, she started setting forth laws to bind your wife to the land, and keep her here against her will. It is great power that our queen has, and the spells are not easily broken. Kristiniva has been healing your wife, but also keeping her from healing. She is trying to slowly drain the power from Celeste without destroying her. She wishes to wield the power of love for herself."

The fierce look on Victor's face only grew stronger as he listened to the tale.

Arik continued, "Your wife figured out a way to break one of Kristiniva's laws. She knows that Kristiniva is afraid of you," Arik pointed to Victor, "So Angelik here," he pointed to the child, "was used in a plan to get them both home. Your wife made Kristiniva believe that you were coming to get Angelik. She asked me to take Angelik to Sark. She fears you and your power of justice, understanding that she has always been in the wrong. She thinks you intend to come here and kill her, to serve her justice."

"I put the lumistone in the basket with the child because I knew that it would allow you to see through some of the enchantments that disabled her memory. I hoped that you would see us, and come to Shea to save her. I have been trying to help her get home, but it seems that things get more complicated as we go."

"Our land is now going to war," Arista explained. "And the goddess will not let Celeste go so easily. She sees her power as a weapon that will expel the evil forces that are at work."

"What evil forces?" Alexandria asked.

"The Shadow," responded Slatkin and Arista at the same time.

The angels now understood the feeling of foreboding in their own land, and why the land itself was becoming black and withered. The Shadow was not just a creature of the void, but the void itself. It was the beast that swallowed all things and turned them inside out. Good became evil, right was turned to wrong and all roads it controlled were destined for destruction.

"Victor," said Slatkin, looking very serious. "I hope you are ready to battle, my friend, for the Shadow is upon the threshold of your kingdom. I'm afraid that it will bring with it our greatest tests."

Victor took a moment to contemplate all that he had heard. "She belongs in Sark!" he said. "She may still want to help your kingdom, but that should be a choice, not a force of your queen's will."

"Yes that is true, I will take you to her now," said Arik. "Kristiniva is away at the moment, visiting her son, but she will be back soon. We must hurry before she returns."

Suddenly Victor's heart leaped at what he was hearing. "Let's go!"

XXV

The Trail of the hunt

Shea, the elves home

Victor started to follow Arik, but Slatkin stalled them just for a moment. "I'm sorry Victor, we can't go with you. We have urgent business in Sark. I can sense it!"

"All of you?" Victor asked, looking at Angelik. Slatkin only nodded.

Victor walked over to his daughter and picked her up. He held her close as he embraced her.

"I'm going to get your mother back and I promise I'm going to bring her home!" Angelik clung to her father, until Slatkin reached out to take her.

"Go, Victor, you'll see her soon enough, and you have my word, I will protect her."

Victor kissed his daughter again and nodded a goodbye, then followed Arik through a wooden door that had been camouflaged in the wall.

Slatkin turned to Arista. She spoke. "I can take you back to Sark, closer to where you need to be than where you entered."

The angels stood still as Arista weaved the spell that transported them back to Sark.

Alexandria looked around, but she couldn't see the elf and didn't recognize where they were. She was sure it was Sark, for the cold winds were blowing and they were surrounded by the kial thieren trees.

Then she understood what Slatkin had felt all the way in Shea. There was work to be done and she sensed that the others felt it too.

They were silent, watching. Their divine perception showed them colorful trails leading through the snow.

Alexandria's were red. There were two of them, unlike anything she had ever encountered before.

Angelik's reached into the East, a blue flame burning across the land. Slatkin stood, calculating all that he could take in of the situation. He was the only one to see all the trails. His trail was green and solid. "Our paths lie together," he said. "We will collect Alexandria's power and follow the combined trails into the East."

"Slatkin," Alexandria was wary. "This is different, it is unusual. I don't know what has caused this. There is no trace of the attacker, only the trail of those who have been wronged. I don't understand it."

"Honestly, neither do I," he responded, "I think we are all about to be tested.

"Tested?" asked Alexandria.

Slatkin nodded and walked forward to lead the way. "Angelik," he said, "Call our horses to us. We'll need them before the night is over. There are miles to travel and we'll need their strength."

"How do I…" she started to say something and then she knew from her instincts what she needed to do. Whispering into the wind, she called for them, knowing that they would hear. She continued calling as the angels walked toward the hunters' cabin.

Slatkin covered Angelik's eyes as they came upon the site of the massacre. Wolves had found the mangled mess of bodies lying in the snow. They were pulling away pieces of flesh with their snouts, and gnawing at the human bones. "Look away, princess, this is something you should not see." He held her away from the scene as Alexandria walked towards it. He could tell she was communicating with the spirits, but whatever she was seeing was for her alone. He walked away with the child until she was far enough away that he was sure she could not see.

They heard the howling of the wolves as Alexandria's

gift no doubt warded them off.

"I may not see what you are keeping from me, but I do see some things," Angelik said, as she seated herself on one of the tree roots. I know that I have to help that little girl. She's so scared...," she started fidgeting with her coat. "She has to be helped. She's being taken further and further away, and she's so sad."

Slatkin seated himself beside the smaller angel. "I know, but we will help her. You and I together will see that she is safe, but we have to be careful about the way we do it, or we will be of no use to anyone. The hunters know our weaknesses, so stay close to me and your aunt."

"I will," she promised.

They waited patiently, watching a herd of Valka beasts moving slowly across a clearing farther down the mountain until Alexandria came back to them. She looked tired and she had red stains running in trails down her cheeks. "I'm still confused," she said, "about who did this, I mean. Whoever it was...she was unlike anything that I've ever seen before. She was not human." She stared off, shaking her head. "...and the means by which these people were killed, it was...something different. I don't know how to describe it...it's like the woman was the weapon. She could grow weapons the way trees grow leaves, only it happened so quickly! These people were slaughtered and there is no reason for it. It seemed senseless...and there's no trail..." she whispered to herself.

"It's the Shadow. That is why there is no trail, and that is why it is such a strange feeling," Slatkin said. "Will you be okay?" he asked, seeing that she was still visibly disturbed by what she had just been through.

She nodded her head. "I still have to give them a funeral." Her voice was solemn and drained.

"Of course," he agreed. "Put something over the bodies and then we will help you. I don't think the child should see it."

Alexandria nodded her head, then walked back to the cabin.

When the funeral pyres were successfully lit, Alexandria once again used her spells to control the wind. Angelik started singing. She had never needed to sing a funeral song, and did not know any, so she sang one of the lullabyes that her mother had sung to her every night before bed. Her voice rang out high and soft, as the flames leapt into the air.

When the song was finished, she wrapped her arms around Slatkin, wishing she was hugging her father or mother instead, but needing the comfort from someone. She shed tears, feeling the girl's sadness and hoping the dead people would find some peace. Alexandria said a few words about the people, but Angelik's mind was feeling numb. She couldn't concentrate on what was being said for too long, but she heard what was important enough to pass onto the girl when she saved her. Her parents loved their daughter more than anyone else, and she gave them the most joy and hope that they had ever had in their whole lives.

Everything around her seemed to be slowing. She felt herself being lifted onto a horse. She rubbed her eyes, aware that she had accidentally fallen asleep from exhaustion. She heard Slatkin and Alexandria talking in quiet tones, she assumed so that they wouldn't awaken her.

"She's just a child. Exhaustion wears on her quicker than it does on us. We have our horses now, so she can sleep on the way. Her trail leads the same way as mine. It is a troubled place, the barren lands. That is where we are being led. It will not be easy for the child to do what she must do. We will aid her all we can."

There was a lengthy silence, and then Alexandria spoke. "They were cheering," there was a quiver in her speech, as she thought again of the hunters who had been so brave, falling so quickly and so violently as the hunters shouted in delight at their deaths.

"Like I said, it will not be easy. I fear for her safety, so we must do what we can to aid her. She's never been on a hunt and although I know that she is well equipped with the instincts that she needs, the hunters are mighty enough to take on an angel if they are all together. Look what they did to her mother."

There was silence for awhile, with the steady rhythm of horse hooves beating into the snow and the smell of burning kial wood blowing on the wind. Angelik was soon asleep again; her head rested on the horse's mane.

When Angelik awoke, Alexandria was standing beside her unicorn, staring down the mountain at the vast desert beyond.

"Where's Slatkin?" the young angel asked.

"He's on his way," Alexandria said, as she walked over to help the child down. "He's changing."

XXVI

Reunion

Shea

Victor admitted to himself that this would have been a lot more difficult without the elf guiding him. He was getting turned around in a labyrinth of underground tunnels and winding forest paths. Finally, they stepped through tangled undergrowth into a circular clearing, in the middle stood a towering stone. Victor had seen one similar in the Astrid territory. It was grey, towering to at least ten feet in the air, and was polished smooth, so that it showed a reflection.

"We'll get a Quiriel soon," said Arik. "The castle is floating this way."

Victor looked up to see a cloud floating towards them, and then right before their eyes, there was a woman standing on the rock. She had blue skin and long white hair.

"Oh, it's you!" she exclaimed when she saw Arik. Her voice sounded excited.

"Hey Starla, we need to get to the castle," he motioned toward Victor.

"But the queen isn't there right now," the sky elf said.

"Even better," Arik said. "We want to go now."

"It sounds urgent."

"It is!" Victor said, reaching for his sword.

"Don't!" exclaimed Arik. "She'll take us! Right, Starla?" he asked annoyed at the delay.

"Yes, but why the hurry if the queen isn't home?" She sounded offended.

"Because we don't want her to be home," Arik said, with irritation, while reaching out to the stone. "We're in a hurry!"

"Oh! Okay. Put your hand on the stone, stranger, and

I'll take you to the castle," she said, looking to Victor.

Victor reached out to the stone and they were suddenly standing in a large room, with a mirrored floor. He took his hand away from the stone, he could feel Celeste. Without waiting for the elf, he dashed away, following his senses.

He did not see what he passed. He only followed Celeste's traces until he found her. It was a sweet scent. A pulling tug led him through the halls and rooms. He was reaching out to open a door in one moment, and embracing Celeste in the next, feeling her softness and her heartbeat. He could feel her shaking as she wept. He could not stop holding her. Having lost her touch for so long it seemed better than he remembered.

"Victor," she wailed with joy and sadness. "Don't look at me, don't look!"

He couldn't say anything. He just held her until she pulled away, covering her face, keeping it hidden. "Please, don't look at me, just get me home!" she said as she turned away. She cowered in the farthest corner of the room.

He could feel the pull, the call that he had been waiting seven years to feel. "Celeste," his voice was now calm, holding back the surge of power he suddenly felt. "I will get you home, but I need you to calm down, so I can take away the fire."

When he said the words, there was a pause. She shook her head. "No," she said full of panic, as she realized what he meant.

Victor's eyes already stung from his own emotions, but he had been called to answer the injustice done to his wife and he fully intended to set things right. He knew she was upset, and he could not blame her. He knew how bad it must be by the way she was acting. She didn't want him to face what she had gone through.

"I haven't spent seven years away from you just to have you pull away from me," he said sadly.

"I don't want you to feel this!" she screamed.

"I have to, Celeste. It's the way to bring you home." His words came out in a strained whisper, as he tried to keep himself together. It would take all his strength to do what he was about to do and it would be easier if she would accept it.

As if she knew what he was thinking, she turned around, slowly forcing her face upwards and pulling the hood away from her scars. Then he saw her face for the first time after seven years. She could see the anger and bitterness in his expression, not at her, but at those who had hurt her. He crossed the room, and pulled her to him.

"I'm sorry I left! I should have stayed with you." The words did not come easily, "I thought you would be safe. I thought that you would be protected." There was silence as he looked at her, his eyes moving over the scars. Though he only saw them physically for a moment. He could now only see her soul. It was still the same shining gold and white light he remembered, though there were new red lines running through it. "You're still the most beautiful thing I've ever seen," he pulled her closer, carefully placing a tender kiss on her burning lips.

He reached out to her face with his hands, letting his power take over, feeling every imprint left on her soul that he had missed.

There was so much there to absorb! The labor pains, the worry when he had left, the panic when the castle walls came down. There was desperation when she heard the shouting and fighting outside her door. She begged Carmina to hide, but the nephilim stayed by her side, not willing to leave her queen. When they broke through the door, Carmina fought them, but there were too many, and she was overpowered. The midwife was thrown from the window. The hunters grabbed Celeste, pulling her outside the castle. She heard Carmina screaming for her. Victor felt the horror Celeste had felt as she had been pulled outside.

The leader threw her on the ground, laughing. Victor

felt her humiliation. The hunters kicked her, spat on her and beat her with their fists. Victor felt every wound. She shielded her belly. If she had not been in labor, she could have fought back, but at the moment she was helpless and the hunters knew it. They counted on it. Her attackers shouted insults at her unborn child as they tied her to the stake. She was listening for the little heartbeat fluttering in her womb and that was all that kept her aware as the hunters struck her again with lashes from their whips.

Then the fire was lit, accompanied by a chorus of cheers. By that time she was too weak to struggle for consciousness. She could not feel the child anymore. Of all the things that had struck her, this was the hardest.

Flames crawled up the right side of her body and she heard herself scream, but she could not feel her throat make the noise. The angel could only feel the flames burrowing into her flesh. She was at the end of what she could endure. She blacked out, and then there was a long troubled sleep.

She drifted in and out of consciousness while the goddess delivered Angelik. This was followed by a slow healing, a painful healing, as Kristiniva nursed her back to health. The years dragged by torturously and power was slowly drained from her each morning. The pain was almost too much to take in at once, but Victor dared not let go, for fear that Celeste would be left with it. He held on, taking it all away. He wanted nothing more than to rid her of these scars. He concentrated, taking it in, turning it into power that he could use. He held her long after the pain had subsided.

He could only see with his divine perception now and as Celeste pulled away, he realized that she was even more beautiful than he had remembered. The red lines were fading slowly. He leaned down, planting a kiss on her mangled lips which no longer hurt then her cheek that had been scarred, and her forehead.

"I'm taking you home," he said, pulling her close

again, wrapping his arms around her, "You will be alright now," he said.

She nodded her head, "But I'll be better when we get home."

Victor nodded. "Arik will take you. I have something I have to do and then I will meet you there," he said.

Celeste tightened her grip on Victor. "She's coming, Victor, I can feel it."

Suddenly, the door burst open and Arik ran in trying to catch his breath. "We have to go now!" he exclaimed. "She's here and if I am discovered getting you home, then my punishment will be harsh indeed!" he exclaimed as he glanced out the window.

"Arik, get my wife home and I will take care of Kristiniva!"

"We can't leave without you!" exclaimed Arik.

"Then get her out of the castle!"

"Alright, Celeste," said Arik, "Let's go!" He held out his hand to her. "We have to go find Starla and get out of here!" he exclaimed.

Celeste kissed Victor a quick goodbye and then her hand was in Arik's as they raced through the castle. As they rounded a corner, they ran into Starla.

"Take us back!" he demanded.

"What?" she asked. "But that's the servant. You can't just take her out of the castle. Kristiniva will be furious!"

"Starla!" Arik caught her gaze. "I beg you to please help us get back to the ground. We can't leave Shea without Victor. You're right, Kristiniva is not going to be happy about this, so we're going to leave."

"So your guest…that was her husband?"

Arik nodded his head. "Yes, now you've always been a good friend to me Starla, so please help us!"

"I can't!" she said. "I'm sorry, but you know I could be punished for helping you!"

"Look," pleaded Arik, "I know that you are afraid of

being disobedient to your queen, but if we're not gone when the other angel gets back, you and I will be in trouble with him! Is that what you want?"

Starla sighed, "Okay, grab the stone," she said, finally convinced.

XXVII

Shadow Lands

Sark, edge of the barren lands

Slatkin, now in his beastly form, stared down at the darkness below. He could see nothing with his mortal eyes, but his angelic senses showed him miles of black sand stretching into the distance and a structure, seemingly man made. It towered high into the sky, black as the sand. The trail he was following led him there. He could feel the void. It was strong here and it was something he feared. It had the power to swallow everything, even himself and twist it into something different.

"Here," said Alexandria. He turned to see her handing a knife to the child, whose eyes lit up.

"Where did you find this?" Angelik asked. It was the Valka bone the huntress had given her daughter. Angelik now knew her name; it came to her as she reached out for the bone.

"Kaila thought she had lost it!" Angelik was suddenly overcome with emotions. "It is all she has of her mother." A tear slid down her face. "Why do the hunters have to be so mean?" she asked. "Why can't they just get along with everyone?"

Alexandria shook her head. "I don't know," she responded. "She'll know how to use that, so make sure she gets it, and then I have this," she said, reaching for another small knife that she handed to the princess. "This one is for you," she said. "The hunters are dangerous, so you have to be able to save yourself in case they try to capture you. It is only to be used in defense and I've enchanted it to never miss, so I know you'll be safe."

A small smile stretched across Angelik's face. "This is

213

pretty," she said, wiping her face with the back of her hand before taking the blade.

Alexandria smiled back. "Yeah, it is!" she agreed. "That's why I bought it." She turned to Slatkin, "So, swords or axes?" she asked, pulling both out for him to see.

"I won't need either," he responded.

"Slatkin, don't say that to me," she pleaded. "I know you have sharp claws, but when you change back, you're going to need a weapon." She had a cool look on her face that showed him she did not intend to back down from the argument.

"Axes then," he decided.

Alexandria thrust an axe onto the ground. It landed heavily in a snow drift. "You're the only one who will be able to move it, so if you come back here, you'll find it."

Slatkin laughed. "Have you been speaking to Belle?" he asked.

"I have," she said. "Why else would I have reminded you to strip at least out of your coat before you transformed? I wouldn't have thought of it otherwise."

Slatkin chuckled again, but it came out as a deep growl.

"You know she'll be glad to hear it when we get back home."

"Back home..." he said, "Well, we'll see, won't we..."

"What do you mean?" asked Alexandria. "Do you have other plans?"

Slatkin nodded his head. "For a while," he said. "There is work to be done, depending on how well we succeed here tonight."

Alexandria nodded her head and sheathed the sword she had been holding. "Well, either way, let's do this!" she exclaimed, grabbing her staff from where she had left it standing in the snow.

Slatkin looked seriously at the child. "Angelik," he said. "We will have to separate for you to do your task. There is someone that I have to find, too. Try to stay close and when we separate, follow your instincts! They will not lead you wrong and keep the dagger that Alexandria gave you close. You may need to use it. Try to stay hidden. That will be the easiest way in and out."

The young princess nodded her head. "I understand." she said, reaching up for Alexandria to pull her onto the unicorn.

He smiled as they descended the mountain, remembering Belle's worrying over the furs. For a mortal, she certainly had a way of seeing into the future.

"Keep going," he said to Alexandria as he stopped. "Stay close to her!" he said, quickly motioning to the light angel. "I'll be above you." He kicked off the ground, soaring into the sky.

Alexandria urged Vortex closer to the darkness of the Shadow. The angels could feel its pull grow stronger as they rode closer to the towering structure that lay beyond in the darkness. As Slatkin circled above, Alexandria kicked Vortex into a quicker pace and they raced further into the black sands.

Trost, inside the citadel

Shekley had left the hunters to discover the city of Trost on their own. He had the girl, pulling her down a corridor, laughing aloud as she continuously fought him. A wicked grin curled his lips back over his teeth. "You're going to be fun to break!" he said. "Though, I regret not leaving you with Volkhan. I would enjoy seeing what he would do with you!"

The girl kicked him hard in the knee, but he laughed even harder. "I hope you retain some of this once I'm done with you. As willful as you are about killing, you could be one of my best fighters. I'll have to thank that irritating boy later for convincing me to keep you."

He continued to pull her down the dark hallway, seeing

through the blackness with the Shadow's vision. When he came to the door he was looking for, Xandra was waiting.

"The machines don't have enough power to work," she said, "But we can still lock her down and get her ready. When the sun comes back up, we should start getting power."

"Very minor setback!" he exclaimed. "I can be patient. I can wait for day. Patience..." he pulled the girl along and Xandra reached out, quickly grabbed her up, and placed her on one of the experimental tables. She held her down, while Shekley chained her body from head to toe. The girl was panicking, still trying to escape, though she could no longer scream. Her throat was dry and sore. The Shadow was savoring every moment of her desperation.

Trost, outside the citadel

They moved forward, seeing hunters outside the towering structure. Alexandria suddenly stopped Vortex to let off Angelik. "Your work is inside. See if you can slip in," she said, before kicking off again. Angelik spotted the entrance and ran as fast as she could, hoping to make it to the girl in time to save her.

Alexandria was racing the unicorn forward. The hunters were slowly gathering things from their horses and laughing. Some, she noticed were discussing the earlier slaughter as they smiled and laughed. She ran straight for them, knocking them down with her staff before they could see what had hit them. Others readied weapons and ran forward to kill the yellow haired angel. She spun Vortex around to face them. She pulled out her sword, and deflected blows. One came at her with an axe as she dismounted. She used her staff to bring his axe to the ground and when he fell forward, she kneed him forcefully in the face, while she deflected another sword with her own. She heard a howl from Slatkin above her and the sled dogs started turning on their masters, clawing and biting. The horses bucked and kicked their riders, and sped off to the mountains.

The hunters who were quickest on their feet started aiming arrows at Slatkin circling above them. He managed to dodge most of them, but missed two. They were now lodged in his wings. He let out a roar and swooped down onto the sand. He flapped his wings and stirred up a great cloud of dust, keeping his eyes fixed on his target. He pushed hunters away as he walked forward, throwing them into the air and further out into the sands, scattering them.

"Galan!" he roared, walking forward.

The young hunter's face lost all color as he looked up at the massive creature, but his father's voice sounded out behind him. "Kill it! Kill it! You have its eyes, aim for the heart!"

The boy grabbed his sword and thrust it deeply into Slatkin's thick fur. Slatkin roared out in pain and broke his gaze, but when he caught the young hunter's eyes again, Galan could not look away. "Sleep," Slatkin demanded. The boy's hand released the sword that still stuck the beast and he collapsed in the sand, sound asleep.

The beast turned to face Volkhan, and growled fiercely, before reaching out with his claws. Slatkin knocked the hunter away. He landed further out in the sand with a thud and a painful yell.

Alexandria was still fighting when Slatkin yelled to her. "We need Angelik, I have my target. Go find her! I will handle these hunters."

Alexandria forced her staff into the sand and suddenly the men she had been fighting started falling. "They're dizzy," she yelled, as she made her way toward the entrance. "It won't last long!" she said before disappearing through the door at a quick run.

Trost, Shekley's quarters

The Shadow was planning, preparing for the busy day

tomorrow when something painful weakening him. Whatever it was, it was coming closer. Shekley curled up on the floor, covering his ears. There was a high pitched squealing, getting louder, making him sick and sending sharp pains all over his body.

"What are you doing to me?" he yelled aloud at the Shadow, but he couldn't hear his own words and he couldn't hear anything other than the terrible screeching all around him.

Xandra knelt down beside him. "Shekley, what is wrong?" He answered with struggling breaths and grunts of pain as he writhed on the floor. He looked as if he were trying to tell her something, but when his mouth opened, it stayed open and his hands would fold over his ears again. Xandra didn't know what to do so she stayed where she was, hoping that this latest fit would end soon. She had to help him, but she did not know the way, she reminded herself.

XXVIII

The Rescue

Alexandria ran through the entrance, but was faced with more opponents. She fought them off with her staff. One was hit in the ribs and then knocked away with a kick. He stumbled into the others. She tripped another and darted toward a stairway to her left. They were following. She turned with her staff raised in the air and shouted "Veheil stavik!" Suddenly, the hunters were falling and slipping, not able to gain their footing. She dashed up the stairs, searching for Angelik's trail.

Angelik let her senses guide her forward. She wasn't used to being so blind. The darkness in the building was unnatural to her. The only instinct that seemed to be any use to her was the trail itself. It was her guide. The bright angel gripped a blade in each hand, wondering how much further it would be. She could feel she was getting closer.

Then she rounded a corner and saw Kaila through a doorway. Her soul was blue, with deep scars of red. She could feel that the girl was asleep. Angelik could hear Kaila's heart beating, rapidly throbbing in her chest. She shifted both of the knives to her left hand and reached out, feeling the chains that held the huntress down. She pulled on them but they did not give. Her heart fell as she realized that she was not strong enough to break them. She felt in the darkness for the girl's hand. When she found it, she placed the Valka bone in it.

The angel climbed onto the table and then reached out to kiss the girl on the forehead to awaken her. The girl smiled in her sleep. Angelik could feel it. She ran her hands over the chains that bound the girl, when she felt something awaken in her. Her fingers started to feel funny. She ran them across the chains, feeling them break and snap beneath her touch. Sparks lit up the room with each snap. When they were all broken, she gripped her dagger in one hand and Kaila's hand in the other.

"Wake up Kaila, we have to leave now," she said. The girl sat up. She was weak and her body was beyond exhausted, but she managed to grip the Valka bone firmly in her hand. The pull of flesh started her wrists to bleeding again.

"What is happening?" she asked.

"I'm getting you out of here," the young angel said. "Come with me and you will be safe, I promise." She leapt from the table and landed lightly on the floor.

The young huntress slid off the table, trying to stand but failing at first. Angelik was pained to know the girl was crying.

"Come on," she encouraged, "I've come to help you."

Kaila nodded her head and stood weakly. Angelik grabbed her free hand.

"Let's go," she said. "We have to get back to Slatkin and Alexandria." She pulled the girl along. It wasn't long before she could make out Alexandria's trail coming closer to her.

"Alexandria!" she yelled.

At the sound of Angelik's voice, Alexandria suddenly felt a wave of relief. She had been worried for the child. "This way!" the dark angel called.

The two girls moved forward, but Kaila stumbled several times. When they reached Alexandria, the dark angel reached out to the huntress. "You are too weak to run," she said, pulling the girl towards her and lifting her onto her back. They ran forward, trying to reach an exit.

"We're getting closer, I can see Slatkin," Alexandria announced. They ran forward and then out of instinct, Alexandria turned around in time to see Xandra fire her gun. She covered the girl and pulled Angelik down to dodge the bullets that buzzed by their heads. "Run, Angelik!" The dark angel shouted. "I'll hold her off!" She pushed Kaila into Angelik and stood in the same motion.

Alexandria was already thumping her staff and shouting spells to form a shield between them and Xandra, before the second round of bullets reached them. Angelik raced away, pulling the girl along.

Alexandria kept her attention on the creature through the clear barrier her spell had made. She could not feel a trace of anything when she looked at her. The angel wasn't sure how to fight something like this. She had seen the woman fight in Khabria's memory, but she had not gained the strength to defeat her. She slowly backed away, thinking of spells to cast. The shield would not hold for long and the angel could see that the woman was intent on having a fight. She was already pounding at the shield, trying to break it. Alexandria needed more time to prepare. She turned and ran, following the traces of the light angel.

Slatkin was waiting for them outside the main entrance, with Galan gripped safely in his claws. There were more wounds on Slatkin, including large parts of his leathery wings, which were ripped and shredded.

"I'll have to heal you when we get safe," Alexandria said.

Slatkin just nodded his head, panting. Alexandria met Vortex and lifted the unconscious children onto him. She grabbed the reins and the three angels made their way across the expanse of sand toward the mountains.

The angels found a cavern in one of the mountains and decided to rest there. The children were still sleeping, except for Angelik, who lay watching over the two humans. Slatkin had gone off to be by himself through his transformation, but Alexandria worried while he was away. She had seen the blows he had taken and she wasn't sure if she could have held up so well. It was a time before she saw the outline of his shaggy Valka fur moving closer, slowly, to the caverns. The axe she had given him was clutched in his hand.

She got up and ran to him. "Let me help you," she said, as she reached out to support him. He shivered, barely able to stand. "Come on," she coaxed, "I'll mend you." She walked with him to the entrance of the caverns and helped him sit.

"I will be fine," he said, "I only need to rest."

She pulled the fur off him and pulled his coat from his back. Blood streamed from his shoulders. The skin had the same rip as his wings. The wound was deep, all the way to his bone. Alexandria did what she could, but her healing spells could only help so much. The bleeding stopped, but the wound remained open and ripped. She then turned to where the sword had plunged into his chest. Again, she did what she could, but the wound was deep and could not be completely healed. She dug into her bag for a bandage. Slatkin spoke weakly, "It will heal in time," he said.

She nodded her head. "I know," she said, leaving her bag and ripping off the bottom of her own shirt. She wrapped it around him and tied it tightly. "Your Belle could do better," she said, "but this will have to do for now."

Slatkin smiled weakly, and nodded his head. "When you get back, tell her that I am well. Do not let her worry needlessly."

"I will, Slatkin," Alexandria said, helping him put his coat on again. "Now have a rest while I go find us something to eat. Angelik will watch over you all. She'll not let anything harm you." Slatkin chuckled, remembering the promise he had made to Victor. He had not expected her to be looking after him.

Galan awoke to the smells of cooking meat. He sat up groggily, and noticed his sister lying beside him. "Kaila," he whispered, gently reaching out to touch the scars on her wrists. She clutched the Valka bone tightly in her sleep.

"She is still scared," Angelik explained. "She doesn't understand that the danger has past. She'll be okay when she awakens."

Galan looked at the angel, and then at the other two who were sitting by a fire. "What happened?" he asked.

"You were rescued!" exclaimed Angelik, smiling brightly.

"There is no need to fear us," explained Slatkin. "You have been very good, Galan."

"Where is my father?"

"I do not know," said Slatkin, "but I must say that I could not rescue him. He is part of what I saved you from. You gave him love and respect. He deserves neither."

Galan hung his head and said no more, feeling both relief and loss.

XXIX

Confrontation

Shea, Kristiniva's castle

The goddess stood frozen as she stepped through her door. She was staring at the angel before her. Victor was standing in the main hall. He was as still as a statue, silent. Only his hair moved as the wind passing through the castle whipped it around his face. He had come here for Celeste, Kristiniva knew and she understood, as she always had, that his intent was full of so much more. He meant to kill her as punishment for keeping his wife from him. She knew it, and yet, she could not find it in herself to attack him. He was perfectly made, as beautiful as his wife. Kristiniva could feel his power. Justice. She felt it building in the air around her and she knew she had met a worthy opponent. She could only stare at him. She could find no words to express the fear and awe that coursed through her.

She was frozen in her tracks, not able to move or speak. She felt unable to defend herself or oppose him. Minutes passed with only the sound of wind blowing gently through the castle.

Finally, Kristiniva spoke. "You will kill me." Her voice sounded loud and crisp as it broke the silence.

The angel shook his head, the first visible movement he had made. "No," his voice filled the room, "but I must make things right," he said, keeping his voice as calm as he could.

"You expect me to let her go?" she asked, thinking this would be worse than her death.

"No," said Victor, "I've already taken care of that part."

He was amused at the expression on the goddess' face as she realized what he was saying to her. She felt an angry

224

panic and suddenly the room turned dark, as ominous clouds rolled over the sun. The goddess' eyes went from electric to black. Within seconds, the whole castle began to shake with thunder and lightning illuminated her hair turning it from blue to black.

"You cannot do this!" she shouted. Her voice boomed in thunder, as the reality of loss stirred within her.

"I will do whatever it takes to make things right." Victor growled as he crossed the room quickly, putting his sword to her throat.

"How can you ever think that they can be right again?" she asked, a smirk now lining her deep blue lips. "You should have saved her, but you left her alone. You couldn't save her. So I did."

Hatred surged through him, filling his thoughts shadowing his reasoning. He shook his head as he reached out, grabbing her slender neck in his fist. The angel was trying desperately to counter the human nature still clinging to him. He wanted to kill her now, but he knew he couldn't. Too many of his people depended on her. He fought with himself to stay within the confines of the binding laws of angels. He released her neck, placing his sword over her chest. "I have already suffered for my mistakes, so do not remind me. I know more than anyone that I could not save her and I do not like to be reminded." The power he had collected from Celeste surged through him. He pushed the blade through her chest hard, feeling the tissue give way to the pressure. Blood gushed out, staining her marble skin. Lightning flashed and the wind gusted in chaos, as thunder shook the castle. The goddess fell to her knees, gasping in shock.

Kristiniva grabbed her chest in disbelief when the blade slid out. She couldn't breathe. She began convulsing.

The dark angel wiped the blood from the sword and licked it from his hand. It was revolting and bitter, but he found the sweetness he needed. Victor grabbed her face with his blood drenched hand and stared into her cold, shocked eyes. He spoke with gritted teeth. "You have something I need!" The power she had taken from his wife was there, beating in her heart. With no mercy left for her, he put his hand inside the wound gripping her cold heart. As lightning flashed outside, the goddess collapsed to the floor. He could feel the power leaving her and entering him. It filled him with an indescribable power, a surge of warmth and care, something unlike anything that he had ever felt. He wondered briefly, if this was what Celeste felt all the time. He held on to Kristiniva's beating heart until there was no more power to drain. Then he withdrew his hand, feeling sympathy for the goddess.

He wanted to kill her as much as he wanted to save her and he halted for a moment, considering what he would do with her. The surge of care won.

As quickly as he had struck her, he was able to heal her wound. It closed up and the goddess was still. She lay, gripping her chest, breathing heavily, as she had never breathed before. Only a light scar remained across her pale breast. Her eyes were vacant and white. The storm that raged turned from hail and thunder to a fierce blizzard. Kristiniva pulled herself into a sitting position. Her hair turned white as ice plummeted from the sky.

"Now, listen carefully," he said pointing the sword to her chin. "Your Sarkian followers, the Astrids, have suffered because of your decisions. You need to listen when they pray. The hunters are out of control and they are causing the tribe to diminish. They need you!" He slid the tip of his blade to her throat.

Kristiniva nodded her head. "Yes," she said through her troubled breaths.

"If you help them, you can gain back some of the power you try to wield, but you will have to earn it rather than taking it." As he said the words, he felt the warmth of his sympathy fading, remembering what she had taken from him that he could never have back.

"I will do what you ask," Kristiniva said. Her voice was raspy.

Victor leaned down to her, "I know you will," he said coldly, "because if you don't, I'll come back for you." He pressed his sword harder against her neck, "Be warned too, that if you ever come near my wife or child again, I will go against all the binding laws that I follow, and I will kill you!"

The goddess stared up at him, speechless and shaking. He stood there a moment longer, with the sword pressed next to her skin. Then with narrowed eyes, he pulled the sword away and turned to leave, sheathing the sword, and wiping blood on his shirt. Now that he had what he needed, the blood seemed tainted. He wanted to be rid of it.

When he was out the door, he dashed back to the stone. Starla was standing atop the rock, ready to take him back. They exchanged no words as he touched the stone and found himself in the clearing. It was dark under the swirling storm clouds. Celeste and Arik were waiting at the edge of the trees, soaked from the rainshower and shivering from the ice. He ran towards them.

"Thank you," he said sincerely to Arik, yelling over the roar of the wind. "If there is any way that I can repay your kindness in the future, I hope you will let me know."

Arik nodded "I will."

"Now, take us as close to the castle as you can, she wants to go home," he said, smiling down at his wife.

Arik nodded his head, "Very well," he said, "but I do have one request," he said, "Take care of one another," he said, smiling, as he weaved the spell to take them home.

Kristiniva pulled herself up from the floor, clutching her chest, still shocked by what had happened to her. She shakily walked forward and then floated, unable to keep her footing. She glided through the air, searching for the angels. Someone had helped them escape, probably one of the elves.

How else was Victor able to get here? Her thoughts were dark. She would find the one who helped them and see to it they paid for her pain, not just from the sword of Justice, but from the separation from her own angel. She threw the doors of the castle open with a mighty wind and then she descended through the clouds. She could feel it already, the sting of loss that was unbearable. As these thoughts filled her head, her eyes lit a glowing orange and her hair swept out dark grey behind her.

She floated down, and spotted Arik. He was closing the gateway back, before running into the thickets. Thoughts started churning in her mind, thoughts of hate. He would pay for taking away her love, her power. She summoned a lightning bolt, but then cast it aside. No, she would have something special for him and she would summon the strength of the Mountain Trolls to help her.

XXX

Home

Sark

As Celeste looked around, happiness flowed into her expression. She shivered in the biting wind. Victor took off his wolf fur and wrapped it around her shivering body. They embraced, and then gazed at each other, each one taking in the other, before making their way towards the outline of the castle on the next mountain.

Celeste sniffed the air, smelling the sweetness of the kial trees and the cleanness of the snow. She felt the wind in her hair and the crunch of ice beneath her feet. She sighed with relief and joy.

"I'm home," she said, with excitement and relief flowing through her.

"Finally!" pronounced Victor.

Celeste laughed as she noticed the torches burning brightly in the tallest tower. She wasn't surprised that he had used torches instead of candles. "You kept a vigil!" she said, her heart feeling warmer than it had in a long time.

"Of course!" Victor laughed at himself.

When they finally arrived, Celeste felt sadness as she took in the condition of the castle. The gate was thrown down and the walls were crumbling. It wasn't how she remembered it, but her heart was still glad.

"Victor," she said, as she walked towards the door, "Do you think that it will ever be the same?" she asked.

He shook his head, "I don't think so, but I think that it will start getting better soon… I hope so, anyway."

"I think that you might be right," she said, as Victor opened the door. Immediately, Carmina came rushing into the room. "Celeste?" she asked in a whisper, her voice was quavering in her excitement. She ran to Celeste, hugging her.

"I can't believe you're back! You're back! You're back!" she said, and then she pulled away. "Your scars..." she began, but did not finish her solemn thoughts.

Celeste smiled, "They'll heal," she finished for the nephilim. "Look at you, though," she said, surprised. "You've grown!" she exclaimed. She marveled at just how tall the nephilim was. The last time that she had seen her, Carmina was an adolescent and the same height as Celeste. Now she towered awkwardly tall above her and Celeste was hugging her stomach, instead of her neck.

"Where is everyone else?" asked Victor.

"Well," said Carmina, "Belle's here and Evingh, but no one else. We thought they were with you."

"Evingh?" they asked in unison.

"Yes," said Carmina. "I guess he's the latest addition to our family. Apparently Belle made some kind of promise to Slatkin that she'd take care of him, and...well, you know how Belle is. She's treating him like he's her own child. He's not very responsive to anything. He likes music and from the way we cleaned him up, you'd never know he was a hunter. He's kinda handsome and much younger than the way he looked at first...well, just come see! Belle will be so glad to know you've returned!" Carmina started walking and they followed her. She kept talking as they followed her.

"I knew you'd be coming soon, I just didn't know when. The kraelvins came to me again. They told me you'd return. I was so excited and I still am of course."

Victor was laughing as he followed. "I can tell," he said.

They peeked into Belle's room. She sat by the hearth reading a book to Evingh. He sat blankly before her. She looked up as Carmina walked in and when she realized who else walked in, she threw the book onto the floor and ran over to give them both hugs.

She half laughed and half cried, as she squeezed her queen in a hug. "You're back! Oh, welcome home!" When she saw the scars, she pulled away, and said more solemnly, "Welcome back." Then she turned to Victor, "Oh, I'm just so glad, so excited!" She was almost jumping up and down in her joy. Her smile seemed to brighten the whole room. Victor thought about how happy Slatkin would be if he could see her so joyous. She turned to Evingh.

"Evingh, the queen has returned, come see her." She spoke as if speaking to a small child. Evingh did not respond. "Come," she said, walking closer to him, and reaching out her hand to help him up. At the touch of her hand, he stood and walked with her over to the two angels.

"Evingh," said Celeste, her voice was full of sympathy, understanding what he had been through. She took the hand that Belle was not holding and held it gently. "You'll be alright, if you continue to be good. I can see all that is good in you and you have great potential. You've been given a second chance and Belle is trying to teach you how to use your skills to help others. I cannot relieve you of your nightmares, they are of your own making, but I can tell you to cast them aside and see what is in front of you. This new life is going to be full of love, if you will let it in."

The young man smiled at her words and his eyes seemed to awaken somewhat, but he said nothing back to her.

"He's been like this since he's been in my care," said Belle, disappointed. "I'm supposed to teach him how to be good, but I don't know if any of my words are getting to him. I mean, he'll hum with me, but nothing else. He looks so blank sometimes. I can never tell what he's thinking."

Celeste smiled at Belle's worried look. "You're doing wonderful," she said, "Slatkin knew what he was doing. You are like a mother to Evingh now, something he never had as the hunter Chase. He has never had a guiding hand or a loving embrace, until he came here. You have helped him more than you realize. Slatkin will be proud." She smiled at the beaming look on Belle's face.

"Chase was his name?" she asked. Celeste nodded.

"Well, my name is better. It fits him." She giggled. "So where are the others?"

"I'm sorry," said Victor, "they had work to do. I thought they would be back by now, but apparently they have been caught up in it."

"Oh," said Belle, her disappointment showing, "Well, that's alright, maybe they'll be home soon. It's almost daylight," she said. "I was just getting ready to go to bed, but if you want to eat, I'll be glad to get something started for you," she said.

Victor laughed, and Celeste shook her head. "Actually, with all the excitement I'm pretty tired," she admitted. "I think I'll turn in," she said, "but I look forward to breakfast at dusk," she said, smiling.

Belle nodded her head, "Well alright then," she smiled back and embraced the angel again. "I'm just so glad you've returned."

Celeste received another hug from Carmina. "Have a good rest," the nephilim smiled, "and if you need anything at all, I will see to it."

Celeste nodded, "I know," she replied, "and I thank you."

She turned to Evingh and hugged him also. "You sleep well, too," she said. "We're all here for you." She felt him awkwardly lean in to hug her, and she laughed. "See," she said, "it's not so hard, is it?"

Belle giggled beside them, and then pulled him away. "Off to bed, we need to be now," she said. "It's time to sleep."

Victor pulled Celeste through the threshold into their chambers. She leaned into him and he fell against the door, shutting it. "I have something for you," he leaned down, kissing her lips, running his hands across her warm skin. She pressed herself against him, feeling the power Kristiniva had drained from her suddenly returning. She felt the wounds on her face healing. Overpowering all other senses, she felt the passion she had been missing for seven years. Victor lifted her off the ground and the angels quickly made their way to bed.

Epilogue:

Arik had stopped struggling and was forced to his knees. He stared straight ahead. He refused to look at the goddess. He was afraid of what seeing her would make him do. Anger was surging through him. It was taking over all other thoughts and he realized that as an elf, he had the power of killing in him. His heart beat loudly in his ears and his breathing was heavy, filling the silent room.

Two rock trolls, creatures made from stone itself, held him firmly down by his shoulders. He was aware of the goddess pacing in front of him. Her deep purple robes created breezes as she walked past. She stopped suddenly, glaring down at him. He still would not look at her. There was unbearable silence, and even the trolls became uncomfortable.

Finally, the goddess spoke. "I do not want to hear your excuses, for I am certain they are nothing but lies." As she spoke, there was an annoying numbness in his throat and he realized she had taken his speech. The spell was so strong, it sealed his mouth shut. "I do not want to know your thoughts. No doubt they are full of darkness." With these words, came an excruciating headache and he knew that his telepathy was gone. "I do not want to ever...and I want to stress that word...EVER...see you again. You are useless to me and a hindrance to my subjects. In fact I want you so far away from me and my kingdom that we lose all thoughts of you ever existing. I am banishing you, Arik, and your name shall not be uttered without consequence from here on after. I don't want you seeking revenge, so I am stripping you of your power. You will be in a place so dark and deep that the moonlight will never grace your skin again."

At these words, Arik's anger became unbearable. The thing which she did was forbidden. Moonlight was his gift, his birthright as an elf. He felt his expression changing. He was full of hatred for this woman. He had only helped Celeste get back to her home and though he knew there would be consequences, he was not ready for them. He could take the banishment...but the moonlight? He had never considered that she would take that from him. He was an elf! Moonlight was not a right she could take away! He was shaking in his anger. He struggled under the grip of the stone trolls, but as he tried to rise he found himself lying against the floor, his face scraping the rough tile.

Kristiniva turned her face to the trolls. "I will show you the place to take him. It is in Sark." She then summoned one of her Quiriels into the room. The creature came in obediently, bowing to the queen.

"You are to go to the moon elves, and have Arista come here. I want it to be her that opens the doorway to Sark. I am setting an example for his kind and I want them to know what happens when they disobey me."

The Quiriel glanced at Arik and a sympathetic look came over her face, as she realized who it was the trolls were restraining. He saw her distress, but gave her a look to let her know that she should save herself. She turned to the queen, bowing. "Yes, my queen, I will do this thing you ask of me."

When Arista arrived, she was not shocked when she saw her brother wrapped in chains between two stone trolls with his face rubbing the tile. Nevertheless she felt somewhat responsible for it, and she was angry at the goddess.

"Arik!" she exclaimed, running toward him. The trolls pulled him back up to his knees and he shook his head as she came closer. Kristiniva raised her arm and Arista was thrown against the wall in a great wind. She fell breathless to the floor and then stood slowly, collecting herself. Kristiniva glared at her. "I never want to hear that name spoken again! Do you understand?" Arista just looked at the queen, shocked at everything that was happening.

"What has he done?" Arista asked, looking the queen

in the eyes.

"He took my servant from me and he has broken almost every law that I've put into place. He is arrogant, disrespectful and rebellious. His acts are nothing short of treason."

Arista looked sympathetically at her brother and then at the queen. "May I speak on his behalf?"

"No," the queen answered coldly. "You can, however, open the doors to Sark, so that these trolls may do what I have asked them to do."

"My queen, surely there is a better..."

"Silence!" The queen yelled, and Arista found that she could no longer speak. With quivering lips, she walked forward and knelt down before her brother. She spoke to him mind to mind. *"You know I don't want to do this. I can't rule alone, and we should share this punishment!"*

She waited for a response, but there wasn't one. She didn't understand that Arik had also been stripped of his telepathy. With tears in her eyes, she reached out to hug him, but a third troll pushed her back.

Arik stared straight ahead, showing no emotion. He knew that he could not break down in front of the queen. He would have time to plan his vengeance later, but for now he had to be strong. He could not look at his sister. It would be too painful. It already was painful as he realized that his punishment would fall on his kin as well.

With a bowed head and a defeated look, Arista waved her arms in the spell that would open the door. His last image was of her kneeling on the floor, head hung low, her hands folding back to her face and then he was in Sark with the three stone trolls.

Somewhere in Sark

The trolls had apologized to Arik many times over, but they were not about to disobey Kristiniva. They chained him up as she had asked, with black chains of iron. One of them offered him water, which he appreciated, but could not drink for his mouth was still sealed shut. The other left his torch to give Arik what he could of light, which Arik was grateful for. Then they walked away through the long, twisting tunnels of the cave. The echoes of their footsteps slowly faded and then there was a loud, crashing sound far away. He knew he was sealed in. There was complete silence, except his breathing and the sound of the flames crackling from the torch. He tried to scream, but Kristiniva's spell of silence still had his voice. His chains clanged as he struggled in them. He wondered if he could get out and if not, how long it would be before he was driven mad by darkness, or silence. He thought this as the torch flickered out and the injustice, the anger, and the darkness settled in.

Dark Angel Wars: Glossary

Adrianna: The Shean goddess of the sea.

Alexandria: Dark angel of vengeance, sister of Celeste of Trealon and a knight of Chimrion.

Amicus: Shean god of communication, messenger between the humans and the gods.

Angelik: Light angel of innocence, princess of Sark, daughter of Victor and Celeste.

angels: (protectors of Shea), children of Saigolai, god of life.

> ***light angels:** these angels are only granted powers of goodness, they are bred only from the pairing of two dark angels.

> ***dark angels:** these angels are given dark powers to do aid humanity. They are given their gifts by Saigolai upon dying from a mortal life.

> ***orostiro:** these high-ranking angels are the direct descendents of Saigolai, the god of life. They are granted powers of both darkness and light.

Arik: The prince of the moon elves.

Arista: The princess of the moon elves.

Astrids: A Sarkian tribe of women who live separate from their male relatives. They worship both the Shean and Sarkian gods.

baika vine: a vine that grows wild in Sark. It has a pleasing mint aroma, and the leaves can be crushed and used as both a painkiller and an antiseptic. (Belle uses this in healing Chase)

Barren Lands: (Sark) The barren lands are the cursed desert lands that lie to the East in Sark. Nothing lives there and the inhabitants of Sark avoid it.

Barrett: Horse-keeper of the Scithronians, human

Basilla: Saltook's daughter, bar maid, and werewolf

Belle: A mortal earth-witch, Victor's cook.

Binding Laws: Laws set forth by Saigolai to govern his dark angels.

caib soup: A soup made from sea mussels fished from the Sarkian coast. It is a favorite at The Howling Wolf Tavern and Inn.

cairag flowers: pink and red flowers that grow in the clearings of the Sarkian forests. They are rare and are used as an antiseptic. Belle uses ground cairag flowers to heal Chase.

Carmina: A nephilim, the personal guard of Celeste.

Celeste: The angel of love, queen of Sark, wife of Victor and mother of Angelik. She spends seven years held captive by Kristiniva.

Chase: A hunter that is saved by Slatkin, renamed Evingh by Belle.

Chimrion: A land far to the South of Sark. Alexandria resided here until she came to Sark.

David: A leader of the Selbdes, brother to Shekley. His gift is to project memories and thoughts of others into a life like illusion.

Dexon: Victor's horse.

Elise: A tavern wench who is forced into marriage by the hunter Markus, and then killed by him. She appears in spirit form to Alexandria, who releases her from her curse.

elves: Creatures who are born of Shea, and who

live in both Shea and Sark. They each have unique gifts and are the only creatures that have the power to open doorways between the worlds. They are telepathic and highly magical. The orders of elves are as follows: moon, sea, sun, plains, star, snow and sylvan.

endless dust: a medicine created with elven magic to cure all wounds. It is extremely rare, and something that only their kind are aware of.

Evingh: This is the name that Belle gives to the hunter Chase. It means young one in Ulmira, the land of her birth.

Faeries: creatures that exist both in abstract and visible realms. There are many kinds of fairies. They are spiritual creatures that aid in the everyday goings on of Shea.

   ***fairie wine:** A gift made from the fairies out of their magic and Shean fruits.

Fausti: A formal Shean greeting

Galan: A young hunter who saves his half sister's life and is in turn saved by Slatkin.

Gazevi: An informal Shean greeting

gnome: creatures that burrow in the ground, often near mushrooms or moss. They are good natured creatures and are often very crafty with small tools.

Havink: Kaila's step-father, a hunter.

Haz: A hunter whose jaw gets broken by Alexandria

healers (selbdes): These are a particular kind of selbdes that have the ability to heal others when locked into their minds.

heith: an evergreen bush. The leaves are ground and used as a flavorful spice in many Sarkian recipes.

Howling Wolf Tavern: The only tavern in Sark, it is owned by Saltook, the alpha werewolf.

hunters: a tribe of Sarkian humans that worship the god Khanhine. He is the hunter god.

James: A selbdes with the power of healing.

Kaila: a young huntress, daughter of Khabria. Her paternal father is Volkhan, leader of the hunters.

Khabria: mother of Kaila, a huntress and tribal leader.

Khali: Volkhan's current wife, stolen from the Astrid tribe.

Khiel: A Scithronian who aids Alexandria.

Kial Thieren trees: Trees native to Sark. They have charcoal-like bark, and they produce and hold fire inside them.

    *kial brew: an alcoholic brew made from the kial theiren trees

    *kial fibers: thick, tough, soft fibers stripped from the inside of a kial thieren tree. The fibers can be used for many things, including sewing clothes.

    *kial twigs: These are broken from the limbs of kial theiren trees and are used to smoke. They have a sweet flavor.

Kialo: The Shean god of Earth

Kim: A pselbdes

King's Mountain: The highest mountain in Sark, the rulers of Sark have made this their home for countless ages.

Klarrisa: A seer that lives with the Scithronians.

kraelvins: Birds native to Sark that communicate with Carmina, and bring her news of other worlds.

Kristiniva: The Shean sky goddess who is worshipped by the Astrids.

Lazaris: A werewolf that works in the kitchens at The Howling Wolf Tavern.

lumistone: A very powerful weapon, given to the Sea elves by Luna and Selfirin in the before time.

LUMVEREN SUMABILA: A spell cast by Alexandria. It is powerful, but non-lethal

Luna: The Shean goddess of light

Mahldrusecs: Creatures that Shekley makes to serve the Shadow. They are half-humans that he distorts to serve his will.

Malah: Queen of the sylvan elves

Markus: A fierce hunter

Michael: A Selbdes with explosive powers.

Mondlif: King of the sylvan elves

Noggle: a gnome from the mushroom gardens, he is the first to confront the Selbdes when they arrive in Shea.

Nometheog: god of the void

Pegasus: winged horses that pull Kristiniva's carriage.

Quirials: sky elves

Raffie: A Pegasus who befriended Angelik

Saigolai: The god of life and death

Saltook: owner of the howling wolf tavern

Sark: A cold island nation that is in a state of decline. Currently it is ruled by the hunters, it is rightfully owned by the dark angels.

Sassy: A selbdes who is skilled at mind manipulation and visual distortion

Scithronians: A tribe of thieves that live in the Sarkian Forests. They are the orphans of Sark that were once taken in by Celeste.

Selbdes: Psychic creatures that live in Tahln. They have vast powers, and each is unique.

Selfirin: The Shean god of creation

Shadow: The god Nometheog
shareen: a shean drink
Shea: a land with varying climates. It exists as an alternate world for Sark and was created by Selfirin.
Shekley: Creator of the Mahldrusecs, brother of David, possessed by the Shadow
Shiana: co-leader of the Selbdes, girlfriend of David. She has the ability to manipulate matter.
Sigh Reen: A water fairy that resides in the summer stream of Shea.
Slatkin: An orostiro, personal attendant and best friend to Victor, king of Sark.
soul connection: A connection of the thoughts of two dark angels when they are at long distances from one another. In Shea, this has consequences, such as making the angels sick. However, in Sark, it empowers them.
sprites: Like fairies, sprites deal with the everyday goings-on of Shea. However, they usually cause mischief, such as spiking punch, or causing others to drop things or misplace items.
Starla: Quirial and friend to Arik.
Teri: A psychic blessed with communication and understanding between those of other cultures and languages.
Tahln: A land that is much like the modern day world, but somewhat altered. It has been destroyed by Shekley and the dark god Nometheog.
Trealon: The homeland of Celeste and Alexandria. It is ruled by a gypsy king and is a major trade port West of Sark.
Trost: A city built and commanded by Shekley and the Shadow
unicorn: Battle steeds of Chimrion Knights.

Valassa: A scithronian.

Valka Beasts: creatures that would be similar to wooly mammoths with tusks and antlers. They have black, shaggy fur and are usually gentle creatures, however they become violent when threatened.

veheil stavik: A spell used by Alexandria to make the hunters lose their footing. The spell causes a slippery spot on any surface.

Victor: dark angel of justice, rightful king of Sark, husband to Celeste and father to Angelik

Volkhan: One of the elder hunters (although he is only about 35 years old: hunters do not have a very long life span). He is one of the leaders.

Vortex: Alexandria's war unicorn

werewolf: This is the term world-wide for what the hunters and other Sarkians call the khanhine-lupa. Depending upon the tribe or nationality depends whether or not they are seen in a good or bad context.

Xandra: Shekley's girlfriend and first-born mahldrusec. She does whatever she is commanded by Shekley and the Shadow.

Zouphi! A Shean greeting used only by gnomes, and usually implies to stop and wait for them

Angels and Shadows

Acknowledgements

Thank you to my husband for everything you do for me. You are my great adventure in life! I love you!

Thanks to all the editors who helped me pull this together. I couldn't have done it without your help.

Robert Grant Mozingo, thanks to you for the wonderful map.

Thanks to my family for putting up with me and my characters through all these years. Your support has kept my dreams soaring. Love you all!

Thanks to Katie Floyd, Ashlyn Smith, and Vassa Falls for your great contributions to this project!

Thank you my readers for taking the time to explore these worlds with me. I hope you enjoy my characters and lands as much as I do.

Thank You Reimann Books for making it possible to share my dreams with others.

K.L. Stewart grew up in Four Oaks, NC. She currently resides in Richlands, NC with her husband and stepdaughter. She loves Writing, reading, music and movies. Most of all, she loves her family, both related and chose.

Visit K. L. Stewart's Dark Angel Wars website:
http://www.darkangelwars.com/

Read more about K. L. Stewart on her blog
http://klstewartsdarkangels.blogspot.com

Follow her on Facebook and Twitter:
https://www.facebook.com/klstewartbooks

https://twitter.com/writerklstewart

www.ingramcontent.com/pod-product-compliance
Lightning Source LLC
Chambersburg PA
CBHW061617170626
46811CB00001B/448